All That's Left

Book 1: The War Within the Wall

Jeff Carr

DEDICATION

To my family and friends for supporting one ridiculous idea after the next.

To my parents and to Sarah, Anna, & Kami, I love you the most!

To all of my amazing students – Especially my first class: the PVE class of 2027. I am so lucky to have been your teacher, and you will always hold a special place in my heart.

To the film director who ghosted his crew after signing a distribution deal and stole my laptop. Thank you for reminding me I have trust issues.

P.S. I still want my laptop back.

Table of Contents

PROLOGUE

"I'll never forget the day the world changed. Our President built a hundred-foot wall around the entire country and then told the rest of the world to go to hell.

What'd he think was going to happen?"

-     Penny Wells, July 5th, 2029

Five years ago, our President and fearless leader cut the ribbon on the self-proclaimed 'Freedom Wall,' which provided anything but. Structurally, it was a four-million square foot eyesore that encompassed the entire United States' mainland like a fishbowl. The purpose of the freedom wall was to keep everyone out, though, in hindsight, it achieved just the opposite. The President took immense delight in the monstrosity. He often used any excuse he could to stand before it and gawk. It was indeed the pride and joy of his self-imposed third term. He even attempted to move Camp David to the site where the first section of the wall had been erected. And, yes, I do mean the entire camp.

Once, during a photo shoot, the President posed with the immigrant contractors who built the wall. Approximately ten seconds after the bulbs flashed and popped, our Commander in Chief had the workers deported to Mexico, despite the fact they were from Portugal. At that moment, the President made a vow that no one, and he meant no one, would ever reside in this country without extreme and unforgiving vetting. We're talking DNA testing, which uprooted family trees until our cultural lineage was nothing more than a twisted hole in the ground.

Our overall population was cut by 39 percent as government actively exported people, rather than goods, from shipping ports and, ironically, from Ellis Island. Soon after, anyone who remained in the country on a work permit or student visa was sent packing.

Needless to say, our mass deportations and the concrete and steel security blanket didn't sit well with others. As a matter of fact, it downright pissed everybody off. The few friends who remained weren't too keen on the USA closing down shipping routes or limiting imports and exports. Our amigos to the south lost the ability to supply our workforce with ambitious dreamers, and within two years the Latino population went from a close second to Caucasians, to a measly twenty-first, right below the Albanians.

As for our former chaps across the pond, our new way of life stripped them of their most potent and reliable ally; all but guaranteeing anytime a down-and-out Jihadist decided to blow himself up inside a Euro-Walmart, America wouldn't be there to lend a hand or flex muscle. It got so bad that we even stopped offering thoughts and prayers via mindless social media posts.

El Presidente even sold Alaska back to the Russians for a bottle of Vodka and declared Hawaii a sovereign state. All of this was so he could strip Old Glory of two stars and pin them to his chest like a decorated war General.

After the Freedom Wall was complete, the country's foreign interactions were minimal at best, and the need for a strong military was nullified. Our armed forces, which previously housed 2.1 million souls, was cut to a measly one-hundred thousand active-duty members and less than ten thousand reservists. Bombers and Battleships were scrapped for parts or turned into a living history museum. F-16s were stripped clean and used as decorative lawn ornaments for public parks and city halls. The bulk of our military force either guarded the wall or turned their attention to the turmoil and civil unrest that ran rampant in metropolitan areas. Protestors took to the streets, looted and burned fast food establishments, dollar stores, and fired Molotov cocktails and urine bottles at the newly anointed peacekeepers. Some even took to the highways for sit-ins, but those would only last a few hours. Our courageous champion in the Oval Office immediately promised full pardons to any "patriotic" citizens who'd run through them with their vehicles. Within a year, the United States fell under its thirteenth declaration of martial law.

Yet, throughout all this, inconceivable as it may have been, somehow, some towns, some communities, remained unchanged. One could have given credit to simple folk with simple values. Some said it was the Lord's work. It also could have been dumb luck. Whatever the case, whatever it was, towns like Sutton, Nebraska, endured as a piece of land that time forgot.

Our story begins as we fast-forward to the present—a hair over eighteen hundred days later.

PART ONE

THE FIRST STRIKE

CHAPTER 1
THE SMALL TOWN OF
SUTTON, NEBRASKA

July 5th, 2029

The sun was setting in the one-horse town. A barbershop pole twisted with mesmerizing spirals of red and blue. The neon clock in Grant's Five-and-Dime read 7:35 pm. Sutton, Nebraska was a vision straight out of an Ed Hopper painting–Or maybe Rockwell or even Winslow Homer if you're willing to use your imagination. The point is, Sutton was one of those small towns where the train tracks sliced straight down the middle of Main street, or in this case, Saunders Ave. A street that was lined with storefronts of pure Americana, dressed up for a celebration.

There was, however, one thing in this nostalgic version of America that was missing: the people. Not a soul was in sight. For some peculiar reason, this slab of Sutton was a ghost town. Not a shop was open, nor a car present–minus a beat-up pickup truck parked

1

outside the hay-n-feed, but even that had a flat tire and hadn't been moved in weeks. To a passerby, one would ponder if Sutton had fallen victim to the Rapture. They'd wonder if the Mayan prophecy of twenty-twelve was just a tad on the tardy side. And although Sutton had no shortage of Bibles or Mayans for that matter—with there being a family of ranchers from Guatemala—this town was no result of the rapture, nor was it a playground of an ancient God. No, there was something ordinary at work here. Something far more pedestrian and far more American had driven the fine folks away from the center of this hopping farmtropolis.

An eerie breeze conducted a symphony of wind chimes. Homemade banners stretched from building to building; they flapped and whipped about in the wind's wake. All of the signage displayed the same headline:

NEW INDEPENDENCE DAY - CELEBRATE 5 YEARS OF FREEDOM BEHIND THE WALL

FIREWORKS DISPLAY AFTER THE STATE CHAMPIONSHIP

Roughly a quarter-mile from town-center, as the crow flies, clapboard houses decorated the mottled landscape. Forties architecture. Barns. Silos. All quaint and well kept. One home was nestled on the end of a dirt and gravel road, backed by a storybook barn and herb farm. It had a fresh coat of paint plastered over decaying wood as the sun's dying light accentuated a rose-colored glow. Vivid streaks of Windex dimmed the picture windows. The name on the mailbox read "Dixon".

A couple of miles past the Dixon property sat the pure heart of Sutton: a baseball diamond which was blanketed in pristine Kentucky bluegrass. Local advertising speckled the outfield wall, which backed up to a cornfield that lined the earth as far as the eye could see. The stands that flanked home plate sat two-tiers high, and the stadium itself seated just over five thousand souls, which was nearly the entire population of Clay County. This vision of a stadium, originally built to house a minor league baseball club, was an actual field of dreams that would have made Shoeless Joe Jackson regret wasting his precious afterlife in Iowa.

The floodlights were beaming down and projecting a whopping forty-thousand lumens under dark churning clouds. A dirt and gravel lot funneled toward the stadium. It was jam-packed with SUVs and trucks equipped with monster towing capacity and storm chaser equipment. Whatever you could conjure up about Sutton's residents, one could never dispute their mantra of *Utility over Status*. It might as well have been engraved into their DNA.

Droves of people packed the ballfield's grounds. The stands were overflowed with the town's entire population, like biscuit dough overflowing out of a freshly popped canister. Some patrons sat in the outfield bleachers, with a handful in terrace seats. Others doubled up along a chain-linked fence separating the field from the crowd. Even more, Suttonites lined a row of lawn chairs on the grass and down the baselines that butted up against bright blue porta-potties. And the rest? The rest were buying up all the concessions their feeble paychecks afforded them, ranging from novelty foam fingers to snow cones.

A towering, hunter-green, hand-operated scoreboard cast long and silent shadows over much of the outfield. The scoreboard, like much of Sutton, was a throwback from days gone. And while it wasn't a day less than eighty years young, it still looked as good as new.

The scoreboard operator, a pimpled-faced teen named Shane, with shaggy red curls atop his head, barely took his eyes off his cell phone as he placed another zero under the bottom half of the sixth inning. A swarm of mosquitoes circled above him like a plague of locusts ready to suck him dry. The game on the field was, as a local broadcaster described it, "A bit of a nail-biter." One run on five hits for the home team. And for the visitors, it was a double snowball, zero runs on zero hits.

A rousing set of cheers and jeers came from the stands, and all eyes were on the field where a between-innings contest took place. Two grown men wore hot dog costumes as they raced around the outfield warning track. One man was wearing a Chicago-style dog outfit with all the trimmings, down to the celery salt. The other had on more of a traditional hotdog costume, sporting yellow and red streaks down the side of his washed-out bun. The Chicago dog darted ahead but stumbled ten feet before the finish line. He face-planted awkwardly as the traditional dog made up ground; both participants were clearly under the influence of an alcoholic adult-soda or two. The crowd went crazy as both costumed men crossed the finish line at nearly the same time, a photo-finish. When the line judge declared the race a draw, the mystery-meat encased combatants engaged in a heated shoving match that drew a boisterous bout of laughter from the fans. The skirmish was quickly put to an end when a security officer grabbed both men by their poppy seeds and hauled them away. With that, the stadium's public address announcer bellowed out a live commercial in a deep movie-trailer voice, "Hey sports fans. After the game, be sure to visit Walnut's Discount Emporium and Doomsday Prep Center. Your home for all your survival and home security needs. And remember: You never know who will be... Wa-tch-ing you?" The PA announcer inquired probingly as his voice echoed into the ether.

CHAPTER 2
THE HISTORY OF PENNY, REGGIE, AND THE ROACH

In the home team's dugout, a brigade of high school softballers corralled their gloves. They snagged handfuls of salt-laced sunflower seeds and wads of big league chew as they darted out onto the field. They sounded off with interspersed, cliché words of encouragement as their cleats hit the dirt and pounded dust and sand heavenward. The girls wore white tops with matching white pants which had a thick crimson stripe that ran down both sides. Their hats, socks, and the numbers on their jerseys were similarly crimson but with blue pinstripe trim.

One girl remained seated at the end of the bench. Her name was Penny Wells, the team's sophomore star pitcher. Penny was fifteen years old, but on most days, she'd pass for twenty-five. She wore black streaks like war paint beneath her smoldering green eyes while her silky onyx-black ponytail flowed out the back of her ballcap. Her skin was delicate and shimmered like the winter snow, and her pale pink lips resembled a budding rose. She was radiant and terrifying. Classmates didn't know whether to ask her to the homecoming dance or avoid making eye contact altogether. Penny had a small scar beneath the left side of her bottom lip, a souvenir from a past encounter given to her by a man she wished she'd never met.

She sat poised and determined to end the game with a flurry, running her finger down the stitching in her glove–a glove she'd had since the fifth grade when it was two inches too long on each finger. She kneaded the palm, then caressed a slight tear in the seam like a mother bird nursing her hatchling back to health. This glove was more than a piece of leather with five holes. It held history.

"C'mon, Penny, three more outs. Three more outs and this is all over," Penny whispered to her glove, Reggie. Penny would often talk to Reggie, whether anyone was around to hear it or not. On a cold day in the fall of 2024 was when she had named him. Only he was not named after baseball legend Reggie Jackson. Reggie, the glove, was named after Reggie the cat who was Penny's first pet, a grey British Shorthair with yellow eyes that looked like reaping hooks. Reggie, the cat, was a stray that Penny had found one night meowing, stuck in a storm drain. Up until that point in Penny's life, she had hated cats. She thought they were selfish little beasts that did nothing more than parade around your bedsheets after emptying their bowels in a messy box. But Reggie was more like a dog to her, less narrow-minded and self-indulgent and more selfless. Reggie was also spirited and, most importantly, loyal. However, none of this stopped him from relieving himself in a box and parading around Penny's bedsheets.

Penny would often play fetch with Reggie, just like a dog. She would take Reggie for a walk, just like a dog. The townsfolk would whisper and shoot her odd, judgmental looks, but Penny didn't mind. Reggie was hers, and she was Reggie's; they were inseparable. That was until Vernon Weathersby, the town drunk, drove home after he polished off a bottle of whiskey at the local drinking establishment aptly named *The Watering Hole*. Vernon took his eyes off the road for a split second and placed them on the back of his eyelids.

It was then that Vernon hit a ditch, rolled his pickup seven times, and crashed it through Penny's gate. He crushed Reggie against a tree, leaving pureed brain matter mashed into the stitching of the cat's collar.

Devastation quickly set in for Penny, but not in the way one would expect of a child. More than anything, Penny was calculating and hell-bent on revenge. Her mother expected Penny to cry when she and some friends and neighbors threw Reggie an impromptu funeral. But Penny stood stoic and stared at the lump of dirt nestled beneath her bedroom window.

"Your face is kissed again and again.
And you look once more into the eyes of your trusted friend.
So long gone from your life, but never absent from your heart.
Then you cross the rainbow bridge together, never to be separated."

Penny's mother finished reading a poem that was supposed to help with the coping of a lost pet, or so she'd read in a parenting journal. To Penny's mother's surprise, Penny's eyes were brimful of fury rather than overt sorrow.

"Can I go to bed now?" Penny requested in her most monotonous tone. She collected her blanket and stuffed bear and walked away without as much as a goodnight hug or kiss.

One crisp gloomy night, six short months later, Vernon Weathersby arrived home, dropped off by a cab after he served an abbreviated prison sentence for his drunken misadventures. Vernon made a direct path into his garage to kick back and watch a little college football while he waxed his most beloved possession: a cherry red 1967 Ford Mustang GT.

To his surprise, Vernon found the word MURDERER etched into the hood of his ride. Vernon scanned upward in astonishment, where he spotted Reggie's leash, still covered in the brown desiccated blood, as it dangled from the rearview mirror like a Christmas ornament.

Vernon fumed as steam rose from his ears, and he looked as if he were about to combust spontaneously. He phoned the local sheriff to investigate and demanded justice. Unfortunately, Vernon's prime suspect had an alibi. She was a ten-year-old, in elementary school, with pigtails and dimples.

The very next morning, Vernon stormed out of the police station and knocked over a stack of parking tickets on his way out the door. When he exited the building, Vernon was stunned to see Penny waiting for him outside. She sat on a pink and blue bike with handlebar ribbons that flowed in the wind. Vernon stared at Penny with a wicked gaze and watched her innocent smile turn into an evil scowl. And only once Penny was sure no one else would see, she made a tight ball out of her tiny fist and slowly extended her middle finger.

Ω

Now, like so many other times before, Penny sat fixated on the history woven into the fabric of her mitt. She often thought back and remembered things besides her decapitated feline. She would reflect on every minute sacrificed to reach this moment. Every strike, every ball, every run scored, and every line drive off the shoulder or thigh muscle.

She would recall every bruise, every cramp, and every extra mile she was forced to run after mouthing off to a coach–Which happened quite frequently, as the only thing quicker than Penny's fastball was the speed at which she'd disregard authority–And then, when those memories would fade, she would think of one thing. One singular focus burned deep in the furnace of her gut and that was of her biological father, Clarence Ray Wells.

Clarence Ray was a career criminal and professional dirtbag. He was appropriately nicknamed 'Roach' on account of his grimy, black meth-stained teeth. Not to mention his trademark ability to scatter like a cockroach anytime the police investigated the scene of one of his infamous drug store heists. And it should come as no surprise as to how easy it was for Roach to take on his daughter, Penny, as an apprentice. He taught young Penny how to cook a pure batch of meth by the ripe age of seven. One would be surprised by the amount of methamphetamine you could make with some cold medicine and a couple of Dove soap bars if one had the right amount of motivation and a helper with tiny hands.

When Penny's mother was away at one of her two full-time jobs, Roach would tell little Penny that Daddy needed her assistance. He would say it was just family bonding time. Being in primary school, Penny aspired to make her father proud, so she took to Meth-making as a moth takes to a flame. She was so good that she once tried to submit a mobile meth lab, aka her Crystal Rock Candy exhibit, into the school science fair. A science fair in which the DEA made a surprise appearance and, needless to say, was one Penny did not win.

Roach always looked to score, both in and out of prison. Every once in a blue moon between lockups, Roach would stop by the old home to abuse his ex-wife, Penny's mom, Jess. Then, after he finished with her, Roach would head out back, clutch a bat, a ball, and drag Penny by the hair, and say, "I'm gonna make a ballplayer out of you, one way or another." And that he did, but it came at such a price.

During their softball lessons, Roach tormented Penny for each swing and miss. He threw profanity-laced tantrums for every errant pitch. And if that weren't enough, there'd always be the belittling and the black eyes. And those were Penny's good memories. For when Clarence Ray Wells had enough with spousal abuse and sports, the true cruelty would begin. It wasn't uncommon for homework hour in the Well's home to end with Roach throwing Penny down the cellar stairs. But as is the case with most monsters, Roach could never stop himself there.

"What are you crying for?" he chastised as he slid his belt through the loops of his pants. "You better not bleed on my carpet again," he'd scold Penny as he walked down the steps toward her. His steel toe boots hammered down on each plank with a bone-tingling clunk. Each plant of his foot made Penny cringe as he drew nearer. She feared the pain that lied ahead.

Penny learned to compartmentalize her emotions at a very green age and created a safe space in her mind to escape her father's brutality. Her safe place was a room with four walls, no doors, and no windows. There was only one way in, one way out, and she had the key. In her innermost sanctum, she shielded herself from Roach's berating and insults. She'd block out the sight of his fists as they pummeled down violently upon her. Most of the time, Penny was alone in this room, in her mind castle. But occasionally, on the worst of nights, she invited her mother into her sanctuary. Together they would laugh, smile, and cry. Only not tears of pain and anguish, but tears of merriment and togetherness. They'd have tea parties like an ordinary family would. Sometimes they just sat and read, and that was good enough. For Penny, most of her real-life outside of this room was nothing short of a nightmare. But rather than throwing herself the grandest of pity parties, Penny used the pain to her advantage. She knew she wouldn't always be able to stow away in her subconscious. So Penny found new ways to overcome. She found solace in competition and in being the best.

Material goods never seemed to motivate Penny. Her ego wasn't stimulated by thoughts of dating, getting her license, capping one-hundred likes on social media, or taking tasteless selfies. Nor did she give two-shits about ninety-nine percent of the yokels in the crowd who groaned with anxiety and awaited her arrival; awaited Sutton's third straight Championship. Penny was driven by winning. Anything, anywhere, at any time.

Penny's blood boiled with a hunger to be the best. It flowed through her coarse veins like molten lava. Everyone knew it, and by God did most everyone stay out of her way. If Penny Wells survived a childhood full of bludgeonings by Roach, she would surely find no challenge in dominating gauche teens on a mid-American softball field. This perseverance drove Penny to play division-one college sports and finish top of her class. At that same time, her friends would be Snapchatting topless photos and dropping Molly at frat parties. And this is why Penny would accomplish anything she set her mind to, and nothing would interrupt—

"Wells. Hey, Wells." a voice interrupted her thoughts and violently snapped her out of her trance. Penny's coach walked toward her expectantly. His cleats crunched against the plywood dugout floor in a similar cadence to her memory of Roach lumbering down the cellar stairs. The coach stopped and tapped his foot impatiently in front of her. Coach Roswell was a stout man with a wiry mustache, rosy red cheeks, and thin hair that poked out of the back and bottom of his fitted ballcap. "You good there, Penny?" he asked in his Fargo, North Dakota laced accent. Roswell leaned back, sucked in his stomach, tugged upward on his belt, and awaited her reply.

"Fan-freakin'-tastic," Penny scoffed.

"Then whadda you say we go out there and we finish this thing, yah?" Roswell boomed. He slapped his hands emphatically against his budging stomach and smiled with a chunk of sunflower seed stuck in between his front teeth.

"We?" Penny snarled and inhaled furiously through her nostrils like a roided-out prize-fighter preparing for the final round at the MGM Grand in Vegas. "We?" she said again as if it would help drive home the point.

"Well, I mean…Yah, like the royal we…Us…Our, uh…Our team. Ya know…We," the coach stammered as his red cheeks grew even redder. The temperature of his skin rose with each breath. "I mean, I know technically you hit the home run, and we wouldn't even be here if you hadn't pitched a… ah…Well, what I'm trying to say is—There's no 'I' in Sutton—There's no I in—"

"Relax, skip," Penny stood as she placed a reassuring hand on the coach's shuddering shoulder and patted him. "I'm just fuckin' with you. We got this."

"Great. Yah. We got this. Good attitude, Wells. I like it," Roswell exclaimed and clapped again as he let out a sigh and un-puckered his butt cheeks. "But, uh, can you maybe try and clean up the language there, Wells?"

Penny squinted, mulled it over, and without a word walked past her coach like he wasn't even there, or worse, like he was irrelevant.

CHAPTER 3
THE RANGER AND THE WALNUT

The crowd roared as Penny emerged from the dugout. She charged toward the mound at the tail end of the third-grade choir's rendition of "God Bless America"; a horrid performance that was apparent to everyone except the third-grade parents, who stood at the fence line and snapped photos. Shortly after the song ended, the student section started to do the wave. An ebb and flow of timeless cheers surrounded the stadium within seconds.

The wave lost a fraction of momentum as it made its way past a tier of juniors and seniors, their faces glued to their electronic devices. It rounded the curve at section one-hundred-and-one and whipped past a portion of the stadium designated for parents and siblings. All of the softball moms, dads, brothers, and sisters alike stood and flailed their arms about like those inflatable air dancers you'd see in front of a used car lot—all except one man that remained seated.

15

This man was Luke Dixon. Luke was a transplant Suttonite, a decorated war vet, and Penny's shiny new stepdad. Luke grew up an Army brat and likely couldn't tell you where he was born or even which continent he had spent most of his childhood birthdays on. However, he could recall every officer and their rank at each station when he himself served in the armed forces.

The look on Luke's face spoke volumes, with a perpetual squint in his eyes. Luke was infuriated by public acts of communal stupidity, such as the wave, and crowds in general annoyed the living crap out of him. They caused an uncomfortable stir in the pit of his belly. Whenever a friend or colleague would invite Luke to a gathering, he would immediately ask how many people were going. To Luke, six people or less in the same room was a small get-together. Seven to twenty was a crowd. And anything over twenty was just asking for trouble.

If Luke's square jaw, buzz cut, and protuberant pectoral muscles didn't tell you he was ex-military, his semi-permanent scowl surely would. If one needed any more convincing, they would have to look no further than his wardrobe. Luke, a minimalist, had seven shirts in his dresser, one for each day of the week. Three of them were plain white Hanes crew neck t-shirts. The remaining four were matching authentic Army Ranger tees, all gray. And with today being a Thursday, the gray Ranger tee was predictably Luke's weapon of choice.

Luke looked younger than his thirty-seven years let on, that is except for his eyes. His eyes had seen a great many things he'd rather soon forget. When Luke stared into the mirror, he'd often have a hard time recognizing the face that peered back at him. And sometimes, if he stared long enough, he swore there was someone else behind the glass. A doppelganger maybe, he hailed from another dimension. Someone that would move or twitch ever-so-slightly out of line when Luke's attention was diverted.

Unlike Penny, Luke's past was not chocked full of receipts filled with beatings and abuse. Though, during Luke's time with the Rangers, he quickly soared through the ranks. Eventually, he settled into his comfort zone as Chief Interrogator for the Anti-Terror Task Force, the ATTF. There, Luke was the abuser. With as little as a stopwatch, a Pez dispenser, and a nine-volt battery, Luke extracted information from even the most hardened war criminals. His regiment would often refer to him as the MacGyver of counterintelligence. They told tales of Luke's handiwork and spoke of him as if he were Chuck Norris reincarnate.

One rumor that made its way around the base like a chilling campfire tale or folklore was the legend of Dmitri Konstantin. Dmitri was an infamous Bulgarian warlord that bombed a supermarket supposedly because they were out of his favorite red pepper hummus. This craven act killed over one hundred souls, many of whom were women and children. Dmitri was ruthless, to say the least, and cowered to no man. That was until he met Luke.

Those closest to Luke detailed that not only did Dmitri admit to the bombings, but he signed a full confession to countless other crimes; even ones he didn't commit. He also turned on the ranking members of his regime, and all key players were executed or incarcerated within weeks. That, however, wasn't the worst of it. After Luke's cross-examination of Dmitri, guards found the Bulgarian tucked away in the far corner of the room. Dimitri reportedly shivered as his knees knocked together like chattering teeth. He cried out for his mother and wet himself from the space his genitalia used to inhabit.

All of that being said, this was a much different world for Luke. Since the completion of the freedom wall, our enemies, while not few, were very far between. America sat nestled within its comfy new sanctuary and traded the fight against terror for a politically correct battle against small-time gang-bangers. The National Guard took up arms against a group of Caucasian, fedora-wearing hipsters who pretended to sympathize with minorities and the oppressed. These social justice warriors only had one real purpose: hypocrisy. Indeed this was a world that had little use for a man with talents such as Luke's. After he retired from the service, life in Sutton, and his marriage to Jess, had softened Luke; but only just barely. He traded his M4 Carbine in for a Dewalt Lithium-Ion Cordless drill and his torture kit for a socket set.

Luke would often go hunting with his army pals to keep his gunplay on point, and he'd watch old DVDs of cop shows and reruns of "Live PD" to brush up on his investigation skills. Yet, the number one thing that kept Luke frosty just might have been playing step-father to Penny.

One evening, a few short days back, Luke met up with former comrades at a cowboy bar roughly an hour and a half east, just south of Lincoln. They shared stories of the good old days. They talked about pets, kids, DIY projects, and their new riding mowers.

When it came time for Luke's turn to speak, he confessed that he had recently caught Penny sneaking into the house well after curfew. He described how he sat her down at the kitchen table for a mock interrogation and politely invited her to explain where she'd been and what company she'd kept. Luke begrudgingly confessed that after an hour and a half of trying to discern truth from lie, he was forced to concede. He told his compatriots that trying to break Penny had been more difficult than extracting intel from the most sinister and devout Jihadists.

"Seriously, fellas," Luke said to his friends, shaking his head in defeat. "If you heard two percent, just two percent of the smartassery that regularly spews from Penny's mouth, you'd wish you were back in Kabul looking for WMDs."

His friends laughed and nudged each other at Luke's expense, but they secretly shit themselves on the inside as they knew full well their daughters and sons would soon be teens, and they'd be next.

There Luke sat, his chiseled frame matching the Greek God Adonis's. A trained killing machine spellbindingly transformed into a husband and stepdad. Luke adjusted his position on the piping hot metal bench and nursed the remains of a warm beer. He inched forward uneasily and observed while Penny finished up with the last of her warmups.

Each one of her pitches struck the catcher's glove with a loud pop. Penny's velocity hadn't dropped a hair since the first pitch of the game. And while he couldn't be sure, seeing how he left his radar gun at home, Luke estimated it was only increasing. It was as if actual ice pumped through Penny's veins as she appeared unwavering and unbreakable. Her next pitch was a howitzer that nearly took the catcher's mitt clean off her stumpy fingers. Penny had just ramped things up to a level that most competitors couldn't even fathom. Only then, just as Luke was about to relax, did he spot an anomaly in Penny's delivery. There was a definite hitch in her right leg before her starting toward the plate, but only when she threw her slider.

"No, no, no, no…" he said under his breath. "Not again." Luke held his breath nervously during Penny's next warmup: the same thing, another slider, another prominent hitch. To make matters worse, this topic was one that Luke and Penny had discussed ad nauseam after the semi-finals on a long car ride home. He replayed the encounter in his mind.

"I did not," Penny snapped as she stared out the passenger window, her jersey was covered in dirt, and eye black smeared down her cheek. "And besides, we won, and I struck out fifteen batters. Which happens to be a state record, in case you'd like to know. What does it matter if I kicked my leg out?"

"It matters because it matters," Luke slapped his hand down on the steering wheel as he hauled ass down the winding interstate.

"It matters because it matters?" Penny repeated slowly with a hint of a wisecrack. "That's brilliant, Luke. Real deep. You know what? You should put that quote in your new book: Luke's Guide to Life, Love, and Professional Pitching. You can file it under the chapter, 'Do Good Stuff or Winners Win and Losers Lose'." Penny rolled her eyes violently. "You're a real fuckin' poet."

"Yeah, that's hilarious. And watch your damn mouth, will ya," Luke shook his head in frustration. "Besides, what if this wasn't a game you were winning by ten? What if you were losing? Or, what if they tied you up and–"

"But it wasn't," Penny snapped back.

"But what if it was? Say you go out there next week. It's the top of the seventh. Game on the line. The other team, they're sitting fastball. And you know this, so you shake it off. You want the slider. Then you do your leg hitch and tip your pitch, and they take you deep, and you lose."

"And what if aliens abduct me in my sleep and send me back in the body of a hippopotamus," Penny said.

"Here we go," Luke said exhaustedly.

"And say the hippopotamus version of me had a lazy eye and pigeon wings. But y'all don't seem to notice or even mind the new me. You even change the name on my bedroom door from Penny to Hippopota-Pigeon," Penny said quickly. "Then, no one would think twice to call out a leg hitch on account I got turned into a fat-ass hippo with wings that don't fly and one eye that points directly at the ceiling."

"I'm just saying. I don't want this to come back and bite you during a big moment. And next week is the State Championship. There ain't no moment that's gonna be bigger than that."

"It's a high school softball game, Luke," Penny said. "Not the end of the freaking world." She shook her head.

"Thank you for saying freaking, and not the other word," Luke commented.

"My fuckin' pleasure," Penny answered. Luke rolled his eyes. "And besides, Luke, it's *my* high school softball game. Mine. Why does this mean so much to you?"

"Why?" Luke stared longingly out the driver's side window. He gazed out into the horizon to summon a distant memory. "My daddy, that's why." Luke's voice uncharacteristically cracked. "I never told anybody this, and I don't really know why I'm telling you now, but my dad was a hard, hard man. He didn't give a damn about me or my football career," Luke turned toward the windshield. He flipped his wipers on as a light mist peppered the glass and swished remnants of bug carcasses away. "It was my junior year. We were playing Butler in the conference finals. I go to my daddy, and I ask him, 'Will you please, please just come to this one game? It would mean everything to me.'"

Luke exhaled, scrunched his nose, and fought emotion that he'd typically never succumb to. "I look for him in pregame. He ain't there. End of the first quarter. Halftime... I still don't see him. Then, with ten seconds left, we're five points down with the ball at the twenty-yard line. I scramble, dodge a couple of would-be tacklers, get a block from Peyton, my tail back, and I dive headfirst over their safety and into the end zone to score the winning touchdown. My team hoists me up on their shoulders, and they start carrying me around. And there, right near the edge of the parking lot, I see the old man sitting on the hood of his pickup. So I... I run to him. Fastest I've ever run in my life. The aches I felt in my legs and my back was gone. It's like I was floating on a cloud. So, I finally get to him and hold out the game ball. I don't know why, but I – I - I wanted him to have it. I said, 'This is for you, Daddy.' And he looks right at me. Right in my eyes, and he says, 'Son. You're slower than I thought you'd be.' I died a little that day." Luke bit his bottom lip and fought off emotion. "Then he just got in his truck and drove off," Luke sniffled, shook his head like he was shaking away literal and metaphorical cobwebs. "I don't want to be like him, Penny. I wanna help you be the best you can be. Alright?" Luke spun in Penny's direction only to see she had noise-canceling headphones thrown over her ears and that she'd stopped listening minutes ago.

The pop of another warmup brought Luke back to the present. Back to his internal struggle of calling Penny out for her leg hitch. Luke knew Penny would be beyond furious if he embarrassed her in front of the entire town. He also knew she'd be even more infuriated if he saw her tip her pitches and didn't do anything about it. So, Luke weighed the odds and chose the lesser of two evils. Better to have an angry teen stepdaughter with a medal and an MVP trophy than one without. He stood, put his fingers to his lips, and was about to whistle. But before his lips moistened his fingertips, he stopped, frozen in a stupor as Penny self-corrected. Her next warmup pitch was another slider, and it was flawless.

The hitch was gone, like magic. Luke thought to himself, *"That a girl,"* but then watched in further confusion as she took the ball from the catcher. She turned, stared Luke dead in the eyes, and smiled a mischievous smile. It was at that moment Luke knew that Penny saw him watching. She knew the hitch in her leg would drive him insane. And she was doing it on purpose. "Asshole," Luke mouthed to Penny as she tipped her cap. He let out a deep growl, sunk back into the seat, sulked, and buried his face in his calloused hands.

"Coming through. One side. Clear a path y'all. C'mon lady, move that dump truck," a voice said as it crept down Luke's aisle. Dozens of nearby spectators turned to see Luke's neighbor and proprietor of Walnut's Discount Emporium, Ed Decker. Ed was sporting a bucket hat and had a Hawaiian shirt draped over a filthy, sweat-stained tank-top; a pair of binoculars dangled from his neck. His stringy salt and pepper beard hung just below his jawline and had a thin black stripe that ran down the middle of his chin. Ed, better known as Walnut, looked like the world's worst undercover CIA agent; in a most dreadful disguise with his over-sized nose and flushed-red cheeks.

Ed often wished the nickname, Walnut, had been bestowed upon him for his love for omega 3's, or even because of his stern demeanor and renowned reputation for never cracking under pressure. Sadly neither of these were true. On Ed's name day, his mother handed him over to Grandpa Ben, a man who came to this country from China at the age of twelve and had to work hard for everything; a man who pulled no punches. Ben was so blunt that his children thought he was inflicted with early-onset dementia with a side of Tourette's. Ben would shout whatever came to his mind at any point in time, no matter how absurd or inappropriate. But truth be told, Ben had no medical disability. He was just a foul-mouthed, bitter old man that cursed like a judgmental, racist, sexist, fat-shaming pirate.

As he cradled young Ed in his arms for the first time, Ben stared down at the newborn, scoffed, and with a complete lack of affection, said, "The boy's ugly. And his head looks like a damn walnut." From that day forth, family, friends, classmates, teachers, and clergy members commonly referred to Ed Decker as Walnut.

"Here's your beer," Walnut sat and handed Luke a cold brew.

"What the—" Luke looked at his beverage curiously. Walnut had either drank half of it or spilled it on the way down the aisle. "Where's the rest of it?"

"Rest of what?" Walnut presented Luke with an offering: a stack of stale tortilla chips submerged in a tray of scalding hot cheese. "Want some nachos?"

"Do I have to use the cheese on your shirt?" Luke pondered and pointed to a glob just above Walnut's shirt pocket. "Or can I dip in the tray?

"Dadgummit," Walnut reached into his pants pocket. He grabbed a wad of napkins and feverishly rubbed bright orange nacho cheese into the fabric of his shirt. Once the cheese was dry and his shirt thoroughly ruined, Walnut motioned dramatically toward the scoreboard. "Can you believe this? A no-hitter in the State Championship. Penny might just make ESPN."

Walnut's confident declaration drew groans from nearby spectators and a firm smack on the leg from one Lexi Van Gels, the town beautician. The color of her fingernails matched the plastering of makeup that had been packed into the pores of her cheeks. Dark purple eyeshadow accentuated her ridiculously long lashes, and her hairstyle was nothing short of offensive. Lexi looked like a Sultan who wore a hat made of onions. She held a twisted and rubber band-bound program from tonight's game. Lexi's fingers were clenched tight, locked and loaded, ready to unleash another dose of pain. She eyed Walnut up and down and reprimanded him with a look. "What's your deal, Jafar?" Walnut asked. Lexi huffed, fluffed her hair, and spun back toward the field.

"That was a bit excessive," Luke stated. "You should apologize."

"You kidding me? Any second now, a genie's gonna come flying right outta that weave and grant me three wishes. And you know what my first wish is gonna be?

"A peek at the Kennedy assassination report?"

"Well, yeah. But—"

"A private tour of Area 51?" Luke added.

"Sure, that too. But my third wish is gonna be for Sutton to have a decent hairstylist with, you know," he coughed, "actual style."

The beautician scoffed, lifted her nose into the air, and pretended to ignore Walnut's insult. She imagined herself a lofty individual, of which Walnut was too far beneath her status to care.

"For the record, I wasn't talking about an apology for insulting Lexi's hair," Luke said under his breath. He did his best to avoid unwanted attention. "I was talkin' about you apologizing for sayin' things like no-hitter with three outs left in the dern game."

"At least I didn't say she was throwing a *perfect* game," Walnut drew even more disapproval from the crowd within earshot. "Cuz she is if you hadn't noticed." Patrons delivered a scrutinous and collective evil-eye in Walnut's direction.

"You're an idiot, Walnut. You're gonna jinx us." Luke gazed at the mob that surrounded them. "And you're gonna get us killed."

"Please. You're in the Rangers. You can take 'em." Walnut wiped away at an onslaught of sweat that had begun to bead and pour down his forehead. "And besides, there ain't no such thing as a jinx. That's just a bunch of superstitious hogwash." A reply that coming out of Walnut's mouth was incredibly ironic.

"Hogwash? Walnut, you literally wore a tinfoil hat to the game."

"I took it off, didn't I?" Walnut pulled a crumpled tinfoil hat from his pocket and showed it to Luke. "See." Walnut unfolded the hat and proudly displayed it.

"Only because it's hotter than two rats screwin' in a wool sock in July," Luke contested.

Walnut shrugged and said, "You got a point there."

"You have to be the single most paranoid individual on this planet," Luke said.

"How do ya figure?" Walnut said, doubtingly.

"For starters, you have a podcast called 'The *Paranoia Files*'."

"What about it?" Walnut probed.

"A podcast where week-in and week-out you spew a bunch gibberish about alien invasions and shape-shifters that crash-landed here back in forty-two," Luke smirked.

"Forty-Seven?" Walnut corrected.

"And aren't you the same guy who stood in front of city hall and ranted into a megaphone that Saddam and Bin Laden were still alive? That they were goin' Dutch on a fully equipped timeshare in the Florida Keys? And that they had a Jacuzzi tub?"

"They are alive," Walnut bounced back with certainty. "But I never said they went Dutch on no timeshare or any nonsense about a Jacuzzi tub." He took a bite of his nachos; melted cheese dripped from his lower lip and landed on his lap. He moved in closer to Luke, inching so near that Luke smelled the individual jalapeño seeds on his breath. "I said the Bush family rented them a condo. And it had a lap pool." Walnut backed off, proud of his top-secret intel.

"Anyways, Walnut, I figured that you would know by now that it's bad juju to talk about what could be in sports. Just in case it ain't never gonna be," Luke waxed poetically in a simpleton sort of way and shook his head as Walnut rolled his eyes.

Luke shifted his focus to the crowd. Thousands of souls hung from the edges of their seats, from common folk to Sutton royalty alike. Luke had even spotted Mayor Alexys Brockmann before the first pitch, and she stopped him in his tracks to talk about Penny and the game. Mayor Brockmann asked about Penny's breakfast and inquired about her sleep patterns to ensure her favorite hurler was primed and ready to go. The mayor told Luke that as far as life events went, after the birth of her twins, a win tonight would take a close second place in order of importance. Luke was audacious enough to ask where the marriage to her husband of thirty years fell in the ranks, which only drew a mocking laugh as she walked away. To the mayor and most of her constituents, girls' softball was the heart that kept the blood pumping through the streets of Sutton. And with a win tonight, the team would make history: three consecutive state championships. Luke knew that shortly after hoisting the trophy, the self-righteous boosters would inevitably stumble through the streets. They'd parade around, arm in arm, and slur the words to the school fight song long after the bars had closed.

'Rally, sons, and daughters
Of Free Mason's fame
Sing of glory, glory, glory
Sing and sound their name
Raise the Red and Blue
And Cheer with Voices True
Rah! Rah! Free Mason's fame

Next year's seniors would strut around campus, with their chests puffed out like Crested Penguins, going on and on about how being a Sutton Free Mason softballer was like carrying a badge of honor. Parents and Grandparents alike would undoubtedly bring up names of high school Hall of Famers past and speak of them as saints, canonized in meaningless, Midwest athletic lore. Parishioners of Saint Joseph's Church would rush out of mass shortly after communion to attend the victory parade. They'd wear their letter jackets with polished leather sleeves and shimmering brass pins.

Luke, of course, understood the excitement. It wasn't as if he didn't share their enthusiasm; he did. Luke had a competitive edge, which had no off switch. He did, however, have a difficult time hiding the animosity that caused him to grit his teeth while staring out at the spectacle before him. He refused to suppress the disdain in his eyes when he saw Maddux, the local mechanic, wave a sign above his head that read, "Our Good Luck Penny". He was the same Maddux who threatened to pull his sponsorship when Penny made the team over his daughter, Savannah. Luke knew deep down that most of these people, these ungrateful swindlers and cowpokes, had never struggled the way he or Penny had struggled. They had never faced down a man like Roach or a terrorist willing to die for a God he never knew. But they sure as hell would hoist Penny upon their shoulders like the Queen of Sheba if it meant a third straight title for their town.

"Alright, let's play ball." The umpire kicked off the top of the seventh and swept crumbled remnants of infield dirt from home plate.

Luke watched Penny forcefully dig her cleats into the mound as she broke up chunks of dirt, red rock, and dry spit. When she finished burrowing to satisfaction, she circled the mound several times. She kept her eyes dead square on the batter-to-be, a freshman middle-infielder from Kennedy High School. Kennedy High was a small town with an upstart softball program out of Bernet County. Their jerseys were dark grey with gold trim and gold numbers on the front and back and their mascot was a Titan.

"Bring it," Penny taunted her opponent.

Luke almost felt sorry for the batter, number twelve, Sofie Ayala, as she sped toward the batter's box. Sofie was a precarious chipmunk of a girl who thought she had a fighting chance of reaching first base. This four-foot-nine, one-hundred-pound fourteen-year-old was about to get epically schooled.

Sofie took a few optimistic warmup swings and pointed the head of her thirty-two-ounce bat toward the outfield. To most, this move was completely harmless and possibly a way for Sofie to ensure she kept her elbows in and body square to the pitcher.

A few weeks after Luke had moved in with Penny and Jess, he began to offer up both softball and life advice. Although Penny dismissed most of Luke's teachings and commonly referred to the mid-thirties veteran as *Old Man*, she did secretly latch onto one tip: "*In sports, take everything personally. Use it as motivation.*" Luke knew that Penny would see the batter pointing toward the outfield as an insult.

Luke saw Penny's eyes squint savagely and could practically see her salivating as she leaned back ever so slightly and rotated her shoulders. Penny inhaled, held her pose for a moment, then wound up and fired a bullet directly into the catcher's mitt.

POP.

"Strike one," the umpire called.

Penny's catcher, Pietra, looked up to see Sofie's chipmunk face staring back at her in complete shock. She hadn't swung. She didn't even have a second to think about swinging, as this was the first time she witnessed that kind of velocity. Unfortunately for her, that was Penny's changeup. Penny often did this to unsuspecting underclassmen. She toyed with them if only to give a glimmer of hope.

"Don't worry. It'll all be over soon," Pietra ridiculed, causing Sofie to turn beet red with anger.

The chipmunk-like batter stared nervously at Pietra, then over at Penny. A series of rally cries were bestowed upon her by her coach. Sofie dug back in but was visibly unhinged.

Luke tried to control his breathing. He inhaled slow and exhaled even more deliberately, like a sniper poised to shoot the eye of a bird from one thousand meters. Penny simultaneously did the same. Luke would often tell her that pitching was like shooting a rifle, an act that was ninety-eight percent mental and two percent physical. He saw Penny determinately dig her knuckles into the ball and pick at the ruby red stitches. "*What was going through her mind? Surely she*

31

wasn't nervous," Luke thought. He knew Penny was rarely nervous, although the situation's gravity started to weigh on him. Luke wanted to stand and pace back and forth, to wear a path into the aisle beneath his feet. What he wouldn't give to keep his toes from tapping anxiously on the ground like a junkie in desperate need of a fix. Luke preferred to be in the middle of the battle rather than an observer of one. In the service, Luke favored explosions and shrapnel raining downward, mere inches away from piercing his skin, over the comfortable confines of an office with a satellite view. He put his jittery fingers to his lips and let out a half-hearted whistle.

Penny rolled her shoulders and took another deep breath. She held it in again for what seemed to be an eternity, then delivered another dart that screamed like a steam whistle and zipped just above Sofie's knees.

"Strike two," cried the umpire.

The crowd erupted. The heat that emanated from the second pitch was so intense that if little Sofie Ayala had a bladder full of Gatorade, Luke was sure she would have lost it in the center of the batter's box.

"Woohoo. You see that?" Walnut rammed Luke with a sharp elbow. What a heater."

Luke nodded assuredly. He knew that pitch was child's play and that Penny typically saved the best for last. Luke watched the batter look back to her coach for much-needed encouragement. The coach gave her an inspired yet fruitless sign of support. Penny rolled her shoulders for the third time, exhaled once more, and stared into the dilated pupils of Sofie's eyes. Sofie's knees started to rattle together as she stared right back at Penny. What happened next would haunt the freshman for the rest of her sporting life, as short-lived as it may have been. Luke saw a grin stretch across Penny's face; she smiled at the batter. A cocky, confident, twisted smile as if to say: good luck with this pitch, or better luck next year, kid. And with that, Penny fired an eighty-mile-per-hour fastball right down the middle of the plate for strike three and left Sofie frozen in time. The crowd went ballistic. With a nudge from the umpire, Sofie scampered back to the dugout, her tail tucked firmly between her legs and her over-eager grin replaced with a flood of tears and a quivering bottom lip. Teammates tried their best to console her, but she looked like she wanted nothing more than to disappear.

Luke applauded passionately and shared a knowing look with Walnut. Two more outs. This game was almost in the bag if Penny could just stay composed.

"Told ya she's gonna get a no-hitter."

"Walnut," Luke scolded. Angry fans turned again in Walnut's direction.

Walnut smiled coyly and shrugged his shoulders. "I'll remind you lot once again; there ain't no such thing as a jinx. Or sports juju. Or a curse, or whatever."

"Give it back!" two immature brats, Carter and Cameron, or C-squared as their mother often called them, interrupted. They jostled over their mom's phone in an intense game of cellular tug of war. They were scrawny kids, hair, and clothes, both equally disheveled. The youngest, Carter, clearly wore Cameron's hand-me-down Star Wars shirt and comically long shorts.

"I wanna play!" Cameron said as he flexed his peanut-sized muscles through his miniature tank top.

He yanked his little brother backward and sent him tumbling into Luke's beer.

"Damn," Luke muttered.

Avery, the boys' mom, turned and watched Luke pounce to save every last drop of beer. "Boys. Look what you did," Avery handed Luke a paper towel that she had tucked away in her pants pocket.

"No thanks," Luke politely declined as he cringed and eyed a soiled yellow sweat stain on the toiletry.

"Let me buy you another one," Avery said.

"Can't," Walnut added with a chuckle. "Last call ended fifteen minutes ago. Want a swig of mine?" he offered Luke his beer, which was now mostly backwash.

"No, thanks." Luke tried not to seem ungrateful, but more importantly, tried not to puke.

"I said it's my turn," Carter rudely interrupted again. He kept hold of the phone with a Bruce Lee-like death grip. "Mama said so."

Luke, Walnut, and the battling boys turned to Avery for an official ruling. Judging by the look on her face, she had said no such thing.

"Enough already! The both of ya," Avery exclaimed in her most mom-like voice. "Why can't you just sit there with your mouths shut and watch your sister's game?"

A fair question, Luke thought. Something he wished would have happened six innings ago.

The boys gave this proposal a little less than a moment's consideration, then immediately returned to yanking back and forth on the phone.

"I'm not sharing," Carter said with even more attitude.

"Neither am I," yelled Cameron.

34

"But your sister–" Avery protested.

"Aubrey sucks at softball, Mama, and the coach ain't never gonna put her in," Carter said with a hint of glee.

"You take that back right now, young man," Avery tried to defend her only daughter, even though she knew the little demon-spawn was right.

"It's true, Mama," Cameron agreed.

"How about you take turns playing and stop fighting?" Avery stated.

"Fine, but I go first. Cameron can't even play his game. It needs data, and there ain't no signal." Carter replied.

Cameron took another swipe. "Yer lyin'! Lemme see."

The redneck decathlon had somehow wholly enthralled Luke in a sort of trance where he had all but forgotten about the game. He watched Avery snatch the phone with authority as she jabbed away at the screen. She held it in front of her face; her distorted reflection bounced off the black screen like a funhouse mirror. There was nothing, not even one bar of signal. She contorted like a Chinese gymnast and hoped a different angle would help her locate a nearby cell tower. Several of these poses presented Luke with the undesirable view of her lower back tattoo that read, 'Property of Justin'. She finally conceded and turned back to Luke and Walnut. "Yours have a signal?"

"Sorry, ma'am. Not a believer in mobile devices that operate at or above the two-point-four gigahertz range," Walnut declared with authority. "On account of government-sanctioned geo-tracking and the exponential rise in cancerous brain tumors tearing through the youth population."

After a long uncomfortable moment of silence, Carter reached up and gave a trembling pull on Avery's sleeve, eyes filled with tears like a bathtub full of water, about to overflow. "I ain't got the cancer in my brain, right Mama?"

Avery fumed and whirled back toward Walnut, muttering, "Asshole." She stood, grabbed her boys by the arms, and led them away.

Walnut looked over to Luke and shrugged. "What'd I say?"

Before Luke answered, the distinct sound of aluminum meeting rubber wrapped in yarn and horsehide demanded the crowd's immediate attention. Fans leaped to their feet and blocked Luke's view. *"What just happened? What did I miss?"* Luke thought as he bounded upward to see a ground ball that had made its way up the hole between the shortstop and second baseman. *"Was this it? The first hit of the game?"* With a desperate attempt to preserve Penny's no-hitter, perfect game, or whatever else Walnut was sure to ruin, the shortstop dove. The ball skipped off rocky infield dirt and somehow stuck to the edge of the webbing of her glove. The shortstop jolted upright, got to her knees, and fired a laser over to first. The runner stretched and lunged for the bag. The ball smacked the first baseman's mitt a split second before the runner's cleat hit the base.

"Out!" the first base umpire pumped his fist.

That was two down, with one to go, and despite Walnut's prediction, ESPN crews were nowhere in sight. Those in attendance mostly remained standing for the final out. Egotistical boosters hugged and cried and stared into their front-facing cameras, being sure not to miss an opportunity to live stream to their six and a half followers who were all most likely at the same game. Some even bellowed the fight song, which sounded more like a choir of dying cats. Vendors stopped serving food, drinks, and trinkets and positioned themselves at the top of their respective aisles. The mayor even stood arm in arm with her loving husband. Throughout all of this, something peculiar piqued Luke's interest. His inner Sherlock Holmes was on full display as he intently eyed a handful of teens, scattered randomly throughout the crowd. They swiped away at their phones with their faces glued to the screen. They all looked like frantic squirrels scouring for a winter's worth of nuts. Luke turned to the student section and saw the same behavior. It wasn't necessarily that teenagers were buried face deep in their smartphones that concerned Luke. In this day and age, it was considered their natural state of being. He was more troubled by the fact that they all did it at the exact same time, a most inopportune moment, and they all had that same look on their faces: the one that's midway between constipation and confusion.

Luke slipped his cell phone out of his Wranglers. Of course, being Luke, he still had his flip phone, which was as close to off the grid as Jess would allow him to get. His eyebrows shifted curiously, and he looked up and saw Walnut, who watched him intently. Luke peered toward the horizon. The last beam of the angry red sun was barely visible, and the dark clouds that rolled in were even more hostile. A distant clap of thunder echoed.

"Maybe just the storm?" Luke thought out loud.

Walnut nodded. He seemed satisfied with the deduction. "This is precisely why I still have my Ham Radio."

The cell phone was deposited back into Luke's jean pocket—squeezed between his quartz-strength thigh muscle and the cheap denim. His eyes returned to the action on the field, but only for a moment. Something wasn't sitting right with him. He'd been back in Sutton for nearly two years now, and since the introduction of 10g service, they hadn't had a single cell or data outage. Not one. Not even this past April when a tornado touched down on the middle of Main Street. *"What would cause this?"* Luke thought to himself. *"The storm? Maybe, but that didn't make sense. It was too far off. There's no way."* The more he thought, the more his eyes darted as he scanned through the database in his mind. The last time he'd encountered anything like this. The last time hundreds lost cell service at the exact same moment was when–

"Stee-rike one!" the umpire interrupted Luke's train of thought. His hoarse voice strained like a chainsaw cutting through Jell-O.

Fans clapped and hollered; some leaned around Luke as he stood. His massive frame blocked an eleven-year-old's view who stood in the row behind him. So deeply invested in the action on the field, Walnut failed to notice Luke's erratic actions. Walnut put his fingers in his mouth and tried to whistle but mostly spit all over himself.

"Gimme those!" Luke yanked the binoculars over Walnut's head, snagging the strap on his earlobe. The momentum pulled Walnut forward and nearly sent him into the next row.

"Hey!" Walnut yelled out in agony as he elongated his neck unnaturally, trying to keep his balance. "That hurt."

Luke put the binoculars to his eyes, studied the horizon, and slowly panned from right to left.

"What are you lookin' for?" Walnut stood upright and leaned in close as he awkwardly attempted to peek through one of the eye-holes that butted up against Luke's cheek.

Luke lowered the binoculars. His eyes grew as wide as frisbees as he stared into the great beyond past the scoreboard. "We need to go," Luke said in a wavering yet pressing tone, a tone that caught Walnut off guard. "Like right now." Luke slapped the binoculars against Walnut's chest, then stormed away.

"Stee-rike two," another shriek erupted from the umpire.

Walnut fidgeted nervously. He watched Luke move down the aisle without prejudice. Luke kicked over popcorn boxes, purses, sixteen-ounce cups of warm brew, and all with little regard for those who stood in his way. A look of more profound concern crossed Walnut's face after Luke shoved a belligerent drunk back into his seat just before he reached the stairs. One strike left in the game, and Luke was going? This wasn't like him at all. Walnut hadn't seen a look that intense on Luke's face since Delaney-Sue and Allie Bybee's 40th birthday party at the bowling alley. A moment where Delaney-Sue's loser of an ex-husband, Genaro, showed up and mocked a disabled employee. It took three paramedics and the Jaws of Life to wrench Genaro's head free from the ball return after Luke had his way with him.

"What the heck, Luke?" Walnut looked down at the binoculars, shrugged, pulled them to his eyes, and stared out onto the field. Through the zoomed spectacles, he spotted an anxious outfielder spitting sunflower seeds and adjusting her belt. Walnut scanned upward and landed on the statue-esque scoreboard operator, who stood frozen and stared upward. The young man was paying zero attention to the game on the field. Walnut's hands trembled. He tilted the binoculars higher, higher, and even higher. He was suspended in time for an alarming second and then yelled, "Holy mother of Lee Harvey Oswald." Walnut's hands locked, and his joints stiffened like a corpse. He dropped the binoculars to the ground, shattering the front lenses as they tumbled beneath the bench in the next row. He looked to his right and saw Luke flying down the stairs toward the fence behind home plate with vigorous strides. "I told you, Luke. I told you this was gonna happen." Walnut boasted as he regained motion in his extremities. Walnut scurried to follow and knocked over the same drunk Luke had shoved moments earlier. The man had only just made it back to his unsteady feet before falling back over the bench and into a puddle of spilled beer and soda. "Didn't I tell you this was gonna happen?"

CHAPTER 4
THE CROWD GOES WILD

Penny stood facing the outfield, and she took in a deep breath—for, she was just moments away from the day she'd been dreaming of since the first grade. One more pitch and she'd be the softball version of Bob Gibson, with her name etched in the Nebraska School Activity Association record books for all eternity. She adjusted her cap and stooped down to pick up the rosin bag. Its weight was somehow lighter than it had been earlier on in the game, like a feather in her hands. She tossed the rosin about and patty-caked it off her palm and then off the back of her knuckles, drying up the chalky beads of sweat. Her hands resembled those of a baker's covered in a coating of flour. She entrenched her cleats into the soft dirt below in preparation for one final encounter.

The sounds and buzz of softball surrounded Penny as she took a long, deep breath. She heard chants and playful banter on the field between teammates; her coach as he clapped from the dugout, barked orders to the infielders, and directed them to shift; and the fans who had created quite the frenzy— a subtle mix of obnoxious screams and uproarious cries of jubilation. But over the top of all of that, Penny detected a noise that did not belong—one that overpowered even the blaring rock ballad and percussion of feet stomping against metal bleacher seats. She heard a low, deep rumble in the distance and looked down at the earth beneath her feet and saw sediment quaking. Instinctively, Penny turned her attention to the sky. She glared out and cocked her head to the side and eyed a dozen black specks on the horizon that tore through the clouds and was heading straight toward her. Parents' cheers quickly started to wane as the reverberation grew nearer.

"Penny!" Luke yelled from behind. "Penny, get off the field!"

Penny nearly jumped out of her shoes. Luke's voice was different from what she'd heard before. There was distress in his call, and the way he'd said her name startled her. She spun back and spotted Luke. He stood at the dugout fence with his fingers interlaced around the chain links, skin white to the bone as he constricted his grip.

"RUN!" Luke yelled again. "Come to me. Now!"

Out of nowhere, an air-raid siren sounded. An older woman covered her ears. A baby started to cry. Penny whipped back toward the black specks as they charged toward her at lightning speed. With every second, they moved closer, closer, and slowly became more visible. Penny's mouth opened wide. Her chin nearly touched the infield dirt as the figures took shape, and she saw them for what they were—twelve

Xian H-20 stealth bombers with red and yellow stars etched on the wings. She recognized the symbol from her history class: it was the Anti-American Coalition flag. They were made up of a group of countries who dedicated themselves to obliterate the American way of life. And they'd be on her in less than sixty seconds.

Penny dropped the rosin bag between her feet. It landed with a thud and kicked up a canopy of dirt that resembled a miniature powdery mushroom cloud as the bomber bellies opened, ready to unleash a flurry of incendiary cluster bombs.

This would be the moment in a movie where the dramatic music would start to play. Haunting violins and torturous cellos would lament as the composer flailed his arms. Drums would pulsate, resembling an intensifying heartbeat, drawing the viewers in as they'd witness the good people of Sutton scamper toward the exit and dive headlong into their cars. The audience would let out a collective sigh of relief as Walnut would speed away and narrowly escape death by firebomb. Penny and Luke would fall to their knees, locked in a long-overdue embrace, finding a sense of solace in each other as they prepared for the worst... just as the Air Force showed up to save their collective lives. But this was no movie, and the Air Force was nowhere in sight.

The stadium itself had undertaken several remodels, but an effective evacuation route was certainly lacking. Twisting tunnels from the outfield, claustrophobic corridors from behind home plate, and narrow staircases from the terrace section all drained into a lone walkway that fed the main concourse and stadium exits: a plumber's nightmare. To say this arena of sports entertainment was ill-equipped to handle emergencies would have been the understatement of a lifetime. Would he not soon be a stain on a wall, the fire marshal indeed would have lost his license after today.

While some fans scaled the walls in a desperate attempt to flee the confines, others took their chances with the main exit. A stampede of softball players and fans shrieked and tried to claw their way into the singular, small tunnel. The first to escape were off to the races. They sprinted for their cars, pushed, and shoved their way across the dirt and gravel lot; a slew of moms and dads dragged their little ones along. In particular, one man had a set of infants under each arm, hauling them away as if they were cheap luggage. Penny, still on the field, jostled her way past her teammates and tried to escape through the dugout. She kept her eyes locked on Luke, who remained on the other side of the dugout fence.

"Move, Penny," Luke said. He waved her on as if she needed telling.

"I'm trying!" Penny yelled as a thunderous percussion erupted behind her. The first bomb hit and took out dozens down the right-field line. Blood-curdling screams sounded out in philharmonic pain. Penny and others around her fell to the ground and covered their heads as smoke and debris instantly filled the air. Dirt and rocks were sent airborne and sliced the surface of Luke's arms and ripped through Penny's jersey. Penny turned, and through the haze, she saw the giant green scoreboard and its operator burnt to a crisp; her ears were now ringing. She looked back toward Luke as he barged into the dugout, acting as a one-man rescue crew. Luke, joined by several other coaches and parents, yanked players free one by one, indiscriminate of jersey color, filing them out like a factory worker manning the conveyor belt. Finally, he grabbed Penny by the forearm and pulled her to her feet.

"Hey," she whined as Luke threw her over his shoulder and carried her up the stairs like a caveman. Typically Penny didn't give a damn what others thought. Still, having to be carried like a helpless child, no matter the situation, was nothing short of humiliating. "Put me down." Penny kicked and wiggled her way free just as they stalled behind the fleeing masses; another log jam of flesh about to burn as two of the bombers turned to make their pass.

"Luke, Penny, over here!" Penny spun around and saw Walnut standing a few sections away toward the left-field foul pole. He hailed them over like a frantic air-traffic controller. Penny followed Luke's eyes as they danced back and for between Walnut and the sea of humanity, trying to escape through the constricting concourse exit. Penny looked down as Luke grabbed her arm and moved in Walnut's direction.

"But the exit," Penny protested and gave the concourse a desperate glance. They were so close. *Why are we not going to the exit*, she thought. "You wanna follow him? Walnut? And go in the actual opposite direction of where we wanna be?" Penny rattled off.

"You're gonna have to trust me," Luke said.

"Am I?" Penny questioned as they shoved their way through the logjam of proverbial sitting ducks. She was on Luke's heels as they hopped over bleachers, still littered with soft drinks, beer, popcorn, half-eaten nachos, and ice cream served in souvenir helmet bowls. They weaved past a fleeing family who was in such a state of shock that they were running toward the flames. Penny stopped as Luke reached a railing that separated the lower level from the second tier, directly below Walnut's position. Luke grabbed the top bar, looked back, and extended his hand.

"You first," Luke said, ready to hoist her up. Only she didn't reciprocate.

"Luke," said Penny with a breathy exhale. "Do you hear that?" She turned away from him and took a few steps in the direction of the left-field bleachers. She knew that they should run, get to whatever safety Walnut had in mind, but there was a sound that called out to her. A hyperventilating plea reminded her of how she used to cry when Roach would beat her mother. Luke must have heard it too because he moved to her side and followed her gaze to the bleachers' fifth row. Penny's heart nearly dissolved on the spot as she saw a screaming toddler of no more than two years old, decked out in John Deere footie pajamas. The fire from the first blast severely burned the boy's cherub-like face. His hair was scorched, and blood poured from a hole where his right arm was supposed to be. With his left arm still intact, he clutched the lifeless fingers of his deceased mother, who had most certainly been trampled before she was burned to death. "He's just a little kid," she whispered. Penny looked up at Luke.

Judging by his expression, he knew what she was thinking. They couldn't leave the boy alone. Penny tried to decipher the look on Luke's face and figure out the thoughts going through his brain. *"Would he hop onto the field? Scale the wall? Or would he take a long way around through the stands? And what would he do when he got to the boy? Would he carry him back here first? Would he stop the bleeding?"* And then an unforgivably morbid thought crossed Penny's mind. *"Would Luke end the boy's pain?"* Judging by the pool of blood and the glossy look in the boy's eyes, even Penny knew the youngster was on borrowed time. Time they did not have if they wanted live to see tomorrow.

"Get down!" cried Walnut with a trembling screech.

A massive flash blinded them, followed by a deafening blast as another bomb made contact. The explosion was so violent that Penny almost bit off her tongue as it lifted her and Luke off the ground and threw them into the concrete wall of the lower tier. The detonation created a gust of heat, so scolding hot and ferocious that it caused the very hairs on their arms to singe.

Penny landed with a crash and clasped her hands over her ears as a high-pitched ringing pierced her eardrums. She turned over and inspected the carnage. Terror acted as a magnet and begged her attention; no, demanded it. The reflection in her eyes painted a picture of sheer horror, a front-row view of the unthinkable. An orange and black wave of fire shred across half of the ball field as it incinerated spectators in the stands and the concourse, the same concourse route Penny begged Luke to take only moments ago. The blast submerged its victims in a twelve-hundred-degree inferno. The twisted flame consumed them one by one. It burned like the stream of fire from the gullet of a dragon until it finally reached the boy in the footie pajamas and cremated him in a literal flash. This would be a moment Penny would never forget. Still, at the same time, it was also quite possibly the most unexpected act of mercy bombing had ever provided a tortured young boy's soul.

The lead bomber banked left and out of sight after delivering the devastating payload. Still, another persisted in making a direct path right toward them. Penny changed her attention from the sky to Luke, who was surprisingly still frozen, stuck in the fetal position. "Luke!" She shook him by his shoulders as his hands covered his ears, and he rocked back and forth manically. *"What the hell was wrong with him?"* Penny spun around and watched as the bomber encroached. There wasn't time for this. She had heard of PTSD on Twitter feeds and in health class, but she'd never experienced it up close and personal like this. Penny stood and searched for Walnut. Sure he was insane, but he might know what to do.

"Walnut!" she shouted, but Walnut was nowhere in sight. Penny dropped down to her knees and landed at Luke's side. Thoughts raced through her mind. She didn't know if she should slap him out of his stupor or wait until this had passed. Unsure of herself, Penny placed her hand on Luke's forearm. She was surprised to feel the tension as his muscles swelled. His grip was strangulating, yet he clung to nothing as if he were seizing. She gently slid her hand up and down his arm and finally decided to try and coax him out of his shell-shocked state with forced compassion.

"Luke, it's me, Penny... Luke. We have to leave. I need you to get up."

"Negative," barked Luke in a firm tone. Penny startled.

"What?"

"I will not abandon my men."

"Men?" Penny asked, thoroughly confused. She didn't know who Luke was yelling at, but it sure as hell wasn't her.

"Respectfully, sir, I don't give a good Goddamn what your orders are," Luke revealed just as his eyes snapped open. He seemed surprised to see Penny before him, almost as if he expected to be somewhere else, with someone else. Penny watched as he glanced down at her quaking hand, which still rested on his arm. Embarrassed, she quickly pulled away. "What happened?" Luke asked.

"Please," Penny mouthed, not knowing what else to say. Her voice cracked. "Please. Luke. Let's just go."

"They're coming back," Walnut announced with haste as he reappeared and lunged over the rail. He slapped his sausage-like fingers down on Luke's shoulder and pulled him to his feet.

Walnut sprinted ahead with astounding haste for a man with his size and lackluster physical prowess. Penny followed after and looked back at Luke, who quickly caught up with them. He didn't seem to notice the blood pouring from a gash in his thigh. Walnut stopped at a steel blue door with paint peeling from years of neglect. A placard labeled **'PRIVATE'** dangled from a solitary screw. Walnut extracted a set of keys from his pocket and drew an accusatory look from Luke, who reached the door. "My buddy works janitorial. We have our flat-earther meetings in here on Tuesdays."

"This isn't the time, Walnut," Luke muttered as Walnut thumbed through the keys and finally landed on a silver one coated with rust.

"This is the one," Walnut said as he inserted the key into the lock and turned the handle over.

Luke ushered Penny into the stadium's administration office that doubled as a storage shed for promotional giveaways from Sutton's former minor league team, The Kernels. He closed the door firmly behind them. Penny took in her surroundings as streams of orange and red light from the glowing flames filtered into the otherwise dim room. She eyed a row of cubicles, a manager's office, and boxes upon boxes of overflowing memorabilia. The bins were chocked full of t-shirts, hats, and foam fingers. They all proudly displayed the team's mascot, an animated ear of corn in a husk that doubled as a military jacket. How any of this was going to help them, Penny had no clue. She saw Luke rummage around and knew he was thinking the same thing. Dust danced in the fluorescent beams. The overhead lights flickered and buzzed as the building shook yet again.

"We can't stay here," Luke said as he dropkicked a stuffed corn husk across the room.

"Don't you think I know that?" Walnut yelled in a panic as he studied the increasingly claustrophobic space. "Just gimme a dang second, will ya?" Walnut paced. "Where are ya…? C'mon, man, where is it?" he asked just as something caught his eye. "There. It's there." Walnut pointed in a frenzy.

Penny followed his stare to a fortified wall, hidden behind a tower of old furniture and even more boxes. Penny moved swiftly just behind Luke and Walnut and sprinted in that direction. Without knowing or questioning why, she mirrored Walnut's actions and began tossing packages aside, trying to figure out what 'There' meant as she foraged through the clutter. Penny launched a box clear across the room. Two-dozen bobbleheads rolled out and clattered on the floor. One of the bobbleheads, a ballplayer in a batter's pose, landed upright, its head wobbled with a crooked smile.

"You brought us in here to die for bobbleheads?" Penny questioned, incensed, as she ran her fingers through her hair.

"Walnut?" Luke growled.

"I didn't–We ain't gonna die–I mean… Behind the boxes and shelves. There's another door. Or at least, there should be," Walnut stammered.

"There *should* be?" Penny challenged. Doubt and fear started to set in. She wanted to rage. "How I bout I pick up one of these bobbleheads and see how far I can shove it up your–"

"Penny, enough," Luke barked. "Another door to where?" he said to Walnut.

"You'll see. It's behind here. Just help me move these shelves, will ya?" grumbled Walnut as he nervously slid the containers around until he saw it. "It's here. See. It's right here. Just like I said," Walnut stood stoic and proud with his hands on his hips like a conquering soldier.

Penny ran to Walnut's side. "Then how about helping us again, General Patton."

Luke frantically ripped boxes, rugs, floor mats, and old uniforms from the shelves. The trio rabidly tore everything in her path until a hole opened up and gave way for Penny to see another door behind the mess. Walnut was right. But where did it lead?

Walnut pulled on the door handle. "It's jammed."

"Here, let me," Luke said as he nudged Walnut out of the way. Luke wrung his fingers around the handle, braced his left foot against the wall, and jerked. The veins in his arms ballooned as his muscles bulged from beneath his shirt. With a hoarse grunt, Luke pried the door open. Paint, debris, and particles of wood splintered, and finally, the door swung open; after being nearly torn from its hinges. Luke backed away and wiped the dust from his blistering red hands. He looked up and saw Penny stare at the door in disappointment.

"Perfect," Penny said. "This what we came here for, Walnut?" She shook her head as she examined a janitor's closet. A three by three-foot space with two mops, a bucket, a grimy floor drain, and Playboy magazine covers plastered from floor to ceiling.

"No, no, no... It has to be here," Walnut said as he paced the room.

Penny set off to the opposite wall and leaped atop a metal chair. She inched upward on her tiptoes and peeked outside. The people that survived the blasts thus far continued to rush toward the main concourse. It had turned into a stampede. Men, women, and children used human beings as stepping stones. Soles of shoes crunched and crushed limbs into one another. Bodies bent and molded into an unimaginable conglomerate of death.

A black figure lacerated low-hanging clouds and smoke. It was another bomber. Before Penny reacted, a flash of light blinded her, followed by yet another destructive blast. The ground shook again. Penny was thrown from the chair and crashed down on boxes full of printers, keyboards, computer mice, and other accessories. The last explosion knocked out the power entirely. The room was filled with an impenetrable darkness as the walls started to crumble around them.

"Penny," Luke called out.

"I can't see anything," Penny answered.

She heard a scuffling, then was blinded by a beam of light as Luke flipped his phone's flashlight on.

"Your flip phone has a flashlight?" said Penny.

"Take it." Luke handed the phone to Penny. "We need to get outta here."

"Luke, I'm telling you we're in the right spot; we just gotta find the door," Walnut insisted as he pulled an LED headband from his pocket and pulled it snug over his massive head.

"Why do you keep a headlamp in your pocket?" Penny asked, not wanting to know the answer.

"What door, Walnut? All I see is trash, trash, and more trash," Luke said as he turned side to side.

As Luke and Walnut bickered over the legitimacy of Walnut's intel and claims of a hidden door, Penny used Luke's phone light to survey the area. She stepped over boxes, chairs and hurdled obstacles as she made her way to the manager's office. She aimed the beam at a strand of Ethernet cables that pretzeled around convoluted electrical tubing. The wires ran from a server bay, up a wall, and into the ceiling. This room was new compared to the structure of the building and wired post-construction. Penny exited the office, with the flashlight still fixated on the wire strand that zigzagged across the ceiling, as smaller strands branched out and supplied power and connectivity to individual work stations.

"How do you know it's here?" Luke asked, frustrated to the point his temples were on fire.

"My guy. He gave me the keys in case of a day like this. Said there was a bunker."

"Your guy? What guy would that be?"

"You know how this works, Luke," Walnut said. "I can't give the names of my source."

"Source? Walnut, you own a hardware store in the middle of nowhere. You ain't got no source."

"Stop it!" Penny interrupted. Luke and Walnut's heads whipped in her direction. "Will you two old ladies shut the hell up and help me move this?" Penny stood in front of the longest wall in the room. Before it sat a set of shelves, easily twenty feet long, it stretched floor to ceiling, filled with cobweb-collecting containers. Luke watched as Penny directed the streak of light from the phone at the bundle of wires. The strand snaked down the wall and tunneled into what looked to be another room behind the shelf. "There's the door back here. I can see it behind the boxes."

Luke and Walnut locked eyes.

"Don't you even say it," Luke said.

"I told ya so," Walnut said.

Luke snarled, turned to the shelves, and grabbed ahold of the upright. "Move, Penny."

Penny did as he asked as backed away slowly as Luke and Walnut heaved and hoed. They rocked the shelving back and forth until its momentum carried it enough to topple over, causing a flurry of packing dust to fill the air. Penny coughed and choked on the dust as it permeated throughout her lungs. Luke bound over the shelves and covered his mouth with his sleeve. He lifted his knees higher with each step like one would during a boot camp tire drill.

"Keys," Luke said with a muffled voice as Walnut tossed him the key ring.

"The black one. I–I think it's the black one," Walnut said.

"There are *five* black ones, Walnut."

Penny slowly turned her head away from Luke and Walnut. She shined the flashlight to the ceiling. A light fixture started to rattle. Shards of rutted sheetrock and debris began to fall and hit the ground, cascading across the linoleum floor.

"Penny, on me. I need that light!" Luke said.

"But the ceiling," Penny tried to warn them as a roar grew louder. The rumbling intensified.

"Now, Penny!" Luke screamed.

Penny whipped back to him, charged toward the door, flashlight stream aimed right at his hands. Luke fumbled through the keys. He tried one after another after another, yet nothing worked.

"Wait. Dadgummit. The black ones are for *my* fallout shelter."

"Walnut," Luke gritted his teeth."

"I swear to God, Luke, I'm gonna kill him if we get out of here," said Penny.

Luke hit Walnut with a sobering stare. "Not if I kill him first."

"Try the one with the spade on top," Walnut shot back.

CLICK – the key fit. Luke turned and unlocked the door, swung it open, and ushered Penny and Walnut inside just as the office ceiling collapsed behind them.

Penny ran further into the unknown. Further into darkness. Luke was on her tail while Walnut brought up the rear; Penny heard him panting. The flashlight bounced off the floors and walls as she navigated what looked to be an underground maintenance tunnel. Maybe even a makeshift bomb shelter left over from the Cold War or the Iranian nuclear threat of 2023. She ran as fast as her legs would take her and traversed further down, down, down from the surface. She plunged for what felt like hundreds of yards into the earth. The more she ran, the more often she'd check her rear. She feared that one of these times, she'd turn and find herself alone. Maybe Luke and Walnut would get lost or veer down another path. Or perhaps the walls would collapse and isolate her.

BOOM! The world shook yet again; only this time, the impact was much closer, and it came from directly above. The shockwave sent Penny stumbling forward as she slipped and face-planted on the pavement. Luke's phone fell from her fingers and spun out of sight. She shielded her head as the earth pulsated around her. *"Was this it? Was this tunnel going to be her tomb?"* She curled into a ball. She wanted to cry. No. She needed to cry. So many things were left undone and so many things left unsaid. Before Penny's emotions got the best of her, Luke pulled her in close and held her tight against his body, shielding her. Chunks of concrete rained down beside them.

"I got you," said Luke in a soft voice.

His warm breath tickled the back of her neck and sent a surge of chills down her spine, as he acted as a six-foot-two security blanket. If this was the end, at least she wasn't alone. She closed her eyes and clenched her fists tighter and cringed with each blast that would follow—never knowing which one would bring the crumbling earth down upon them. Penny felt the heat from the surface above as a blast of air surrounded her and turned the tunnel into a stovetop. For some peculiar, through all of the chaos, Penny couldn't scream. She couldn't cry. All she could do was burst out into a fit of nervous laughter. A laughter that she, herself, didn't understand and that she was sure Luke wouldn't either. But it only lasted so long, as another blast quickly snapped her back to reality. Luke pulled her in even closer. Walnut panted like an asthmatic in urgent need of a hit of his albuterol inhaler. Yet somehow, Penny was no longer afraid. In her mind, she knew she should be crying like a babbling fool, saying things like I don't want to die, or calling for her momma. But, no. That wasn't her. She wasn't weak. She was going to make it. She needed to survive.

CHAPTER 5
THE LIFE AND DEATH OF NOVALEE BLANKLEY

One Hour Before the Attack

The evening breeze blew and whipped around clean cotton sheets which were pinned to a clothesline. A woman in a white linen dress carried an empty clothes basket. She gingerly walked barefoot down a set of stairs with wobbly wooden planks and exited a two-story brick home as she stepped into a quaint, yet unassuming, back yard. Several stained glass windows reflected brilliant flecks of green, blue, and red against the sheets reflecting that of a kaleidoscope. The woman graciously permitted the warm summer air and long thin blades of green grass to tease and caress the soft skin between her toes as she navigated the perimeter. She hummed a familiar tune, a sort of lullaby, one that she'd sung many times before. Even though it was only a hum, you knew her voice was angelic.

She shifted the basket and tucked it beneath her arm until she reached the edge of the white picket fence that lined the yard, where she set the basket down on the delicate soil. The woman rested her arms atop the white fence post and picked at flakes of dry, peeling paint. She tossed them skyward and watched them flutter down in the breeze like the winged seed of a maple tree.

A steady gust of wind blew through her long, blonde hair, causing it to swirl around like a funnel cloud. Individual strands acted as hundreds of tiny fingers that flicked against her jawline. She drew a white, floral-print ponytail scarf from her wrist and placed it between her clenched teeth. She massaged the soft, delicate strands of hair into a bunch, removed the scarf from her mouth, and tied her hair back into a messy bun. Her eyes squinted in the breeze as she watched as the grass and flowers beyond the property flatten in waves with each billowing gust, only to spring back up. The woman inhaled the welcoming scents of summer, an eclectic mix of sunflowers, bar-b-que, and laundry detergent. Her olive skin soaked up the sun. A constellation of freckles plotted a pattern like Taurus in the night sky just beneath her haunting greenish-grey eyes. She was breathtaking.

The woman's ears perked up as she heard the buzz and roar of a crowd followed by bass resonating from speakers alongside the booming voice of the public address announcer from the stadium. She gazed out at the horizon and saw the outfield lights tower majestically over the softball field. She heard the entire town cheer for her daughter from a mile away, and at that very moment, Jess was sure that Penny stood atop the mound like a triumphant heroine. She envisioned her little girl carrying the weight of the town on her able shoulders as she sliced through batters like a warm knife through butter. Jess imagined Luke's awkward posture, the half-sitting, half-standing pose, yet not fully prepared to commit to either. She even knew that Walnut would be nearby or most likely attached to Luke's hip, like a lost puppy. Jess pulled her pink smartphone from the basket and held it near her lips. "Text Luke: 'I hear them cheering for our girl. Oh, and I got a surprise for you when you get home'."

The automated, robotic voice repeated back, "Ok. Texting Luke, I hear them cheering for our girl. Oh, and I got a surprise for you if you eat bones. Ready to send?"

She laughed, shook her head, and tried again. This time the Siri clone got her message right. Jess hit the bright flashing green send button and set the phone on the squared end of the fence post as she stared into the distance once more. Tonight's sky reminded Jess of the day she and Luke had first met.

Jess's car had just broken down on the side of the freeway as the July sunset scorched down upon her. The dying light radiated over the horizon like God herself was closing her eyes. The glow of fireflies began to pepper the sky, like twinkling stars, as they hovered over a row of American Elms. Jess was miles from the nearest gas station, her cell phone was dead, and not a car was in sight. She laughed at the irony as a twangy country-western song ran through her head, for this moment was just as bleak. That was until a beat-to-hell pickup truck barreled down the road. Jess took this as a sign from the heavens as she heard her favorite George Jones ballad, 'He Stopped Loving Her Today', blast from the truck's stereo. As the pickup truck moved nearer, the rumble of the engine drowned out the music, and the engine sounded as if it had contracted a nasty case of whooping cough.

Jess knew time was of the essence and held a rushed internal debate of how best to get the attention of her would-be rescuer. Would she hail the stranger down like a cabbie on the bustling streets of Manhattan? Or would Jess use her womanly charm and hike up the hem of her skirt and flash the temptatious golden-brown skin of her inner thigh as it glistened with sweat? While clearly, the latter was the more attractive choice of the two, Jess's history of meeting disreputable men made her wonder if she shouldn't go with the former. With her mind made up, Jess slipped a handkerchief from her pocket and began to wave it wildly about as the steam from her radiator billowed in the background.

The driver slowed to a near crawl as the truck brakes whined like a dying mule and the driver-side window rolled down in a slow, jerky fashion. Jess gasped and blushed like a schoolgirl when she made eye contact with the driver, Luke. He cocked a partial grin and flicked the brim of his cowboy hat that sat just above his brow.

"Ma'am," he said in a low, deep voice like a redneck knight in shining armor.

By the time Luke was nearly done working on Jess's car, the full moon had illuminated the highway and acted as a spotlight that shined down directly over him. Jess watched intently and wrenched her hands together, her palms and fingers covered in a sweat that had nothing to do with the oppressive heat.

Occasionally, Jess would catch Luke steal a glance in her direction, which caused a flurry of butterflies to flit about in her stomach. Something was simply enchanting about his country-boy charm and movie-star dimples. And Jess certainly didn't mind the way his jeans fit or how his shredded biceps bulged out of the rolled-up sleeves of a tee-shirt that was two sizes too small.

Jess's entire body melted, and her face flushed with red as he beckoned her over to show her the oil line on her dipstick.

"You should be good to go," Luke said as he replaced the dipstick and slammed the hood shut. "Probably should change that stuff, or at least fill it up every once in a while."

"I feel so stupid," Jess chuckled. She reached into her knock-off designer purse that overflowed with a couple of loose bills, a travel pack of tampons, and a half-used container of ChapStick. "Let me give you something for your trouble."

"Nonsense." Luke gently grabbed her by the hand and looked longingly into her eyes. "I don't want your money."

Instinctively Jess peered at his ring finger as his hand slid away from hers. His touch caused a shiver to travel down the entirety of her spine. Jess cracked a hopeful smile for, Luke lacked a wedding band or the accompanying tan line from one recently removed.

"Well, I have to repay your kindness somehow, sir. Spending all night out here with me and all." Jess paused apprehensively. "I'm sure that your wife is missing you terribly?"

"First of all, ma'am, you can call me Luke, not sir. And second, I don't have missus."

"Okay then, Luke. How about a girlfriend?" Jess teasingly bit her bottom and fidgeted with the seam of her dress.

"I mean, I wouldn't call this a solid first date, but if you really wanna be my girlfriend, I won't object."

Jess snorted in laughter and blushed bright enough to reenergize the sun.

Ω

Three years later, Jess recounted that moment as if it were yesterday. A random encounter with the man of her dreams set into motion by some sort of divine being. She knew then and there; everything was about to change. She had finally caught the break she'd so desperately deserved. She would permanently be able to get out from beneath the literal and figurative boot of her ex-husband, Roach. Jess was whole again, and aside from being Penny's mother, her life had a purpose.

As the sun sank, Jess stared out into the distance. She soaked up the sounds of the stadium and wished she were there with Penny and Luke. Jess imagined each pitch as it happened in real-time until she was jolted out of her daze by a ragged voice that came from the house, a voice that faintly called her name.

"Jessica?" the voice probed again, this time even louder and full of anguish.

Jess backed through the back door of the home and into the kitchen. She scanned apprehensively, then craned her neck and peered down a long, lonely hallway.

"Help me!"

63

"Missus Novalee?" Jess responded with haste. She hurried into the sitting area as her eyes darted laterally. The room looked like an Antiques Road Show episode after the Royal Family's private collection had been raided. There were shelves chocked full of tea sets and silver spoons. The family who owned this two-thousand-square-foot palace had outfitted the walls with proportionate oil paintings of Prince Charles, Princess Diana, and the Queen herself. The images were majestic, though a bit on the creepy side. As guests moved throughout the room, they often claimed the eyes in the paintings would follow them. Twin bookshelves stood along either side of a picture window, overcrowded with various editions of the King James Bible, Shakespearean classics, and other sixteenth-century literary works. Framed doilies scattered the remaining space on the walls. Jess often thought that whoever designed this portion of the home either had an affliction for decorative floral mats or hated wallpaper with a passion.

"You must hurry," the voice lamented.

Jess turned her head instinctively, like a bloodhound who had caught a scent. She rushed into the living room, recently converted into a fully-equipped hospice space. There was a bed beneath a large crucifix with a dry and crackled palm branch tucked neatly behind it. Beside the bed sat a high-back companion recliner and a rolling TV tray topped with warm stew and a half-empty water bottle. In the corner of the room, motionless and hunched over the side of a wheelchair, sat an older woman with greyish-blue hair. She wore a dress that looked to be a remnant of the twenties—the eighteen-twenties.

Jess's eyes opened wide in panic. She slapped her hand over her mouth in shock as she looked down and saw the woman's rigored fingers outstretched and reaching for something that was barely beyond her grasp. Jess imagined the worst. Thoughts of fear and shame filled her mind: Novalee Blankley, the last in a long line of descendants of Sutton's founding fathers, *dead* on her watch. Suddenly Jess's feelings made a hard right turn toward guilt. Surely this was all her fault. Novalee had fretted and sniveled more than once while Jess daydreamed like a teenager as a human life hung in the balance. Jess had worked her butt off to achieve her nursing license and had suffered through working two jobs while also attending medical school. She'd beaten out fifteen other candidates for this position and had cared for Novalee for a smidge under two years. With no other living Blankley sons, daughters, or grandchildren, the talks of scandal would inevitably start to run rampant. Townsfolk would transform into rumor mongers overnight, like a werewolf at the sight of the full moon. There'd be a witch-hunt accusing Jess of murder, or at best, negligence, a shared belief she was vying for the Blankley fortune.

Before another Kübler-Ross stage of grief slithered into Jess's mind, Novalee let out an unexpected moan that bordered on a death rattle. She was alive. Jess hurried to her side and lifted Novalee upright in the wheelchair. She put her fingers to Novalee's windpipe and checked her pulse.

"What in blazes are you doing?" Novalee questioned with a raspy yet regal voice as she pried Jess's clammy fingers away from her neck. To hear Novalee speak, one would suspect she hailed from just

North of London. The truth is, Novalee was an avid Downton Abbey fan who'd only stepped foot out of the state of Nebraska a single time in her ninety-seven years. And that voyage only took place after Novalee fell asleep on a Greyhound bus to visit her sister in Lincoln and missed her stop. Ironically, the bus driver woke her six hours later in New London, Iowa, surrounded by what she lovingly referred to as foreigners.

"Oh, Missus Blankley. You gave me such a fright. I–I thought–"

"You thought what?"

"Well, that you had..." Jess refused to bring herself to say it.

"That I had tragically perished in my boudoir?" Novalee said with a flair for the dramatics of it all, as she had no qualms about filling in the gaps.

"It's just you called for help. You yelled for me. You said to hurry, and then I saw you doubled over."

"Indeed," Novalee declared matter-of-factly. "I dropped the clicker. I can't reach it, and I absolutely *must* change this channel." Novalee motioned toward a nearby table where the remote control had tumbled to the floor. "This program is ever so dreadful."

After Jess fetched the remote for Novalee, she headed upstairs to the bedroom. She carefully tucked Novalee's linens away at the bottom of a timeless oak armoire. As she reached into a full clothes basket to her immediate left, she pulled out a pair of underwear; her finger came in slight contact with an old light brown stain on the backside, which was obviously –

"Shit!" Jess exclaimed. She looked around the room at the treasures and curiosities collected over the years, acquired by the Blankley fortune. Jess eyed exotic trinkets from the Silk Road, from Bombay to Rome, and back to Shanghai. She looked at all of this and reminded herself that no matter how rich or famous one becomes, in the end, we all inevitably go to the bathroom in our underwear and need someone else to clean it up.

Jess tossed the soiled bottoms into a lily-white waste bag that smelled of lilacs. She reached into the laundry basket for another article of clothing when she once again heard Novalee lament woefully from the first floor below. Truth be told, most of Jess's days went like this.

"Jessica," Novalee's voice bleated like a goat.

"What now?" sighed Jess.

"The picture box is broken again." Novalee often referred to the television as the picture box, as if it made her sound more sophisticated.

"Be right there," Jess assured as she closed the armoire doors and tromped down the stairs making it blatantly apparent that the weight of each step emphasized her frustration.

Upon making her way back into the living room, Jess saw Novalee's hands cupped over her ears. Jess winced as she heard the source of Novalee's discomfort. There was a banshee-like shriek coming from the television speakers. The sound was so intrusive that Novalee was near cross-eyed.

"Don't just stand there, darling. Fix it... Fix it!" Novalee demanded as she pointed toward the television. Her face scrunched in irritation that caused her wrinkles to bunch together like the Himalayas on a topographical globe.

Jess stammered toward the television, her hands clasped tight over her eardrums. But before she reached it, the squeals and static ceased and were replaced by a silent screen lined with bars of color. Jess and Novalee cautiously lowered their guard just as the mechanical voice of an emergency broadcast announcer called out, "Attention. If you are in the following counties, please seek immediate shelter. Webster, Adams, Hall, Hamilton, Clay…" With a sinking thud, the television, along with the overhead lights, went dark.

Desperate to troubleshoot the situation, Jess moved to the light switch on the far wall and flicked it up and down a few times.

"Aren't the tornado tests usually on the first Friday of the month?" Novalee inquired as her chapped, flaking lips quaked and fingers trembled.

"They are."

"But, it's Thursday," Novalee said.

"It is." Jess crossed to the windows, unlocked the two latches that kept the right side secure, and lifted it open. She stuck her head outside as the whipping wind gyred the curtains around her like a cyclone. Jess pulled herself back in, swiped loose strands of hair from her face, and looked back at Novalee with uncertainty in her eyes. "Maybe it'll swing north toward Henderson. It seems like every time winds pick up like this, it ends up swinging north."

Just as Jess was about to release the shades, a flash of blinding light pierced the sky, and a loud boom rattled the earth and clattered Novalee's antiquities. Fine china fell from the shelves in the dining room hutch. A cookie jar toppled end over end to the floor in the kitchen. Lady Diana's priceless bust fell from the mantle and broke in two, drawing a horrified gasp from Novalee. "Di. What have they done to you?"

Before she jumped, screamed, or even reacted, Jess was caught off-guard by the air-raid siren that let out a cold and unforgiving scream.

Novalee cupped her hands over her ears once more.

Jess rushed back to Novalee's side. *"What the hell was going on? That boom. It wasn't thunder. And the light. No way was that lightning."* Jess had lived in Tornado Alley for most of her life. She'd spent more horrified hours in tornado shelters than she'd care to remember. When she was young, her family lost everything to an F5 that destroyed her hometown of Joplin, Missouri. But this... This was much worse. Her first thought raced to a possible malfunction in the town's power plant. Names and faces of friends and family cycled through her mind. *"But wait,"* she thought; *"the blast, it was from the west. The power plant was due east... And the hospital? The refinery too...?"* There was no telling. Not from here. And not with Novalee screaming bloody murder with her hands still clasped over her ears.

"Make it stop. Make it stop," Novalee yelped.

"Let's get you downstairs," Jess yelled out as she gripped the handles of Missus Novalee's wheelchair. She knew she had to make a decision and fast.

"To the cellar?" Novalee looked at Jess nervously. "I haven't been down there in ages."

"It's fine. Just a precaution," Jess said as she wheeled her toward a door near the kitchen.

"A what?" Novalee refused to relent the kung-fu grip over her eardrums.

Jess pried a couple of Novalee's away from her ear. "A precaution," she said in a slow and semi-condescending tone.

"Precaution? Do you have any idea how much this blouse costs?" Novalee asked. "There's probably mold, and critters, and heavens-to-Betsy who knows else what down there." Novalee pushed Jess away. As old and frail as she was, she'd at times show the strength of a Silverback gorilla.

Jess swung the cellar door open and moved back behind Novalee. "I don't have time to fight with you right now, Missus Novalee. Raise your arms so I can get you on the lift."

Novalee shook her head defiantly as Jess attempted to maneuver her hands and arms beneath Novalee's armpits.

"I won't go," Novalee declared in a firm tone. Basements had always haunted Novalee. Maybe it was due to childhood nightmares and the fiery face of her menacing furnace. Perhaps it was the dank cellar smell that reminded her of death and her own mortality. Or possibly, it was because of her husband, Reginald Francis Blankley.

One Sunday afternoon, Reginald went down to the basement to work on his model trains. Eleven hours later, he came back up in a body bag after Novalee found him lifeless on the floor after suffering a massive heart attack.

"Missus Novalee, I must insist."

Novalee shook her head no like a rabid Chihuahua fighting over a squeaking chew-toy.

"I promise I won't let anything happen to you," Jess said in a calm, reassuring voice. "Besides, you're the only client I have left," Jess said sarcastically.

"It's a wonder as to why that is," Novalee said with a scornful smirk.

A second blast shook the ground. Dust whirled downward as it fell from the ceiling and light fixtures. Jess lurched toward the front door like a drunk at a pub crawl. She opened the storm door wide and watched in horror as an amber glow reflected in her eyes. A mushroom cloud loomed over the town, five hundred feet high. Jess closed the door in a state of shock, and without a word, Novalee gave her a knowing look. She was right. They needed to move. Jess marched back to Novalee, scooped her off the wheelchair, and hoisted her onto the lift. Frantically, Novalee fiddled with the lift controls and pressed the lever that lowered her into the cellar. She hung on for dear life as if the two-mile-per-hour contraption was a ninety-degree plunge on a Six Flags roller-coaster. The lift motor whined and clanked with every inch of descent. Jess walked alongside the lift, wheelchair folded and tucked under her arm, as the lift moved further into the darkness. If the situation were different, she might have even laughed at the nervous twitch in Novalee's left eye as it flapped uncontrollably.

"There you go. That wasn't so bad, right?" Jess asked, without really wanting an answer, as the lift stopped at the base of the stairwell. She unfolded the wheelchair and shimmied Novalee back onto it.

Novalee's head whipped about in the near-pitch-black nothingness. Only a single strand of daylight peeked through a crack in the foundation. With a grunt, Jess pushed Novalee beneath an overhead bulb. Jess disappeared for a moment and grunted from the shadows. The sound of a chain pulley echoed with each groan until a generator engine kicked on. Jess returned to Novalee's side, reached up, and plucked the dangling light chain between her fingertips, pulled down, and showcased the eerie cellar with a pop and a click. Crumbling concrete walls surrounded them. Reginald's train set still remained intact. It was covered in dust and dirt and served as nothing more than a cobweb-enclosed breeding ground for arachnids. A brown-recluse scampered from the roof of the train's caboose onto the track. Mildew stains streaked the floor and ceiling, and a putrid smell snaked its way into Jess's nostrils as she grimaced and covered her mouth.

Somehow the sights and smells of the cellar, topped with Novalee's incessant whining, nearly caused Jess to forget about the air-raid siren. It was like falling asleep with the radio on, the moment in between deep breaths, in between still and restful REM, where you stop hearing the music and fall into a dream. That was until a third, and the more violent blast hit the town. The shrill of the siren echoed once again. The house groaned and shifted. Even more dust particles came raining down upon them. A water pipe cracked as a steady stream of cold water began to spray overhead, misting directly onto Novalee's blue hair.

"Look what you've done now," Novalee said.

"What I've done?"

"Yes. Jessica. You've forced me into this pit, and now I'm submerged in sewage."

"Sewage? It's a cold water pipe."

Novalee sniffed her moist skin. Maybe Jess was right, but that still didn't wipe the look of disdain from her face.

A fourth blast hit. Somehow this was even closer than the previous three. But with it came a wave of heat that overtook them, even from deep within the cellar. Hot air burst through a dirt-soiled window and shattered it into a million pieces.

"What's happening?" Jess questioned as more glass crashed down from the floors above. The ground rumbled and quaked. *"What is this? What has she done in bringing them down here? Were they going to be buried alive? These shockwaves, heat, and raw power of the explosions felt as if an earthquake, tornado, and wildfire struck all at once. Was it the end of days that Father McCullough had preached about in his Sunday sermons, sans the rapture horns? Or was the siren the horn itself?"*

"We're under attack, aren't we?" Novalee speculated.

"Don't be ridiculous," Jess replied. As soon as the words left her lips, Jess realized Novalee was right. They were being bombed. Paranoia ran rampant through Jess's mind, and it all started to make sense. *"But who? Why today? And why here? A cow town in the middle of nothing."* But rather than reach a definite conclusion or finish playing detective, Jess's heart sunk. She had been so worried about Novalee that she hadn't considered Penny or Luke. Jess stared off into nothingness like she was suffering an absence seizure.

Novalee was disappointed in Jess's decision to turn her attention away and somehow was so self-indulged she interrupted out of the blue with anything less than a prioritized query. "Jessica. Did you ring Doctor Cordingly about my Morazopan refill?"

"Call," Jess said as a lightbulb went off in her brain. "I'm sorry, what?"

"The doctor. Did you call? It's been two days. And I don't think you want me to send a letter in the post. You know what happens if I go without my pills. My feet swell. My hands ache. My…"

As Novalee rambled, Jess tuned her out and patted herself down. "My phone. Where's my phone?" she whispered, flipping her pockets inside out in search of her cell phone. They were empty. "Where the heck did I put it?" she questioned. "I'll be right back."

"Right back?" Novalee asked with fear wavering in her voice.

Novalee's skeletal, vein-ridden fingers grasped Jess around her wrist just as Jess started toward the cellar stairs. Jess looked down at Novalee's as her fingers began to cut off the circulation to her hand. Novalee's skin was soft to the touch, like glabrous satin, but her clenching grasp was unrelenting. Their eyes met. Jess saw the distress in Novalee's gaze. "I promise you, I'll be right back," Jess said, exclaiming with as much conviction as she could muster. With a yank, she wriggled free of Novalee's clutches.

The blasts became more frequent and resembled a cadence of a mid-summer thunderstorm, only more intense. Even more of Novalee's collection shattered around her as Jess ran up the stairs and into the living room. Smoke and dust formed a cloud of chaos which she had no choice but to inhale. Her body was going through the motions as she searched the tabletops and under couch cushions for her cell phone, but her mind was blank. She was in auto-pilot, stuck in fight or flight mode, not knowing where she was going next or why, only that she was. She tossed a love seat and searched beneath. There was nothing aside from a couple of French fries, a lone house slipper, and some pocket change.

Jess ran into the kitchen and began rifling through drawers, cabinets, and even the fridge. She flirted nimbly around shards of shattered porcelain floor tiles. Still, there was no phone. Almost embarrassingly, she paused and whipped her attention toward a faded lime green phone mounted to a wall beneath a quartz wall clock. "The landline."

"Jessica. Jessica, I can't breathe down here," Novalee's frantic cries came from the depths of the cellar below, followed by bellowing hoarse coughs.

"Almost done," Jess lied to appease her as she raced toward the phone and lifted it from its base. Jess put the handset to her ear. Dead air. She mashed the switchhook in a desperate attempt to hear a dial tone with no luck whatsoever. "Dammit," Jess huffed as she threw the handset down. It swung back and forth and rattled off the drywall like a tetherball twisting around its pole. "Missus Novalee, my cell. Have you seen it?"

"Your what?"

"My cell phone."

"The pink contraption you're always fiddling with?"

"Yes. That one. Have you seen it? The house phone is dead, and I don't remember having it on me since I was—" At that moment, Jess's eyebrows raised knowingly. "Outside." Jess spun in a flash and started toward the back door when a noise grabbed her attention like a vicious chokehold. A boom resonated from the front of the home. But this boom was unlike the ones that rocked the house, and it didn't quite fit in with air-raid sirens, glass shattering, and explosions. Instead, Jess heard a primal techno thumping that resembled a rapid heartbeat, a cacophony of orchestrated chaos with trunk-rattling bass that came from a vehicle. Soon after, the sound of car brakes squealed to a grinding halt as gravel crunched beneath tires.

Jess hurried to the front door in hopes of seeing Luke and Penny. She peeked out the peephole and saw a cloud of crushed gravel swirling. A tan and white two-tone, beat-up '84 Ford Bronco parked mere feet from the front staircase. Tire marks had dug three inches into the loose soil and shredded fresh sodding. Rough, grim bullet holes with scorched edges riddled the Bronco's grill. The vehicle was abandoned with music from the rickety stereo system still pumping, and all the passenger doors were swung wide open. The engine purred and grumbled as steam rose from beneath the hood. Jess scanned the property; her eyes darted from fence line to fence line, but no one was in sight. Then, without warning, glass shattered from behind and jolted Jess from her surveillance. Someone was breaking in. She made a beeline to the front closet and hoisted herself up on the tips of her toes. She reached and rummaged about deep within the top shelf. Jess stretched and grunted and willed herself taller and longer but still didn't clutch what her fingers were so desperately trying to grasp.

"Come on," Jess exhaled, flustered and frustrated. She realized she was a hair short of her target and dropped to her knees with a thud on the hardwood floor. Like a dog digging for a bone, Jess tore through shoeboxes and downed overcoats and finally emerged with a small step stool. Jess set the stool beneath her, made her way back to her feet, and stood on the top step. Again she lunged with outstretched arms as she reached and reached and finally gripped her prize, a Remington 870 TAC-14 shotgun. She stepped off the stool and racked the breaching cannon. Somehow this small-town American beauty looked completely natural with cold steel in her hands. It was apparent that Jess was no stranger to guns. Her father, Emmitt, was a professionally trained redneck who used to take her hunting every autumn. Jess bagged Canadian Geese and Northern Pintails before most kids her age were riding bikes without training wheels. But this situation was far different from hunting waterfowl, and the nerves started to kick in.

With jittery hands, Jess started toward the back of the house, toward the noise. Anxiety spider-webbed through her veins like a plague. Her heart pounded through her chest, but at the same time, her senses perked up as the adrenaline kicked in. The kitchen door handle shook and rattled just as another bang came from the side of the house. Someone was trying to kick down the door to the sun porch. An instant later, footsteps came from the roof above. Whoever or whatever was out there was surrounding her. The sounds amplified in her eardrums—an intermittent dissonance of paranoia. Jess had to calm herself. Someway. Somehow. She closed her eyes for a moment and let the fear take over. After a few deep breaths, she dismissed as much as possible and reopened her eyes, now filled with a semi-confident rage. After being classically trained in suffering and abuse, Jess was far too accustomed to the terror that would send most running for the hills. She took another deep breath and made her move as she charted a course straight toward the commotion in the kitchen. She slid against the doorframe and peered inward. A gloved hand swung wildly through a broken pane of glass and fumbled for the deadbolt latch.

"I have a gun," Jess announced her presence and warned of her intentions. Three shots rang out in rapid succession. Jess ducked down to avoid a wild spray of bullets.

"So I do," yelled a gruff smoker's voice from the other side of the door.

Jess analyzed and processed the sound of the gunfire like a supercomputer. The shots came from a handgun. Probably a .22. Her dad had a .22. She remembered shooting it at the farm on her sixteenth birthday, the last day she saw her father alive.

Shaking off a painful memory, Jess looked down at her shotgun and knew she had the advantage. Confident in her chances, Jess gave a once-over into the kitchen. A latch clicked. The door unlocked and creaked open cautiously and whined louder with every gaping inch. Jess had to act. As soon as the intruder's boot crunched down on the broken shards of glass from the shattered pane, Jess lunged across the open door frame and unleashed an unforgiving blast from the Remington. Everything seemed like it was in slow-motion as Jess watched the spray of the shotgun shred through the chest of the intruder, propelling the masked man airborne. His body flew against the wall like a ragdoll. Blood spattered and stained the magnolia-covered wallpaper. She staggered to her feet and watched the plus-sized man slide downward, smearing a streak of dark blood behind him, his body covered in urban camo, head to toe, with cutoff sleeves and a skull tattoo that covered the left side of his neck. The .22 handgun lay by his side. Jess kicked it away and hovered over him. He looked pitiable as he gasped for air and choked on his blood. He floundered about like fish stranded atop a deck and tried to speak. She bent down and leaned in close to the man.

As she got closer, Jess's imagination started to run laps around her usually logical mind. *"Who was he? Did she know him, now or in a past life? He didn't look familiar."* But answers to her questions would never come as the rotund marauder coughed and struggled. A calm came over him suddenly, and before he passed, his eyes widened. Only, he wasn't staring at Jess but behind her. With the chaos and bloodlust boiling, she'd nearly forgotten about the other noises. The person at the side of the house. The car out front. The sounds from the roof. Instinctively, Jess spun around and simultaneously ducked out of the way, narrowly missing the wild slash of a machete.

Jess raised her shotgun, ready to unload another round, but before she pulled the trigger, a moment of hesitation sunk in. A look of confusion morphed across her face. The machete-wielding intruder was a girl who was wearing a mask similar to the dead fat man's, who soiled himself on Novalee's kitchen floor. Unlike the fat man, the girl was petite and wasn't a day over seventeen, judging by her build. Behind the girl's dead eyes and expressionless face mask poured long strands of strawberry blonde hair. Her clothes were a mingling of a chic lumberjack. The long sparkling red fingernails that gripped the machete handle looked to be freshly manicured. Jess's mouth dropped in confusion, and her head tilted to the side. The girl saw this. Taking full advantage of Jess's hesitation and apparent disappointment, she lifted the blade high over her head and started to swing downward. Jess froze in a cloud of doubt.

The machete was going to slice straight through the base of her neck. Jess's death was to be a most gruesome execution. As the blade descended, Jess's mind raced yet again. *"None of this made sense. The explosions. The fire. The people breaking into the home of an elderly woman and trying to kill her. For what? Were they related? Was this a robbery? Were people rioting? Was she going to die?"* Jess's eyes began to mist. The thought of leaving her daughter and husband behind became a stark reality as the blade came closer and closer. It was mere inches away from tearing a gash into Jess's flesh, inches away from a violent end.

"No!" Jess yelled. This wasn't going to be the finale of her story. In a desperate attempt, Jess lifted the gun upward. Her finger started to depress the trigger. Someone was going to die, but it wouldn't be her. Milliseconds before the blade struck down or before Jess could blast a six-inch hole in the girl's face, they were both thrown from their feet as another detonation came from outside the home. A wave of fire tore through the open doors. All of the windows on the western side of the estate burst and shattered and sent fragments of glass airborne like shrapnel.

Canned goods and boxed pasta shells rained down over Jess as she slammed into the pantry, buckling the doors upon impact. The masked girl's skull made a stomach-churning cracking sound, like an egg hitting concrete, as she smacked into the corner of Novalee's granite countertop. The girl collapsed, motionless at the dead fat man's feet; they deserved each other in that moment. Blood pooled around the girl's head and met the man's like that of two oil stains in a garage. Her eyes remained wide open as she stared soullessly into the darkness. Jess reached for the mask.

80

She wanted to see who was behind the veil as if laying witness to the girl's face would somehow make sense of all this nonsense. Her fingers gripped the blood-soaked chinstrap, but as soon as Jess began to lift, a shriek resonated from the cellar below.

"Miss Novalee," Jess sprang upward and bolted toward the cellar door. "Miss Novalee, talk to me," Jess demanded. She dashed down the stairs, skipping two at a time. Over her labored breath, Jess picked up on a gurgling sound, like someone was being waterboarded in the depths of the basement. When Jess reached the bottom stair, she saw... nothing. The single bulb that had illuminated the space was out, but only for a moment. As Jess crept toward where she left Novalee, the bulb chain clicked, and the light came back on for a brief second before going dark again. Again and again, this pattern repeated as power faded, giving Jess a glimpse of something she couldn't yet process, or rather, something she didn't want to process. Strobes of flashing light gave her a slideshow-like view of Missus Novalee's fate. Her throat had been slit as her head slumped over her left shoulder. Her eyes stared straight at Jess, but the light was out behind them. Jess gagged and struggled to breathe.

The gurgling, the snap, the sickening sounds of death, all the sounds began to make sense. A woman she had cared for, waited on hand and foot, and a woman she loved dearly, no matter how irritating, now lay motionless and mangled right before her eyes. Even more petrifying was that Jess saw who had done this. They stood in the shadows directly behind Novalee. Two additional masked men looked to be straight out of a horror film with their gigantic builds and white expressionless faces. One thing was apparent: prison was a vacation for these behemoths. Jess cautiously inched backward into the intermittent blackness as her heart raced and neared the top of her throat. It was like trying to swallow a live frog. Her hands clacked against the handle of the shotgun. Nerves and fear ran rampant through her.

"Why are you doing this?" Jess begged under her breath, but she realized she didn't have time to wait for an answer. Jess mustered all the strength and will available to her, locked and loaded the breaching round in her Remington, and took aim. The lights continued to flicker off and on and off again and created a strobe effect; causing things to appear in slow motion. Jess expelled a nervous breath when a man's voice sung out from behind her.

"The itsy bitsy spider…"

Jess froze in place. A literal statue made of fear.

"Climbed up the water spout."

She nervously cocked her head to the side, afraid to look directly behind her. She strained to catch of glimpse with her peripheral vision and fired wildly into the blackness.

"Down came the rain and," the gravelly voice continued as Jess knew her shot had missed the target, "washed the spider out." As she prepared to fire again, a hand, covered in a spider web tattoo, emerged from behind Jess, covered her mouth, and quelled her screams.

Jess struggled as a man's arm wrapped tight around her head; his bicep gripped her throat and constricted her airways like a massive boa. Instinctively she dropped the gun, clutched at her neck, kicked and swung and thrashed with all the fight she had within her, but it wasn't enough. Jess dipped in and out of consciousness as the man's grip deprived her of oxygen. The song continued as a whistle, and Jess started to fade.

"Out came the sun
And dried up all the rain;
And the itsy bitsy spider
Climbed up the spout again."

An instant later, it was lights out. Jess's body went limp, crumpled, and slapped against the wet cement. Her Remington fell helplessly at her side and landed at the man's size eleven combat boots. Jess's hand slid down the side of her neck and navigated the contour of her chest, stopping at the base of her belly.

CHAPTER 6
THE END OF THE
BEGINNING

It seemed like days had passed since it all began. A plastering of debris, tears, and dry blood crusted over Penny's eyes. The skin of her eyelids burned and tore as she pried them apart. Her vision was blurred, but from what she could see, the area that surrounded her was nothing short of a pitch-black void. "Luke?" Penny muttered in a raspy voice as her lungs filled with dust and smoke. She struggled to her feet and held her head tight between her hands. She put pressure against her temples as they throbbed. Her ears rang like a fire alarm that mated with the screech of a scream queen. She'd had a migraine only once in her young life, but this was far worse. Penny tried to steady herself as her knees shook uncontrollably, either from fright or fatigue; most likely both. "Luke?" she called out again. This time her vocal cords mustered more strength and echoed in the near-empty space. Anxiousness started to grip Penny tight as her breathing began to accelerate. A thought entered her mind that she didn't want to accept. A terrifying notion that she may be alone. That Luke may be… He may be dead.

Penny took one step forward and felt her foot plant down on something hard, but not quite earth or stone. Penny hunched over and felt around blindly with her hands until she grasped it; Luke's phone. Penny thumbed around for the power button with haste and turned on the phone. The no signal indicator covered two-thirds of the screen and flashed off and on in a mocking cadence. Still, Penny was more interested in the flashlight than the signal strength. She switched on the LED beam and held it up; its luminous stream tore through the thick cloud of dust, broken earth, and concrete that surrounded her in the subterranean air. Penny coughed a deep cough. As she cleared her lungs, they sounded like a two-by-four scraping over a cheese grater. She squinted and waved her free hand in front of her face in an attempt to locate Luke and Walnut. They had both disappeared somewhere deep inside the cavernous maintenance tunnel. She scanned to her right and saw a workbench with a variety of rusted tools. Black mold clung to ceiling pipes and support beams. To her left was a stack of old stadium seats, clearly retired from last year's renovations. This room didn't look familiar; it didn't look like where she fell. She wondered if she passed out and someone brought her here, or perhaps she had died, and this was some twisted purgatory for maintenance workers, and her name tag had gotten mixed up.

"Help me," a voice said indistinctly. Penny spun in a circle as the voice seemed to surround her. It may

85

have been a mile away, or a few feet, the echo of the hall and chaos surrounding her made it impossible to tell.

"Who's there?" Penny coughed and asked as she waved the light back and forth.

"I can't breathe," the voice agonized. This time Penny was able to pinpoint a general direction. It came from behind her. She double-timed it and trudged along over downed earth and utilities. She leaped over a toppled refrigerator, the flashlight guiding her along like a ship at sea following the gaze of a lighthouse keeper's glint.

"Luke," Penny's voice cracked. She tried to produce saliva to moisten her lips and throat, but her mouth and tongue were as dry as a desert scraped over with sandpaper. She cleared her throat, and her voice squeaked like a mouse when she said, "Is that you? Please, call out again."

She stopped to listen. Only the sounds of the beat of her heart and her heavy breathing were audible.

For a moment, there was an ill-omened silence. Penny collected herself and tried to calm her breathing. She listened as hard as she could until someone gasped, then coughed—the throes of death. Someone was trapped.

"I'm coming."

With no general sense of direction, only a sense of urgency, Penny sprinted down the hall. In fact, she couldn't remember a time where she'd run faster. Penny didn't know where he was, but she knew he was running out of time. As she saw more debris ahead, she prepared to leap over it but tripped. Her momentum carried her forward as she landed on her right side with a thunk. Her head hit the ground as her cheek skid against the brash surface and left a trail of bloody claw-like marks down the side of her face. The cell phone flew from her grip yet again, this time like a fighter pilot that ejected himself from the cockpit. Without hesitation, Penny hoisted herself up. She didn't feel the blood trickle down from an open wound onto her jersey as it dotted and streaked across the team crest like an odious Rorschach test.

"Where's the phone?" She scanned and finally noticed it facing downward, butted up against the wall. The light, still on, traced a perfect outline around its cobalt casing. Penny bent down and picked the phone up, but before she stood fully upright, she saw what tripped her up: a boot and part of a mangled leg that protruded from the rubble. "LUKE!" Penny's meager cry wasn't even loud enough to produce an echo. She dropped to her knees and started to yank on the leg, but no matter how hard she tugged, it didn't matter; he wouldn't budge. "Walnut. Help me!" Penny lifted rock and stone from atop the body. She couldn't move fast enough. "Please don't die," she begged under her breath.

Penny wrapped her arms around a massive chunk of wall covering what she thought would be his head. She bent at her knees like so many times in the weight room and lifted with everything she had. Jagged edges dug into her fingers. If not for her callouses, it would have torn right through her hands. She mustered a burst of strength and tossed the mound aside, after which she picked up the phone once again and aimed its light down on the face of–a maintenance worker. His eyes were wide open as blood seeped from the edges. A puff of dust still lingered, hovering in the air from his last breath like his soul waiting to move on. But make no mistake, he was undoubtedly dead.

"Poor bastard," Walnut's voice said solemnly from behind. Penny turned in a flash and came face to face with Luke and Walnut. Somehow in the commotion, they walked right up on her without her even noticing.

"We found a way out. But we gotta move now," Luke pointed to his right. "Ground's gonna give way soon."

Penny looked at Luke, relieved for a moment, but then twirled her rapt attention back toward the crushed and deceased worker. She took a couple of deep breaths, then sneered as she peered up at Luke. She repeatedly slugged his chest with a clenched fist until Luke grabbed her by the wrist.

"What was that for?" Luke asked.

"For leavin' me by myself," Penny said as she again turned her attention to the worker's body. "And for making me think that he was you." She turned her back to Luke and Walnut and walked away without another word.

Once outside the collapsed tunnels, Luke and Penny raced toward a double-parked, soot-covered, cobalt-blue Ford F-150 near the edge of the stadium lot. Luke always parked his baby far from any other vehicle. Walnut panted heavily, trailing far behind as he rushed in the direction of his '67 Cadillac DeVille.

Penny glanced back over her shoulder and hesitantly surveyed the scene. Black smoke twisted skyward like Satan himself was winding his finger around strands of hair that dangled from the heavens. Parts of the stadium were still ablaze, while others were missing entirely. She looked over the parking lot. Cars were incinerated while bodies were thrown about like mangled and seared scarecrows. Penny looked back in the direction from whence they came and saw Walnut still running, still a ways off.

Luke must have noticed this at the same time as he called out, "Pick up the pace, Decker."

The only time anyone referred to Walnut by his actual first or last name was when he was scolded; scolded by either his mother or the police, or both at once. Penny saw a burst of life enter Walnut's legs, a second wind, as he double-timed it and reached the passenger side of his car. She cringed as he planted his palm on the hood and soared as he attempted to slide across the front of the DeVille; only he didn't make it. The left side of his hip slammed into the side of the car, and Walnut bounced off of it like a pinball.

"I'm okay," Walnut immediately ensured as he bound upward and limped over to the driver's side. He plopped onto the leather bench seat, slammed his door shut, and started the engine. It purred and grumbled as he cranked down his window. "Get Jess and meet me at the bunker. I'll have everything ready for you."

Luke nodded as Walnut peeled out and left a trail of smoky dust in his path. He was far too familiar with Walnut's bunker. On many occasions, Luke drew the unfortunate straw to help his *friend* restock the bunker's supplies. Penny coughed and waved away the cloud of exhaust as she stepped up into the passenger seat. She spun around and anxiously watched as Luke darted toward the driver-side door and hopped in.

"C'mon," Penny demanded as Luke cranked the ignition. He smashed his boot on the pedal and shot a torrent of gravel behind in their wake. The truck cannonballed out of the parking lot and dodged people, a handful of survivors who had recently crawled their way to safety and the deceased, so many deceased, along with torched cars and a chunk of the concession stand that had been blasted into oblivion and landed hundreds of feet from its home.

Luke fishtailed as he hit Route 6 like a bat out of hell. Well, more like what was left of Route 6. Everything that remained was engulfed in flames or burned to a skeletal core. The concert of explosions continued in the distance. Penny had no earthly clue if the onslaught was a mile away or twenty; all she knew was that wherever the sounds were coming from, death followed. "Mom," Penny said as she fumbled around in her pocket and finally pulled out the cell phone. She dialed and raised the phone to her ear. It started to ring as Luke whipped the steering wheel from right to left and sideswiped a parked car.

"Sorry," he said as he dodged a mail truck immersed in flames in the middle of the road. Penny grimaced as she unwillingly caught sight of a Fed-Ex driver burnt to a crisp in the front seat of his delivery vehicle.

"There's no signal," Penny announced as a police cruiser ripped past, cherries blazing. The sirens dopplered away and faded into the distance almost as quickly as they came.

"Try her again," Luke barked. He turned on his radio and raised the volume as he navigated through static until he found a feed.

"This is not a test. Seek immediate shelter," the voice of the Emergency Broadcast operator droned on and played the same message on a loop.

Penny's panicked fingers dialed again. She put the phone on speaker. After what seemed like an intensifying eternity of ringing, a voice recording connected.

"All circuits are busy now. Please, try your call again later. If you feel you've reached this recording in error, please dial again. All circuits are busy now. Please, try your—"

Penny slammed the phone shut. "What now?"

Luke didn't answer; he didn't need to. The next ten minutes of their drive would be the longest span of his life. He kept his eyes peeled as he entered a freeway. He stared intently at the road ahead. The five-liter V8 engine growled as it passed burning farms and a roadside rest area. Penny looked aimlessly out the window and felt helpless but not yet hopeless. She watched cars pass by, buzzing in all directions, not knowing where they were headed but knew they were all headed somewhere and fast.

"I don't understand," Penny fretted.

"Neither do I." Luke adjusted the side mirror as his view of the small town behind them roasted like a blackened marshmallow on a campfire. "Of all the insignificant, back-wood, dumpster puddles in the world, why here?"

"Maybe it's not just here. Maybe we're just what's left?" Penny said.

Luke saw a shot of seething pain cross Penny's face. He wanted to tell her otherwise, but he knew she had a point. What if she was right? Her bottom lip started to tremble as she looked down at the phone. The word 'JESS' was etched in bold black lettering in the recent call list.

"Don't worry. She's fine."

"I know she is," Penny said as she stiffened her lip and realized she must have let her guard down.

"I'm here, you know. You don't have to…"

"Just keep driving, Luke."

Luke checked his side mirrors, then readjusted the rearview.

"What is it?" Penny asked.

"Nothing. Why?"

"That's like the fifteenth time you've done that. Why do you keep looking back?"

"Just stayin' frosty is all." Luke flicked the blinker downward and yanked the steering wheel to the left as he drifted onto a dirt road and cut off a semi-truck in the process. The semi's horn blared in passing.

"Frosty, huh?" Penny mocked. "Least you used the blinker."

Luke and Penny climbed their way up the dirt road; a dust cloud kicked up from the tires and merged with the black smoke which already filled the air. They passed a speed limit sign that read twenty-five. Luke clocked the speedometer; the needle fluttered between sixty-five and seventy.

"Now, what in the hell is this?" Luke pointed out the windshield. Penny leaned forward in her seat.

An SUV had crested the hill ahead of them and barreled their way as it swerved back and forth across the road. Its high beams caused Luke and Penny to squint as Luke laid on his horn.

"Is he having a stroke?" Penny asked.

"Put your seatbelt on," Luke ordered.

"It is," Penny said.

"Then make sure it's tight."

"Why?"

Penny looked at Luke; his eyes never left the road. Then she looked down at her safety harness and checked the strap for any slack. Luke flashed his high beams a few times and depressed the horn relentlessly like a contestant buzzing in to win a prize on a game show. The SUV was shredding toward them, head-on, like a bullet, and showed no signs of slowing, just the opposite actually.

"Why don't you just pull over?" Penny begged.

"And where exactly do you suppose I do that? Into the trees?"

Penny took in her surroundings and stared out at the giant oak trees that lined the road. There wasn't anywhere to pull off.

Luke considered it for a moment but doubled down. "No way am I backing down." He slammed his foot down on the gas and laid the horn on even thicker.

"Backing down?" Penny chastised as she stared at him and waved her hand in front of his face. "This ain't a testosterone-fueled asshole game of chicken. You need to pull over!"

Luke didn't budge. He wrung his fingers around the wheel even tighter.

There was a break in the trees to her right, about forty feet ahead. It was now or never. "I said," Penny leaned across her body, gripped the steering wheel, and jerked it to the right, "pull over."

The F150 swerved sideways, nearly lifting two wheels from the ground. Luke pulled the truck from a fishtail, slid off the side of the road, and slammed through an antique wooden wagon shattering it into a million tiny thorns. They plowed through a row of bushes and narrowly missed the trunk of a tree. The truck bounced into and out of a drainage ditch, crushing a field of freshly planted hydrangeas, and spun around in a complete one-eighty. Penny was jolted about violently in her seat until the vehicle skid to an abrupt stop.

"What were you thinking?" Luke screamed as he threw off his seat belt in disgust. "You could have gotten us killed."

"Luke," Penny said unusually soft, considering the situation.

"What?" he snarled.

"Look." Penny pointed toward the road. Toward the passing beat-up '84 Ford Bronco which slowed to a near stop. Penny wondered if they were going to check on them, that was until she saw what lay within the Bronco. Her eyes moved from the bullet-hole-riddled grill to the dainty windows and windshield where she discovered a cab full of men, all masked. Dirt, sweat, and blood caked over their expressionless faces. Penny locked eyes with the monstrous man driving the Bronco that, little did she know, had held Novalee at gunpoint only moments before. A mermaid tattoo covered a huge chunk of his bicep. To his right was another, less sizeable, but no less hideous creature whose mask was broken in two, revealing a scarred and mangled jawline. And at the far end, hugging the passenger door, was a man with long black hair whose eyes peered out from behind the masked curtain. There was a sincere menace in his gaze as he caught Penny's stare in passing. As the Bronco sped out of sight, Penny and

Luke turned their eyes out the rear of the truck and watched as the Bronco's taillights disappeared in their wake. "What in the actual fuck?" Penny said.

Luke craned his neck in Penny's direction and, with his most stern and father-like voice, said, "Watch your mouth."

Luke sped up the rest of the road unimpaired and uninterrupted. He slammed on the brakes and brought the pickup to a grinding halt, just inches from Novalee's front staircase. Luke hopped out of the truck and, like a Navajo tracker, bent down and observed the tire tracks left from the Bronco.

Penny scooted across the bench, exited, and shut the door behind her. She stared down at Luke curiously and watched as he picked up a shell casing. He smelled its emptiness. She witnessed a hint of anxiety enter his normally stoic face. Penny's thoughts instantly filled with a sense of foreboding that something horrible had happened. Her arms and legs broke out in goosebumps, and the tiny hairs on the back of her neck stood at attention.

Without a word or passing glance, Luke crossed Penny's path, across the front of his truck, and failed to notice his front bumper barely hanging on by a thread, or more appropriately, a bolt. He jarred open the passenger door, and for a brief moment, he disappeared inside the glove box. Luke marched back to Penny with a small, ladies' purse-sized Glock 42 and extended the gun to her. Penny retracted, not out of instinct but uncertainty. At this moment, Penny realized she'd never handled a firearm before unless playing Fortnite counted.

"Take this, get back in the truck, and lock the doors. If anyone, and I mean *anyone* besides me, your mom, or that old bat Blankley, comes outta this house, you pull the trigger."

"Is it loaded?"

"What would be the point if it wasn't?" Luke waited for Penny to take the Glock. Her reluctance and hesitation frustrated the hell out of him as his face turned red. After what seemed to be an eternity, Luke grabbed Penny by the elbow and ushered her to the truck's passenger door.

"In," he ordered.

"Are you kidding me? I'm not stayin' here by myself."

Luke exhaled and tried unsuccessfully to center his chi.

"Besides. I never even shot a gun."

"Point it at their chest and pull this," he demonstrated, motioning to the trigger. "I thought you was smart." He grabbed her arm again and began to lift her into the truck, but Penny resisted. She squirmed and kicked free.

"No. I told you. I'm not staying by myself."

"We're wasting time," Luke grunted as he snatched the gun from her hands and tucked it into the rear of his waistband. "Fine, then you keep on my six."

"Your six what?"

"Just stay behind me." Luke untucked the front flap of his t-shirt and drew a 357 Magnum from the front of his belt, directly above his hip pocket.

"You had that at the game?" Penny asked accusingly.

Luke snorted like an enraged bull who saw red and moved at a hurried pace to the staircase.

"Wait. You get two guns?" Penny questioned with a hint of jealousy in her voice. Luke habitually ignored her and led the way up the stairs and into the house.

With no time to strategize or survey the property, Luke realized that he might be walking directly into an ambush. He opened the door deliberately with his hand cannon locked and loaded. He peeked around the corner as the door gave a pathetic whimper as it creaked open. Penny watched his every move, absorbed and studied him, noticing his mannerism, the way held the gun close to his chest; it was not like they did it in the old cop shows. She knew he was a real-life badass, but aside from watching him chop firewood, Penny never had the opportunity to see him in action. The way he cleared the room and checked corners reminded her of watching samurai movies and binging Delta Force Chicago.

Luke's wristwatch beeped, an alarm of some sort. He shut it off and turned to Penny. "Try her phone again," Luke commanded.

"It's not gonna work. The tower is probably-"

"The towers reboot every fifteen minutes. Even when they're flooded or tapped into, we still have about twenty-two seconds before they're out of bandwidth and overwhelmed."

"What?"

"Nineteen seconds."

"Seriously?"

"Sixteen."

"Fine," Penny exclaimed as she started to dial. "You hang out with Walnut too much." Penny hit the sizeable green call button. After a second of silence, she said, "I hear it. It's ringing." Penny and Luke's ears perked up. The faint tone was coming from the back of the house. Without hesitation, Penny shot toward the kitchen and ran faster than she'd ever recalled. She even outran Luke as she nearly tripped over the dead fat man and young female masked intruder whose bodies still sat together.

Luke sprinted in after and slid to a screeching halt on the tile floor after he nearly lost his footing on the pools of blood.

Penny's eyes were as wide as saucers, the space kind, not the dining variety. Her hands started to tremble.

"Are they–"

"As a doornail," Luke said.

Penny tip-toed over the bodies and cringed at the splattering of brains that dripped from the granite countertop. She slumped down over the girl's corpse, being careful to avoid the coagulating O-Negative that decorated the linoleum floor. The smell of death and defecation hit her nostrils.

"I'm gonna be sick," Penny said as she dry heaved over the girl. Penny had only seen one dead body close up before today, and that was a great-grandfather whom she hardly knew. Needless to say, her days of watching reruns of cop shows with Luke couldn't have prepared her for this fresh shotgun autopsy.

Luke hunched over the bodies and assessed the situation, reverting back into full tracker mode. He looked at the shell casings that covered the floor and the broken glass that rested beneath the shattered back storm door. "Good girl, Jess."

"Wait, you think… Mom?" Penny wiped the corner of her mouth, looked over the bodies and again nearly lost her pregame meal. "You think Mom did this?"

"Well, it sure as hell wasn't Novalee Blankley. Your mom's a good shot."

Penny, more curious than terrified, poked her finger into the oozing and gaping head wound of the dead girl. It was soft, a soft, warm, pulp-like goo that resembled the innards of a rotten pumpkin. Penny dry heaved a third time.

"Stop touching it, will ya. It's just a dead body."

"Just a de—Just a dead body? Her freaking brains are on the fork drawer, and this fat fuck," Penny said demonstratively, pointing to the fat man, "doesn't have a damn forehead left."

"Still don't give you a reason to go pokin' around?" Luke retorted nonchalantly. "Let's find your mom and get out of here."

Penny stood as a noise from the cellar startled her. She ducked behind a plastic trash can to the amusement of Luke.

"Good hiding spot."

"Shut up," Penny stood and wiped the blood and brain matter from her hands onto her already soiled pant leg.

The heavy tread of Luke's boots echoed in the cellar with each clomping step downward. Penny walked in perfect stride with Luke, only inches behind, acting as his shadow. The space below was as black as before and left only a slender beam of light that bled through the begrimed windows and foundational cracks. The cracks now seemed to scatter in zigzag patterns across the basement. They

99

resembled the scratchings and scribbles of a toddler with an etch-a-sketch.

"Jess," Luke called out but was only met by the reverberation of his own voice that bounced off the caliginous walls.

"Gimme the phone," Luke said.

"It just died," Penny said.

"Then go upstairs and see if you can find a flashlight."

"Here," Penny reached into her back pocket. "Take this."

Luke held his arm out and bumbled around blindly for Penny's outstretched hand, never taking his eyes from the void that lay ahead. He gripped her offering and felt its cold stubby body. Luke held the item inches in front of his face and said, "You smoking now?"

"Are you kidding me?" Penny said.

"Then you mind explainin' why you have a zippo in your softball pants?"

"One, it's none of your damn business, and two, aren't we supposed to be looking for Mom?" Penny replied.

"One... Everything is my business. And two, if your mom finds out your smoking, surviving an aerial attack is gonna be the least of your concerns."

"It isn't mine," Penny said.

"Ain't yours? Then where'd you get it?" said Luke.

"The girl upstairs. It was in her pocket."

"You stole a dead girl's lighter?"

"She wasn't usin' it," Penny stated.

Luke didn't see her expression but assumed that Penny was rolling her eyes as per usual.

"You want it or not?" Penny asked.

Luke didn't dignify her with a formal response; he just flicked the zippo across his ragged jeans. The blue and orange flame of the Zippo provided an ominous display. Penny's eyes were drawn to the spiders that scampered over the model railroad tracks. She had no rational explanation for it, but just seeing this room in the light made the temperature drop twenty degrees. Penny held on to the back of Luke's t-shirt. The same way she had a little less than a year earlier when she followed her best friend, Alyssa, into the town's world-famous haunted cemetery. Her feet shuffled, and her toes butted up against Luke's heel with each tandem movement. Luke waved the zippo from side to side, inching forward, deeper and deeper into the abyss, illuminating bacteria-ridden patches of shag carpet, black-mold-covered joists, and cold walls.

"God no," Luke exclaimed under his breath. "Go back upstairs, Penny."

Obviously, Penny was not going to listen, and the simple fact that Luke thought she'd ever show such obedience was beyond exacerbating. She released the grip from his shirt, almost defiantly to say, I don't need your protection, and she stepped in front of him. Her eyes widened in fright as she stared down at a pool of blood that snaked its way toward a floor drain. "Is it?" Penny's question hung in the air.

Luke begrudgingly lifted the lighter, higher and higher, and followed the blood's path to its source. Penny wanted to turn away but knew she would not permit herself to take the easy way out, not if this was her mom, so she did the next best thing and partially covered her eyes with her hand and peeked through the slits of her fingers. After a few seconds, the puckering of her face quickly relaxed. Her entire body seemed to let a sigh of relief. A regretful yet necessary smile cracked at the corner of her lips, a sign of comfort and hope, as she stared down at the body of one Novalee Blankley. More importantly, anyone but her mother.

Ω

The F-150 shredded asphalt and moved at meteoric speeds down South French Avenue as Luke buried the pedal in the floorboard. Penny held Jess's phone in her right hand and clutched Jess's nursing name badge tightly in her left, which she found in the cellar; dry blood flecked against the plastic casing. She stared down at the picture longingly. Penny remained sanguine about her mother's chances, hopeful that Jess was alive, somewhere out there still fighting. Yet, in the same breath, Penny was contrite in her desire that this badge belonged to someone else. Some stranger whom she didn't know. Someone else's mother and wife, and that Jess was at home, safe and snug in bed, with her feet propped up on a chair, watching daytime television. Alas, this wasn't true, and nor could Penny ever pray hard enough to will these thoughts into existence. Her mind raced as all the scenarios and all the questions flooded her brain at once. *"Who were those men in the Bronco? Obviously, they were part of the same group as the dead girl and the fat man at Novalee's? At least their masks looked the same. And who the hell wears a mask anyway? Was her mother with them in the truck? And why her? Why the attack? Why Sutton? Why now? What do all these questions have to do with each other? Is there a connection I'm missing?"*

Luke must have been on the same wavelength, for out of the silence, he blurted, "I just don't see it."

"Huh?" Penny asked.

"The attacks. Your mother. Don't make sense at all."

"Then, do you think she might actually be—"

"Don't you finish that sentence," Luke scolded.

"Well, what do you think happened to her?"

"I don't know."

"But why do you think—"

"I said, I don't know."

"She wouldn't just leave her purse and phone behind. Unless she ran. But she wouldn't get far. And if they took her, those guys in the truck, I mean, if they took her, then we need to find out where they went," Penny said. "Which could be a million places by now."

"I know."

"And how are you so calm anyways?" Penny shouted. She's out there somewhere, and what the hell are we doing? Driving in circles?

"We're gonna find her. I promise," Luke said.

"You shouldn't do that."

"Do what?"

"Make promises like that. Promises you can't keep," Penny said as flashes of broken vows careened off of the already overcrowded parking lot of images that zipped through her mind. Thoughts of a father's promise to be a better man, a better husband. Someone who didn't turn to the belt at the first chance. A promise from a mother to a weeping daughter, vowing to keep her safe. Assuring her she'd

103

take her away from all the sadness. A commitment from teachers and coaches, from friends and enemies. Promises from a God to protect his children, yet here we are as the world burns. All sorts of folks made promises, but only those with character were ever known to keep them. And Penny; Penny didn't know many folks with a strong constitution. She broke from her stream of rambling consciousness and found herself obsessively scraping away at the blood on Jess's badge. Her mother's blood began to build up beneath her dirty fingernails.

"Then where we gonna look first?" Penny continued to interrogate Luke. "What's your plan, exactly?"

"Penny, I told you–"

"You told me nothing," Penny interrupted again. "You got all these promises, but I wanna hear your plan. An actual plan." Penny demanded. "What if they already killed her? And if they hadn't, what if they're going to? Tell me what we're gonna do about it."

"Dammit, girl, will you just shut the hell up and let me figure things out for a second." Luke's face glowed a bright red. Incensed, he turned in his seat and faced her with a scolding look that sent Penny retracting backward into her chair. "I don't know who they were, okay." She cowered down and tried to disappear. "I don't know what they want. I don't know where they're going. And I sure as hell don't know if your mom, if my wife, is–"

"Look out!" Penny warned, jumping upward and yelling at the top of her lungs as she pointed out Luke's driver's side. Luke whipped his attention one-hundred and eighty degrees just in time to see his pride and joy on wheels meet the full force of an oncoming armored vehicle. Metal crunched and pulverized upon impact. Airbags deployed. The collision sent Penny and Luke into an instantaneous barrel-roll. Penny heard the truck's roof collapse down on her, closer, closer, with each revolution. If Penny had the power to suspend time right now and draw a comparison, she would think back to when she was younger. The day her mother took her to the carnival to ride the zero-G astronaut experience. But Penny's current reality was no carnival ride, and there was no laughter spilling out from her lungs. And unlike the carnival, this experience would certainly not end with a smiling young girl, a hot dog, and a mouthful of cotton candy; but instead, bruised ribs, a concussion, and a mouthful of glass. Penny hung on to the overhead handle for dear life as Luke's 4x4 spun like a shoe in the dryer, stuck on tumble-dry-mode. The windshield spiderwebbed, causing the microscopic cracks to expand. The back window burst on impact and sent thousands of tiny particles of glass flying. Some sliced deep into Penny's skin. After three more violent flips, the truck landed on its roof and skid toward a series of shotgun-style buildings and storefronts amidst a shower of sparks. Luke and Penny hung upside down and dangled from their seatbelts like cheap hoop earrings as they slammed into the world's last free-standing Radio Shack.

Penny saw a myriad of black spots, and the wreck rendered her immobilized. Her limbs went numb, which was a blessing in disguise. A car horn blared, continuous and numbing. Outside of the serpentine metal that formerly held the passenger glass pane, Penny spotted the armored truck that hit them. The impact ejected the driver, leaving a blood-outlined hole in the center of the windshield; clearly, he or she had failed to understand the importance of seatbelt safety. Penny turned her attention to Luke. He dangled like her, but he was out cold. He had a gash on his forehead that dribbled blood like a leaky faucet. Drip-drip, drip-drip, drip-drip, it pittered and pattered with a regular beat against the roof of his cabin hood. She looked back out a hole in the windshield as she fell in and out of consciousness. Her gaze landed on rows of televisions in the storefront display, consisting of a dozen CRT monitors and some flat-panel LCDs. They were all tuned to various news stations. Some local, some national, and all displayed breaking news clips from around the nation.

Going down the line, barely keeping her focus, Penny saw unthinkable chaos. She quickly understood that Sutton was not the beginning; rather, the end of a long list of targets. A sledgehammer of unforgiving destruction which hit America head-on. Penny's eyes darted back and forth between the images displayed on the screens. First, she saw a non-descript downtown ablaze. Then, an office building was decimated, gutted, torn in half, which closely resembled the Oklahoma City bombing. Next, cell phone footage looked to be a live stream of a suicide bomber detonating himself in a packed shopping mall, wiping out hundreds of retail consumers with the push of a trigger. The carnage was relentless.

The following television showed aerial coverage of a naval base. Cameras panned over parked fighter jets as they carbonized on the deck of a submerging aircraft carrier–Pearl Harbor-esque. There were shootouts in the streets—police, firefighters, and EMTs drug bodies from the rubble. The Space Needle toppled over in Seattle. The Gateway Arch in St. Louis had been sliced in two and lay in the muddy banks of the Mississippi. And finally, the last TV, a black and white vintage set, showcased the Statue of Liberty. Half of her face had been blown away and revealed a melted steel globe beneath. The fire smoldered from within her belly as a spackling of dead bodies lay at her feet. The feeds simultaneously cut to static as if someone pulled the plug on our nation. Penny began to fade as the sound of speeding cars, people screaming, and madness filled the air.

"There'd be no warning. No negotiation. No counter strike. No great war of our time. This wasn't an invasion. This was an extermination. A bloodbath of epic proportions... And Gods be Damned if we weren't prepared."

PART TWO

THE SEARCH

CHAPTER 7
THE ARTIST FORMERLY
KNOWN AS COLORADO

Two Years Later

The icy wind howled a haunting wail as a frozen
tumbleweed blew across a lonely stretch of freeway
blacktop that snaked into eternity. A tattered and
charred American flag whipped in the breeze as it
barely clung to the antenna of an equally torched
police cruiser. The antenna bent and bowed from
hood to roof. The freeway was strewn full of broken-
down, abandoned cars with shattered glass, missing or
shredded tires, and permanently rusted open trunks.
The luggage inside had been fully rummaged about
and scattered around the roadside. The remnants of a
charbroiled tour bus lay across the concrete median.

Seared human remains of a pop-star dangled from the open windows.

It was the dead of winter, and this America was no longer beautiful; rather, stark, cold, and unforgiving. Light snow powdered the ground like a sprinkling of confectioners' sugar. The once vibrant landscape and purple mountain majesties now decayed under a slate-gray sky. The fruited plains were dull and stripped barren like an inverted Bob Ross painting. No happy little trees remained for whatever poor souls still drew breath.

The clacking of giant split hooves clattered against the tundra-like frosted pavement as an elk, a trophy bull, to be exact, made its way down the lonesome highway. In the old world, some lucky hunter would have likely mounted the elk's massive rack high above a mantelpiece. In that same ancient world, this behemoth of a land mammal once lived in fear of the hunt, but now he feared nothing. He casually stopped and sniffed the crisp, chilled air. He searched for a scent he'd been tracking for some time. Thick mucus discharged from his nostrils and froze in place before it oozed to the ground. This winter wonderland's backdrop and canopy reflected in the deep earthy hue of the elk's black and brown eyes. He moved on, hooves clacking in a rhythmic cadence until he reached a hatchback with wooden panel siding and four missing tires. He sniffed again, then grunted like a disappointed Shogun. He continued down the road until he reached a beat-down minivan. The elk scanned the tinted rear window; he peered through the fading and flecking vinyl decals that once displayed a family of six, including four girls whose names all began with the letter 'A'. The elk sniffed once more, then snorted abruptly and lowered his nose to the ground. He backpedaled with purpose until his five-inch rear hooves butted up against the gravel shoulder of the freeway. He pawed at crumbled asphalt with his forefoot, scraping and striking it with a beating motion like a bull about to charge a matador. And this was precisely what the bull elk was about to do; only the matador was the minivan. He bolted forward and picked up speed with each galloping step until he saw red and shattered the van's side window with his massive rack with ease.

The eager elk cocked his head sideways and tried to shimmy its way inside the van. Jagged tooth-shaped shards of glass were chipped free from the rubber window seal by the elk's antlers as he twisted and wriggled. His black tongue lapped away as he tried to reach his prize; what looked to have been a can of rotting, lightly-roasted, lightly-salted, and likely stale store-bought peanuts. Adding to the homogenized stench was a patch of fungus that grew from inside the van. It permeated through the vents, the seats, and headrests like a disease. The elk contorted his neck and head like a world-class gymnast, mere inches away from the can. Its tongue reached, desperate for the fungal goodness inside.

The tip of the elk's outstretched tongue flicked against the tin when a stick snapped from outside and begged for the elk's attention. The elk yanked its antlers from inside of the van. They scraped, tore, and clanged against the upholstery and frame upon exit. He was on high alert; his beady black eyes scanned the area cautiously as his heartbeat elevated to a frantic pace. Usually, this would be his time to tuck tail and run. But for the elk, the prize was far too grand, and the distance traveled to reach his payoff was far too long. His eyes probed the landscape for a predator. He whirled left, snapping his neck toward the direction of the endless freeway that led into the mountains; then, after what had felt like a lifetime, he sniffed the air and paused. Not a creature was stirring. Not a mouse, not a bird, not a cougar, nor a three-toed sloth-nothing. He observed the vast emptiness of the land. He listed to the swirling cry of the wind as it picked up momentum as deteriorating leaves danced about in its wake.

The elk, content and convinced that he was still alone, returned to the window and tilted his head. Just as he was ready for reentry, a sharp hiss pierced the air, and before the elk reacted, an arrow slammed into his gut with a thunk. The elk bellowed and screamed out in pain. Within seconds another arrow struck, this one to the shoulder. The elk yowled out again as his feet hit the ground. He slipped and looked for traction as he attempted to bolt far away from the scene, far away to safety. Without warning, another hiss whistled in his direction, and another arrow plunged deep into its backside. The elk desperately gained traction as his hooves steadied themselves on the asphalt. He clumsily and strenuously clacked away from the van. His thick, scarlet blood streamed from his open wounds and stained the dark patches of his fur. His cries echoed throughout the mountainside as he disappeared into the tree line and became nothing more than a shadow.

CHAPTER 8
THE HUNTERS

A mysterious figure, covered head to toe in a soot-stained mixture of tactical and practical clothing, tracked the trail of Elk blood and paused over a red puddle of melted snow. They stooped down and swirled their fingers around in the cooling liquid. They were of average build and average height and even wore average-sized faded black combat boots. Whoever this was, indeed, was in the midst of full-blown survival mode. A modified bow was draped over their shoulder, with freshly carved arrows housed inside a homemade quiver on their back. A black balaclava enveloped their head, along with a menacing gas mask that covered their face. This was the kind of mask that, at best, signified dystopia while, at its worst, represented a clan of cannibalistic psychopaths. They slid their gloved finger from the puddle of bloody muck across their body into a pool of stomach contents. They lifted their finger and held it in front of their eye goggles and took note of the greenish-bile mixed in with the red blood. The hunter shook their head in evident disappointment, then, at the sound of rustling, whipped their attention to the side and took off in chase.

The hunter burst through thick foliage and into a dell. They looked out at a distance and saw the wounded elk as it barreled down a narrow slope into a valley. His dry and dehydrated tongue hung out of his mouth. He didn't have long now, as his fur was utterly stained from side to hoof as it coagulated on the surface.

The hunter sprinted after the elk, but the elk saw them coming. The bull elk picked up its pace once more and dashed toward a neighboring property line, marked by a rickety wooden fence. The animal bent his feeble knees and sprang upward as he attempted to hurdle the fence but was tripped up and planted into the snow. The anonymous assassin was hot on its trail. They followed the path of innards that dotted the snow like a disturbing Hansel and Gretel trail of breadcrumbs. They slid down the steep slope and entered the valley. They bolted toward the fence line and hurdled it in one clean vault.

Just beyond a row of pines, roughly fifty yards past the fence, the elk had collapsed fantastically. It left a trail of broken earth thirteen feet in its wake. The elk's breaths were was few and far between. Its chest expanded and depressed as it struggled for air, for survival, for life. The hunter walked methodically toward the brave, dying beast and observed for a moment, then dropped down to a knee beside the elk as it started into a death rattle. The hunter sympathetically brushed the fur on the elk's head, trying to calm the beast as it drew the last slivers of air into its lungs. The hunter prayed it would pass quietly into the bitter winter day, though it would be a rather unbefitting moment in contrast to this pitiless world they found themselves in. The hunter strained to get to their feet. They gripped the bottom of their gas mask, pulled it from their head, and revealing their identity.

Penny, now seventeen, had her jet-black hair pulled back tight in a braid. She had a three-inch scar on her left cheek from the truck accident on the day of the attack, along with other tears to the fabric of her pale wind-chapped skin. And God only knows where those came from because Penny sure as hell didn't. She looked like a real-life Katniss Everdeen, minus the crying and the dragged-on love triangle.

She stared down at the elk and listened to its suffering. She wanted nothing more than for its pain to end. She wondered if it even felt pain the way she did. She wondered if it clung to life, desperate to spend one more day in the sun. She wondered if it desired to be with its family or child one last time, if it even had children to begin with. Or was this all just part of nature? Cruel unadulterated nature.

"Wanna tell me what you did wrong?" a voice interrupted her train of thought from a distance. Luke shuffled his way over the top of a slight hill in front of Penny.

"Do we have to do this now?" Penny asked. "I'm not in the mood for a lecture." She threw her mask at his feet. "And why am I wearing this stupid thing?"

"Cardio," Luke said as a shit-eating grin crossed his face. He, too, was in black tactical gear as he made his way to Penny's side; his face was less scarred than hers but much more rugged. He had a beard that would rival Grizzly Adams's, had Adams survived to see this day. Luke knelt beside the elk slowly. "This," he said as he pointed at the pattern of arrow wounds. "This is no good." He slid his fingers up the elk's body. "You need to aim here," he declared as he highlighted every vital organ. "Toward the heart. Lungs. It's cleaner, understand?" He paused and looked up at Penny, who was not at all interested in his lesson. Then, he looked back down at the elk, into his eyes. "Less suffering that way." Luke reached for his side and wrapped his fingers around a ten-inch blade tucked into a sheath in his belt.

"No," Penny said solemnly. "I'll do it."

She crouched down beside Luke and the elk and, without hesitation, she unsheathed her hunting knife from an ankle holster. With her free hand, she ran her fingers along the elk's skull and felt around strategically.

"Remember to hit the—" But before Luke finished his instructions, Penny thrust the knife downward. She plunged the cold, sharp, death instrument into the elk's brain stem and ended its pain instantaneously.

Penny pulled the blade from the elk, wiped it clean against the snow, and dried it on her pant leg before she tucked it away in the sheath. She looked up at Luke, and their eyes met. He grinned at her like a proud papa. At that very moment, a civil war erupted within Penny's heart. She was proud of herself, and she knew Luke was proud as well, which made her uncomfortable. Penny had a difficult time processing the information that fired from her synapses. *"Is this what her friends felt like when their dads took them to the father-daughter dance at school? When they hugged them after graduation? When they walked them down the aisle? In this perverse world, was sliding a blade through the brains of a mammal as good as it gets?"* She wanted to smile, but in the same breath, smiling made her want to vomit. She thought to herself: *"He's not my dad, not really."* That thought sent rage boiling through her veins. *"Why did Luke make me hunt and kill and chase down the animals like I am nothing more than his Labrador retriever?"* Penny's internal struggle must have played out live on her face like a romantic comedy full of highs and lows. And it must have been quite the scene, as she noticed Luke's expression morph into one of great confusion.

At the same time, Luke wondered what was going on inside Penny's brain. He saw her face change shapes a half-dozen times: from a smile to a grin, then back to a smile, then a frown, next she scrunched her face in displeasure, and finally a fit of pure rage. When he tried to smile back, it was too late. Luke wanted to say something, anything. Maybe, he thought, he'd try and boost her spirits, but her foul mood festered like an open sore and quickly ended that notion.

Penny now watched Luke with great curiosity. It became apparent that she needed to seize the upper hand and rid herself of this awkward game of charades. She stood and towered over Luke, looked down upon him, and said, "Can we go now, boss?"

Luke stood, relieved, and patted her on the back. "I'll meet ya at the car," he called out. Penny fumed as he chuckled and walked away.

"No freakin' way, Luke," Penny shouted. "That's not the rules. You kill, I carry," she said as she stomped after him. "Now it's your turn. This isn't fair."

"Too bad, grasshopper."

"Grasshopper? What's a grasshopper got to do with anything?"

Luke kept on and paid her no attention. This disregard enraged Penny beyond belief. If she had a top to blow, this would have indeed taken the roof off. "Luke," she called out after him.

"Maybe next time," he said as he marched out of sight.

Penny stomped her foot into the dirt. "I am not carrying roided out Bambi all the way to the car by myself," she told the wind as Luke was far from earshot. "I'm not doing it." She sat down, crisscrossed her legs, and folded her arms defiantly as only a pouty teenager could do.

Ω

Five hundred grueling yards later, through some of the deepest snowdrifts she'd encountered yet, Penny trudged along. She yanked and heaved and dragged the elk along behind her. At one point, Penny heard a bone in the elk's hind leg as it popped out of the socket and dislocated. Penny hated this with every fiber of her being. She hated being alone out here. She hated this new world. And most of all, Penny hated being cold. Nebraska winters were terrible enough, but mountain snow, forget it. No matter which direction Penny looked, she saw a bright, unforgiving blanket of white. White hills, white roadways, snow-covered cars, and snow-covered buildings, white, white, white; it was everywhere, and it was blinding. She squinted now, eyes burning from the wind, tiny teardrops froze at the corners of her eyelids like little icicles as she desperately looked ahead for the finish line. But all she saw was more white. The Rockies were nothing more than snow-capped skyscrapers made of stone as they disappeared into the white clouds that swept upward into the sky. Quaking Aspens, also covered in thick-white-snow, rocked in the blistering wind; their leaves trembled in the breeze and sounded like clog dancing.

Feathered crystals of snow poured over the inside lip of Penny's boots with every step. Her toes were numb, and the fingertips that protruded from her ripped gloves retracted with each kiss of the biting cold. Through the blinding wind that carried snow like a willing passenger, Penny made out an opening in the tree line that led to a clearing where she found Luke. The clearing was what looked to be a pull-off for tourists to take pictures and gawk at the mountain views. Only now, there'd be no gawking. The pull-off was a perch for lonely travelers. A birds-eye view to reflect on better days. A place to survey the wilderness for anyone or anything to loot or kill. Or worse, this was the perfect spot for a lost soul to plunge from the mountain tops and say goodbye to a cruel existence of permafrost, looters, scavengers, and savages: which a few had done.

Penny mustered all of her strength and lugged the elk toward the clearing with a determined grunt. As she struggled onward, Luke appeared from behind an abandoned car. He reached up and slammed down on the car's trunk as it ground and crunched shut, tearing through two years of rust and decay. He slung a trio of canteens over his shoulder and shuffled over to a beat-to-hell Mercedes Benz, where he took notice of Penny and her battle.

"Need some help?" Luke said with an ill-humored look. But to Penny, it was more infuriating than welcoming.

"You can stick your help right up your—" Penny muttered and held back the expletives as she dropped the elk to the ground. She doubled over and put her hands to her knees. At this altitude, the cold air pierced her insides. It felt like a thousand tiny cocktail swords stabbed away at her lungs with each breath.

"Like the new ride? Still not a pickup truck, but it'll do," Luke said as he picked up the elk's hind legs and dragged it effortlessly as he passed the Benz. "I appropriated it."

"You mean you stole it?"

Luke smirked and cocked a crooked Cheshire cat grin that stretched across his weathered face.

"Better than the last one, I guess," Penny grumbled.

"I don't know," Luke replied. "That last one did have a certain *flavor.*"

Penny shook her head in a healthy mix of disgust and embarrassment, rolled her eyes violently, and exhaled, "Jesus, Luke. Really?"

"You get it?" Luke asked. "Had a certain flavor. Because it was an ice-cream truck."

"Oh, I get it. It's just not funny," Penny mocked.

"Well, I thought it was funny."

"You would."

Luke stopped beneath a tree, bent down, and gripped a tangled rope. "I'll hang 'em and gut 'em. You go and fill these up." Luke tossed the canteens at Penny's feet.

"No." Penny kicked the canteens clear across the road; they skid and bounced off rocks like a soccer ball on a choppy field. "I'm so sick and tired of this," Penny shouted.

"Sick and tired of what, exactly? Doing your share?"

"My share? More like the lion's share."

"Oh please," Luke replied.

"Penny, do this. Penny, grab that. Penny, shoot the damn Elk, but not where you shot it… Somewhere better. Penny, chase it down."

"Watch your tone," Luke demanded, but the order fell on deaf ears.

"Now drag the two-hundred-pound beast up the hill both ways in the snow and then go fill up our canteens like a good little girl," Penny screeched and paced back and forth until she wore tracks through the snow and into the ground beneath. "I'm just sick of being you're little bi—"

"Now, I done told ya, watch your–"

"That's another thing. I'm not a damn kid anymore, Luke. I don't have to watch my mouth."

"That's where you're right. You see," Luke mansplained, "you *are* grown up, and grown-ups have responsibility. And filling the canteens—that's yours.

"Well, my job sucks ass," Penny stomped over to the canteens and picked them up. She wiped debris from the side and nursed a scuff on one of the chrome lids.

Luke tuned Penny's hysterics out, turned to the elk, and brandished his hunting knife. He held it loosely in his hands. Everything about it was precise. The handle was made from an olive tree, and the blade was fixed stainless steel. He tossed it back and forth between his palms just to feel the weight. Luke ran his index finger over the edge. It was so sharp that he was confident it would pierce the heart of the frozen mountain.

"And while we're at it… I have a proposal," Penny rambled on and on as she wrung her fingers together and looked like a stern businesswoman, "why don't you start doing all the–"

Before she completed her offer, Luke impaled the elk with his blade. A backlog of bile and blood sprayed across his face and spurted into his eyes and mouth like an erupting geyser. "Dammit!" Luke exclaimed as he got to his feet. The blood and muck streamed down his shirt and onto his pants. He wiped feverishly and spat what appeared to be an endless stream of black saliva from his mouth.

Penny stared blankly at him for a moment, then gagged at the sight and smell. "You know, on second thought," she said as she made an about-face, "I'll just go do my job and fill the canteens." Penny laughed out loud as she walked away. She got a kick out of the barrage of obscenities that flowed from Luke's mouth. He genuinely expanded his vocabulary game from average country boy to foul-mouthed sailor in less than five seconds.

Penny cherished this moment for other reasons. It also gave her all the ammo she needed to mock Luke for at least another week, maybe more. Insults and jabs raced through her mind as she marched on. Thoughts like: "*Wanna fill the canteens, Luke? Why does your shirt have bile on it, Luke? Are your pants supposed to be that color? Your breath smell like a dead elk. Want me to raid a Bath and Body and find you a loofa? How'd it taste when the elk waste sprayed into your throat?"* flooded her head as she snickered to herself.

CHAPTER 9
THE KING

Luke finished tying the dead elk to the hood of the Benz. He ran his finger over a bullet hole that burrowed its way into the door frame; then, he orbited the rust that built up around it. He peered at a slew of dents and scratches, which each likely told their own story. "It's a shame, you know," Luke directed his commentary toward Penny. She ignored him as always as the windows inside the car quickly fogged. "This car, a few years back... woulda been worth a small fortune." Luke patted the Benz like a pet who'd just performed admirably for its owner.

He opened the driver's side with a creak and slammed it shut as he sat down on the cold leather seat. He huffed a blast of hot air into his hands and rubbed them together to keep warm. "We'll find a place to make camp, then tomorrow we can—" Luke's nose twitched as if someone held a feather beneath his nostrils and tickled him with it. He sniffled several times, then sneezed. Luke lifted his head like a bloodhound and sniffed the air again. "Is that a—? No. Unh-uh. Absolutely not. No way." Luke twisted in his seat and looked to the back of the car, where he spotted a German shepherd. Its wet, matted hair dripped all over his seats. The dog barked and panted as his giant tongue dangled from his mouth like a yo-yo. He splayed out across rusted five-gallon gas canisters, his mastodon-like paws spread as he stretched and let out a whimpering yawn.

"C'mon," Penny said with an appropriate gleam in her puppy dog eyes.

"I told ya last time. No. Damn. Dogs."

"You told me no Yorkies. Because, how'd you say it? They ain't real dogs anyhow. But Elvis. Elvis is a real dog," Penny said as she turned her attention to the canine. "Aren't ya, boy?"

"Elvis?" Luke replied as the dog, apparently named, Elvis, wagged his tail with ferocity and thumped it against the canisters. "When did you find time to name it?"

"He's a he, not an it, and that's what his tag says. Elvis."

Elvis sprang up, tilted his sideways, looked at Penny, then to Luke.

"I don't give a good goddamn what his tag says. Get rid of it. Now."

Penny scrunched her nose and folded her arms across her chest, then literally put her foot down as she stomped her boot damn near through the floorboard. "No."

"This ain't a negotiation," Luke countered.

"I realize that. Glad you do too," Penny said as she twisted in her seat. A high-pitched squeal rang out as her pants rubbed and scraped against the leather cushion. She opened the door with vigor and started to climb out of the car. "Looks like I'll just find my own camp tonight."

"Don't be so naïve," Luke said as he grabbed Penny's wrist. "You know what's out there."

"Which is why I'm bringing Elvis," Penny replied as she pulled away, desperate for separation, desperate to prove her point. Perhaps she was bluffing, but Penny would be lying if she said she hadn't wondered what things would be like if she were on her own. Alone to make decisions, find food, sleep where she wanted to sleep, travel when she wanted to travel. A life, or at least a day, without Luke, couldn't be so bad. In this case, Luke had such a stranglehold on her jacket's sleeve that she couldn't break free. He pulled her in closer as she unsuccessfully lunged toward the open door.

Luke slid his grip downward and grabbed hold of Penny's gloved left hand. He squeezed it tight with purpose. "You're not going anywhere, kiddo."

She spun back toward him and shot him a scolding look. "Kiddo? Do I need to remind you that you're not my father?" Penny squirmed and wiggled free from his clutches as her hand slid out of her glove. She gripped the open frame and was milliseconds away from bursting out.

"So you keep reminding me."

Penny refused to turn back toward Luke. She sat on the edge of her seat as her feet dangled over a dusting of fresh snow.

"And you're right. I'm not your father," Luke said with angst in his gravelly voice, his southern drawl as coarse as sandpaper.

A tear seeped from Penny's eye. The bitter winds from the mountain pass nearly froze it onto her cheek.

"But I am here, Penny. And while I may not be the family you were born into, I'm all you got left. I stuck by you through all the fire and hell and death we've seen. I covered you up on cold nights. I watched your back, and I've cleaned your wounds. I wiped your damn tears when you slept and made your food when you was hungry. I stuck around, Penny, because that's what real family does. Family sticks. And this," Luke gestured, "you and me, it's all we have left right now. You got me?"

Penny hesitated, then swung her legs back inside the car and slammed the door shut. She knew Luke was right, but by God, she was seventeen and full of piss and vinegar and just had to make her point, so she looked him dead square in the eyes and said, "Fine, Luke. That's fine. But if I stay, so does Elvis. You got me?"

Luke sighed, looked down at her hand, at the scars that covered her knuckles, then he looked back at Elvis. The dog had a dumbfounded look that stretched across his face, and a sliver of slobber dangled from his mouth. "I guess we're all in this together, huh boy?" Luke said. Elvis perked up and unleashed a pathetic attempt at a bark.

Night had fallen, and a campfire threw otherworldly shadows over a graffiti-riddled wall beneath a dilapidated highway overpass; this acted as an overnight rest stop on Penny and Luke's travels. The post-apocalyptic wall art included your typical end of the world slogans, such as 'The End is Nigh,' to more imaginative and colorful four-letter words.

The freshly skinned and gutted elk carcass hung from an exposed piece of rebar with Penny, Luke, and Elvis nestled around the comfortable campfire. Penny warmed her hands while Luke gorged himself on the venison feast.

"You think we'll really find her this time? I mean, you think she'll really be there?" Penny asked as she used her hunting knife to dig dirt from beneath her fingernails.

"Only one way to find out." Luke spit out a sliver of fractured bone. "Besides. How many tan and white Ford Broncos with Colorado plates are in this God-forsaken country?" He sneered as he tore into another bite—eating as if this was his first, or possibly last, meal on earth. The venison was a tad on the over-cooked side; the outer layer was burnt and blackened to a gritty crisp. Though the inside was somehow juicy and way better than any can of beans or corn they'd found in the previous weeks.

Penny was more selective with her eating. She picked off the burnt ends and tossed them to a more than receptive Elvis. He lapped up every morsel as he caught them in mid-air and chewed with the side of his mouth, bringing a smile to Penny's face each time.

"Figure'n we should make another supply run on the way tomorrow, seein' as how we're eating for three," Luke remarked. His tone lacked a sense of urgency. One would think that the prospect of finding Jess would have them in desperation mode, yet here they were, two years into the search, and each failed opportunity dulled their enthusiasm and severed strands of hope.

Penny kept her focus on Elvis and his chewing. The dog smacked his gums together with each bite and gnawed on a fatty piece between his molars. "Does that sound good, Elvis? Huh, boy? We'll pick up some food, maybe a chew toy? Oh, I know, we can get you a sweater."

Elvis looked at her with a sideways stare. Luke did the same. The coordinated grins and the way they simultaneously cocked their heads were almost comical. "Sweater?" Luke pried.

"He'll look cute."

"Trust me," Luke said. "If that dog still had his balls, cute's not the adjective he'd choose." Luke took another bite and began to speak while he munched on his meal, "I knew dogs that were fightin' wars when they was his age."

"A lot of dogs in the Navy?" Penny asked.

"Army."

"Same thing," Penny rolled her eyes and looked away. She knew what branch of service Luke was in, and she knew full well that getting it wrong would piss him off beyond belief. She heard him growl at her over his food as he inhaled more.

Penny continued to pick at her dinner. When compared to Luke, she ate more like a bird. In between brief moments of blissful silence and the random crackle of the campfire, Penny was annoyed by Luke's obnoxious lip-smacking. She never realized it until their time together in the wilderness, but Luke had this thing; this tick. This habit of where he placed his tongue over his front teeth and orchestrated a high-pitched squeal while he cleaned out the millimeters of space between his incisors. Penny found it to be maddening. The ear-piercing screech caused her to cringe, and to make matters worse, Luke looked ridiculous. His tongue jabbed away at his teeth and swelled his top lip like a monstrous Botox patient.

Penny tried her best to ignore Luke's feeding habits. She looked out at the endless sea of darkness, a soulless sky in a soulless land. She traced the path of a constellation with her index finger.

Luke took notice and watched her etch a pattern into the air. He followed her gaze toward the heavens and said, "That's—"

"Orion," Penny finished his thought.

"That's right. Orion," Luke replied as he swallowed his bite, "the hunter."

"And that star," Penny's eyes focused as she moved her hand to the right, "that's Rigel. The hunter's knee."

"I forgot almost forgot you were a space nerd." Luke laughed to himself, then continued, "You know, in the Middle-East, they call him al-Jabbar, the giant. And you see that star up there?" Luke elevated his arm a notch higher and pointed. "That's saif al-Jabbar."

"What's it mean?" Penny asked.

"Sword of the giant."

"Where'd you learn that?"

"Ranger camp," Luke said, averting his gaze back to the fire. "Studied practical astronomy, trajectories, and—"

"Space nerd stuff?"

"It appears that way," Luke laughed again, but this time his chuckle trailed off. He lowered his eyes and stared into the glowing blue and orange flicker of the flames. Luke got like this whenever he spoke of the Army Rangers; quiet-like. His look, his mannerisms; he was avoiding a conversation, and Penny always noticed.

"You don't talk about it much. The army, I mean."

"Ghosts don't talk. Only listen." Luke returned to his meal.

"You're real fuckin' weird sometimes, Luke."

Ω

Some three hours later, in the middle of yet another seemingly endless night, Luke remained statue-esque. He was seated upright at attention. His eyes and ears fixed on their perimeter, the fire still blazed bright as the embers glowed in the darkness.

Penny snored, back to back with her new best friend, Elvis. Elvis ran in his sleep; his legs galloped in the air as he chased a rabbit, squirrel, or another yard varmint. At the same time, Penny spasmed and flinched, her eyelids twitched rapidly. She was in the midst of yet another nightmare. Her dreamland often shifted violently between different states of her mother's wellbeing, fictional or otherwise. Some of rescue, some of a near-miss that led to more pursuit (which mirrored reality in many ways), but most others ended in Jess's tragic demise. This particular nightmare was one of reoccurrence…

Ω

It was months after the initial attack. Our world was decimated. Cities burned. Small towns resorted to primitive territorialism. Politicians ran and hid inside bunkers, only to be infiltrated, executed, or plagued with paranoia, which would often result in catastrophic loss and murder-suicides. Families were separated, businesses looted, and all the while, the doses of violent visits from our enemies were frequent and relentless.

From time to time, Penny and Luke would stop by their home in Sutton. They'd catch a few hours of sleep in a familiar place, meet up with Walnut, and pray that one of these return trips home would find Jess waiting for them as if nothing had ever happened. Most often, though, they would utilize Walnut's bunker full of dehydrated food, crates of ammo, and his ham radio in hopes of making contact with any of Luke's former military buddies. During their most recent trip to Walnut's bunker, Luke received word of Jess's potential whereabouts from one of his trusted contacts. Rumor had it that a domestic terror group, more of a cult actually, had been taking women and children and hunkering down inside secret locations across the country. They were called 'The Flock', and they were led by a madman known only as 'The Prophet'. The story goes; the Prophet was a former preacher turned psychopath. He built a following in the Deep South, in the Bayous of Louisiana. He diluted his followers' minds with vows of riches, resurrection, and eternal life. Some say he drank the blood of nursing mothers. Others claim he was brought back from the dead himself and chosen to lead. And according to his closest followers, the Prophet foretold great devastation to our country that would leave us stranded and hundreds of millions deceased. When the attacks came to fruition, he instantly gained credibility. His status was ultimately aggrandized, as he overtook the Pope himself as the nation's most iconic religious leader.

Initially, most of the Prophet's sanctums were crude, wet, unassuming locations: caves, abandoned factories, or ramshackle churches. He and his followers held rituals, which often included the sacrifice of a non-believer. They alleged the Prophet demanded mothers and children's souls for they held the power of innocence and life, the power to build a new, better world. They planned to hold a ceremony of epic proportion on the next lunar eclipse. A ceremony where their captives' blood would turn rivers red and stream down the mountainside like the flowing tears of God herself.

Before the attacks, a gaggle of misfits followed the Prophet and tuned in weekly to his streaming channel for a live sermon. His clan consisted of an eclectic mix of feeble-minded folk, born-again psychopaths, criminals, and the clinically unhygienic who watched way too much YouTube. But now... Now it was different. Word of the Prophet's predictions and Nostradamus-like visions had spread and spread fast. Those desperate for sanctuary, security, and some who wished to fulfill primal desires, were eager to join the Prophet's cause. Luke's source claimed the Prophet's Flock had reached tens of thousands and stretched from coast to coast, and they had created a network of railways, compounds, strongholds, and trading posts.

Walnut even chimed in and confirmed that the Prophet had taken complete control of the Union Pacific Railway. He and his Flock moved from community to community in platoons, bringing food, clothes, and aid under the guise of humanitarians. On the surface, their intentions seemed admirable. The elderly, the sick, the weak, men, women, and children would follow the Prophet subserviently across the land like rats that trailed behind the Pied Piper of Hamelin. He made promises of food, shelter, and salvation. But they were all of them deceived, for the Prophet's sole purpose, his primary objective, was not to build an army of followers but acquire them as slaves for trade. In a land where money was worth less than the paper it was printed on, one needed something of real value to thrive, to rule. The Prophet saw this and built his dominion on the backs of those less fortunate. And he had more demand than he had supply. People simply wanted to buy people—and lots of them.

Now, before you'd judge, understand that in darkness, life is the element that shines the brightest. For a grieving parent who'd lost their son or daughter, what better to fill that void than an orphan? For the widow in mourning, who better to keep them warm at night than a partner who'd lie in their bed and find comfort beside them? For the mentally deranged, what better prize than a young man, woman, or child to claim for their own, for whatever twisted purpose came to their imagination. He was revolutionizing the slave trade, re-monetizing humanity to the highest bidders. And in exchange, the Prophet's clients would offer their allegiance, land, or natural resources to his cause. As with most cults, the Prophet's followers were loyal, easily manipulated, and most of all, dangerous.

None of that mattered to Luke. The only thing that mattered was finding Jess, and he would follow any and every lead to that end.

Most of the time, Penny and Luke went on scavenger hunts for Jess on their own. But every once in a blue moon, Walnut would join them, which was the case in this instance; hell, he even drove. As Walnut hauled ass down winding country roads, Penny shifted in her seat. She stared out the window in a trance-like state. She noticed that nearly every tree along their path had burn marks up their trunks, and their tops were symmetrically scorched. Her hands shook, her palms dripped with sweat, and her toes tapped with fear and anticipation.

"You gotta calm down," Luke took notice of Penny's near maniacal state.

"Easier said than done, boss," Penny's voice trembled.

"Luke's right. You're gonna give yourself a UTI," Walnut added confidently.

"A what?" Penny asked.

"A UTI. Back in '02, I had me the worst stomach pain I ever felt in all my days. Doctor said it was just stress. Or anxiety. I don't recall which. But one of 'em had me doubled over in pain, like a bowline knot that wouldn't stop twisting my insides. Yessir, it was brutal. But she just prescribed some Motrin and a muscle relaxer, and I was as good as new." Penny and Luke turned to each other, then turned and stared a hole through Walnut as he continued. "Now, I know what you're thinking... Walnut, I didn't reckon you trusted doctors, not to mention Big Pharma, but I'll tell you what —"

"Walnut," Luke interrupted.

"Yeah?"

"I think you mean you had an Ulcer," Luke said.

"I don't get it," Walnut said.

"Stomach pain. Stress. It's an ulcer. Bowline knot..."

"A UTI's a bladder infection, ya moron," Penny took a stab at Walnut's ego as Walnut sat in silence; the wheels in his brain were clearly in motion.

"Young lady, I believe you may be right," Walnut concurred.

Most days, most drives, were like this. Luke, Penny, and Walnut searched, scoured, and survived. Most days ended with Walnut sharing an absurd conspiracy theory of world domination, alien invasion, or the Illuminati; sometimes, he talked about all three at once. Penny often grew tired of the banter, but she knew deep down, the alternatives would be much, much worse.

"Are we almost there?" Penny asked. Every lead so far had ended up a dead-end. Or, at best, a clue that led to another, which ultimately led to another. Her dread would intensify and then dissipate. Hope ebbed and flowed like a roller coaster scaling and descending camel humps with each new day.

"It's right up here, on the left," Luke said as he pointed to a sign that read 'Alexian Brothers Hospital – 1949'. "Park on the side of the road, behind them bushes. We'll go the rest on foot."

Luke stood aside a weathered fencepost and depressed a strand of loose barbed wire down into the moist earth with his boot. He pulled a parallel row upward with a gloved hand. He created a space for Penny to squeeze between, similar to a wrestler entering the ring between the ropes at a WWE event. Wispy clouds marinated the dense woods, providing little to no visibility. Penny ducked down and squeezed through the wire. She emerged on the other side of the barrier that guarded the condemned hospital grounds.

"After you, sir," Luke eyed the microscopical space he intended Walnut squeeze through.

"You're kidding me, right?" Walnut huffed. "I couldn't fit through that when I was a teenager, let alone now."

"Fine." Luke pulled out a pair of industrial-strength wire-cutters from his back pocket. He snapped the top strand of barbed wire in two; the tension jerked the wire in the opposite directions and sent it spooling and coiling like a metallic rattlesnake.

"Wait, why'd you make *me* squeeze through?" Penny wondered.

"Probably to fat shame me," said Walnut.

"Or to laugh when I cut myself doing the barbed wire limbo," Penny added.

"Maybe a little bit of both," Luke said, amused. He walked on with fiery purpose and led the way to the decrepit structure that stood before them. He left Walnut and Penny scowling as he passed.

The inside of the neglected hospital was somehow in worse shape than its exterior. Someone stripped all of the copper from the building, and the once dove white walls were now a hue shy of nicotine yellow. Penny tiptoed over the occasional rat. The creatures scurried circles around the beams of their flashlights. She aimed her light upward at the ceiling, which was missing dozens of its polystyrene ceiling squares; giving way to ductwork, exposed wiring, and years' worth of accumulated cobwebs. Tree roots and blades of grass peeked through crumbling asbestos floor tiles.

Penny's light beam followed a faded sign that led toward the emergency room's waiting area. She, Luke, and Walnut sidestepped rusted gurneys and wheelchairs that seemed perfectly at home within the confines of the building. Broken glass, plaster, and debris crunched beneath their feet. A hole in the ceiling caused water to drip from a leaky roof and orchestrated a soft, melancholic beat.

"Where did he say she would be?" Penny started to question just as Luke threw up a clenched fist. Although Penny was never in the military, she had seen enough of it on TV and in video games to know that Luke wanted her to hold, or at the very least, shut the hell up. He outstretched his index finger and gave a stern point to his right. Penny followed Luke's gaze that landed on the cafeteria. She gave an affirmative nod and moved out.

The cafeteria was, for some reason, in worse shape than the rest of the facility. Significant scratch marks clawed their way across the flooring. Paint peeled from the walls. A thick layer of dust covered everything in sight and danced in the ray of the flashlights like an apocalyptic ballet. The smell was just as horrific as the sights. A rank odor reached Penny's nose. She pinched her nostrils in a failed attempt not to gag. She was about to take another step when Walnut blocked her path with his tree trunk of an arm. She looked down at the ground to see the toe of her boot inches from the exposed stomach contents of a dead raccoon. Its head was sunken in, and its fur was matted. Scavengers had picked at its eyes, brain and had made their way to its intestines.

"Thanks," Penny whispered. Walnut grinned and nodded as Luke's head emerged from a doorway at the dining hall's end. He waved them on and disappeared as fast as he arrived.

Luke corralled the trio outside of the administration offices and spoke in a calm voice. "I'm going in alone. If I'm not back in five, you get out. Get to the car. Don't turn back."

"But," Penny started to argue.

"No buts, Penny." He turned to Walnut, "We clear?"

"As sparkling water," Walnut nodded.

Luke inched forward, his .357 Magnum at the ready. Rows of cubicles lined the office maze. Luke turned every corner tightly, clearing them with precision until he was face to face with the Director's office. Luke caught wind of a commotion inside. He took a reluctant yet necessary gulp, gripped the handle, and in a single burst, he swung the door and took aim, but he didn't fire. Instead, his eyes opened wide and began to mist. His tight jaw loosened, if only for a moment. His gun lowered to his side and eventually fell to the ground. He stared straight ahead and saw a woman's body splayed across a corner desk. Rats feasted on her flesh and tore away at the skin beneath her long blonde hair. Luke's eyes panned over her body. He followed the contours of her chest and waist. He scanned her elbow, covered in bruises, and up her forearm, which was covered in cuts, primarily self-inflicted. He ended on her hand that rest across her stomach. A fraction of optimism struck him as he noticed the woman wasn't wearing a wedding ring, although there could have been a million reasons for that.

"Is it… her?" Penny's voice rang out.

Luke spun back around to see Penny standing behind him.

"Is it? Luke, is it my mom?" Penny bolted for the body. Luke reached out to grab her. He clutched her fingertips, but Penny wiggled free. She reached the corpse and ushered the rats away. She swiped the hair from the woman's face, but her features were unrecognizable. Chunks of rotten flesh dangled, half-chewed, and the woman's eyes were missing. Penny ran her hand down the woman's arm until her fingers caressed the woman's clenched fist. "She's holding something."

Penny pried the woman's fingers apart and ripped a faded and torn wallet-sized photo from her rigored grip.

"What is it?" Luke asked.

Penny fell to her knees and sobbed uncontrollably; her body convulsed as tears flowed from her eyes like a river.

Ω

Penny's eyes snapped open as she levered upright and awoke from her nightmare.

"Woah, calm down, Penny. You were dreaming up a storm." Luke watched Penny's rapid upper body rise and fall with adrenaline-laced breaths. Penny's pupils doubled in size as she got her bearings. "Same dream?" asked Luke.

Penny nodded, "The hospital." As soon as she uttered the word, a lightbulb went off. Penny's hands raced as she felt around in her pockets until they finally clutched something. Penny slid a photograph from her pant pocket. The picture she took from the woman, although now it was crumpled and ripped like sun-dried buffalo hide. She stared at the faces; a woman in

141

her mid-twenties. A man was stood behind her, presumably her husband or fiancé. Their hands interlocked on her pregnant belly. Penny looked at the faces, the man hoping to be a dad and the woman who dreamed of one day being a mother. Just not Penny's mother.

"You still have it?"

Penny nodded and wiped a tear from the corner of her right eye. "I still feel guilty, so I carry it with me."

"The guilt?"

"The picture. The guilt. All of it. Every day."

"You got nothin' to feel guilty for," Luke said.

"I was glad she died, Luke. I didn't even know her, but I was glad she died."

Luke shook his head, gripped his knees, and rocked himself upright. He moved to Penny's side and took a seat.

"It's a matter of perspective, Penny. You weren't glad she died. You were just glad that it wasn't your mom."

"I saw her body; I saw she wasn't breathing. And when I saw all of it," Penny held up the photograph, "I was happy. I mean, I smiled. I laughed," Penny blubbered and fought back a bout of tears. "What kind of person does that?"

"The kind of person who would give anything to be with her mother again."

Penny turned away. She looked up at the sky and stared at the stars. She hoped beyond hope that they'd give her a sign. When all they did was twinkle mockingly, Penny pulled a necklace from beneath the collar of her t-shirt. She ran her fingers across a golden crucifix. While Penny wasn't the praying type, her mother was. Hence, she held the pendant tight between her index finger and her thumb, desperate to feel a closeness and affirmation. Desperate to feel God's presence.

"Luke." Penny slowly tilted her head back toward her him, "What do you think dying's like?"

"Where's this comin' from?"

"I don't mean like getting killed, or the pain or anything like that. More like, what happens when people take their last breath."

"I reckon it's like taking a mid-afternoon nap. Only one you don't wake up from," Luke said without thinking about how his words would affect her. Instantly, Penny turned pale as a ghost. "You know what?" Luke said with instant regret. "We shouldn't be talkin' about this."

"Yet here we are. So, go on. Tell me what you mean."

"Well, I guess I'm sayin' it's probably a lot like sleeping. You close your eyes, and things flash through your brain, memories, people, places, just like a dream. Then there's... Well, nothing. Just quiet and darkness. And hopefully, some peace." Now Luke stared at the black sky.

"What about heaven? You think we go somewhere?"

"I guess we'll all find out on our own. When the time comes."

"Mom took me to a preacher in town once. For Sunday service. The preacher said, 'For those who believe, no proof is necessary, but no proof is possible for those who don't believe.' And that scares me. Not knowing until it's too late. And what if they're wrong.

Everyone who believes. What if it's just a lie or a story to make you feel better or less scared of death?"

"It scares me too, Penny." Luke put his hand on Penny's shoulder. "Look, I don't know the first thing about the afterlife, God, heaven, hell, or any of it. But I do know that your mom is the smartest, most caring person I've ever met." Luke took the pendant from Penny's hand and stared at the fire's reflection that glowed in the crucifix. "And if she believes, then–"

Luke stopped abruptly as a *howl* echoed in the distance. A howl that wasn't completely animal, nor was it entirely man. It was a howl that was primal, rabid, and pure evil; a howl that was all too familiar for Luke and Penny. Even Elvis knew something was amiss as he bolted awake and backed away from the fire. He snarled, and his teeth chattered while his hackles raised.

"That was *really* close," Penny choked out as Luke dropped the pendant. Penny tucked it back into her shirt and let it fall to her chest.

"We need to move," Luke said.

CHAPTER 10
THE MILE-HIGH CITY

Luke tucked his hand into his sleeve and feverishly wiped the fog from the windshield as the wipers raced back and forth. The soft splash of raindrops hit the car windows as he navigated through the mountainous terrain. The morning sky was a blanket of grey, so much so that Luke barely differentiated between the road, the mountains, and the clouds. His eyes were heavy and black. Purple skin drooped beneath them like full, plastic grocery bags. He briefly drifted in and out of consciousness. The world blurred behind him as he tried his best to focus. He shook himself and slapped his face a few times to snap out of the dream-like state. He looked over at Penny while she slept. She had a blanket snugly tucked beneath her chin and looked so content beneath its warmth, blissfully unaware of the world that surrounded them... if only for this moment. Luke looked back at Elvis, who snored; his upper lip vibrated like a seismograph with each breath. Luke said to himself, "If I only I could sleep so soundly." A smirk, daresay a smile, morphed across Luke's face as he twisted in his seat. He looked back out the windshield porthole he'd cleared just in time to see a massive pothole carved out of the pavement, which had to be at least three feet deep and six feet around.

Luke swerved to the right and narrowly missed the crater. The sudden jerk of the wheel sent Elvis toppling over in the back seat and Penny headlong into the armrest.

"What the heck was that?" Penny came to and rubbed a fresh mark on her forehead.

"Sorry," Luke said, now wide-awake after the adrenaline boost from his near-miss, "somethin' in the road.

"Where are we?" said Penny, mid-yawn, as she stretched out in her seat.

"Look." Luke pointed out the window as the Mercedes crested a hill. They roared past a sign that read:

"DENVER
CITY LIMIT–
ELEV. 5280 FT"

Penny dabbed her sleeve on her side of the windshield; the heat from her breath fogged the glass as soon as she wiped it away; it was like digging in sand. She finally made enough progress to catch a quick glimpse of the Denver skyline, a shadow of its former self. With the snow-capped Rockies to the west, the once towering and majestic downtown skyscrapers were reduced to skeletal frames and piles of rubble. "It's much smaller than I remember." Penny sat back in her seat and looked out the passenger side as Luke rumbled down the broken interstate and they zoomed past an ironically torched fire truck. They gawked at corpses suspended from trees, human and animal alike.

"I took your mom here a little after we started dating."

"You did?"

"Yep," Luke said.

"Why don't I remember this?" said Penny.

"You know that pitching camp you wanted to go to in St. Louis?"

Penny whipped her attention from the apocalyptic scenery, glared at Luke, and said, "You mean the pitching camp you *made* me go to? The one where my team's bus got carjacked?"

"That'd be the one," Luke smirked.

"'St. Louis. City on the rise,' you said. 'It'll be fun and totally safe.' Yeah, right."

"Yeah, well, anyway, back my story. Your mom had the weekend off at the hospital. So I surprised her and packed the car. Got her up at 6 am and made it to Denver by lunchtime. I took her shopping, we saw a movie. It was terrible, though. The movie, not the shopping. A romantic comedy about a guy losing his man-card or some crap."

"Fascinating," Penny said sarcastically.

Luke paid her no attention and kept on. "Then, for the rest of the day, we just walked around, people-watching. We held hands like a couple of teenagers. My palms even got sweaty."

"I'm gonna be sick," Penny interrupted and fake dry-heaved.

"Don't be jealous."

Penny pondered for a moment, then emphatically slapped her hands down on her thighs. "So let me get this straight. You guys send me to some second-rate pitching coach who didn't teach me diddly-crap in some third-world country with a giant silver McDonalds sign by a disgusting brown river. I get mugged and almost die. And you two... You two parade around Denver on a romantic getaway? Why didn't anyone tell me?"

"Figured you'd get pissed off like always. Try to sabotage our relationship again."

"That was just one time."

"I spent the night in *jail*, Penny."

"The judge dropped the charges," Penny shrugged.

"And I couldn't go within five-hundred feet of a park for eight weeks."

"Don't forget about Chuck E. Cheese either," Penny gloated.

A wry sneer crossed Luke's face as he looked at Penny and said, "You were a real pain in my ass; you do realize that?"

"Were?"

"Are. That better?" Luke asked as he jerked the wheel and dodged debris, and sped down an exit ramp toward what used to be a thriving business district. "We're almost there."

Luke pulled the car off the main road and parked alongside a shopping center parking lot, a strip mall of sorts, which had been stripped of most everything of value by now." Luke's door scraped fully open and

148

locked in place with a clunk. He lifted and tugged in an attempt to close it behind him. "Damn hinge is rusted again," he said as he deposited his boot in six inches of fresh snow in an effort to gain leverage. He grunted and swung the door shut. It slammed with such force that loose snow powder bounced off the hood of the car and nuzzled down its sides like a wedding veil.

Penny flung shut the trunk and adjusted her backpack's straps. She patted her leg and summoned Elvis to join her. As they emerged from around the back of the car, Penny handed Luke his two-strapped, government-issue, olive drab, Cordura duffle bag. The bag was the kind of gear you'd see soldiers with at the airport or upon deployment. Or possibly the style you'd seen rednecks tote about on camping trips.

Luke tossed the bag over his shoulder and made his way to a breach in the chain-link fence that bordered the entire shopping plaza. The fence, most likely a deterrent for would-be looters, was ten feet high and made the center look more like a prison than a retail Shangri-La. Luke strode toward a break in the barricade and held it open for Penny and Elvis to pass through. The trio crossed the snowy tarmac; the sheer size of the ghost-mall dwarfed them. From a distance, the birds and God alike saw how alone Penny, Luke, and Elvis really were. They were vulnerable, exposed, as they weaved in and out of stripped cars that stippled the destitute landscape.

They passed an empty Finklang's Fried Chicken fast food joint. Looters had smashed out some of the windows; still, other windows were covered in graffiti-laced plywood. Next, they chugged past a discount clothing store, then a burnt-down Bank of the West.

They trudged on and passed beneath a crooked overhang that sheltered a concrete hole, where an ATM was magnificently ripped from the ground.

The first stop on their scavenger hunt was Jake's Auto Shop. Like most of the establishments, the windows and doors were non-existent. Luke cautiously surveyed the exterior and peered inside. This wasn't their first rodeo. At this point in their dystopian lives, they'd looted through too many places to count: Stores, homes, doctors' offices, pharmacies, fast-food chains, and veterinarian clinics, even before they had Elvis. After scanning to his satisfaction, Luke took off his sack, plopped it down in the soft snow, and pulled out a .44 Magnum Colt Anaconda. The dreary skies reflected off the stainless steel as Luke wrapped his calloused hands around the rosewood grip. He spun the six-round cylinder for good measure before he tucked it into the left side of his waistband. Luke reached back into his bag and pulled out a .9mm Beretta, chambered a round, and tucked that hand-cannon into the opposite side of his jeans.

Penny watched in a sort of awe and jealously. She wondered which weapon she'd soon brandish. Her anxiety was short-lived, and her question answered as Luke reached into the bag a third time and presented a pocket-sized P380. This beast was a whopping four inches in length and weighed just under ten ounces without the magazine. Penny stared down at the minuscule black polymer frame and matted sides with a sense of misery and displeasure. It may as well have been a NERF gun. Her dismay intensified as Luke placed it gingerly in her hands as if the sheer act of her coming in contact with the firearm would somehow make it go off on its own.

"Seriously?" Penny whined.

Luke shrugged as if to say, *what's the problem? Just take it.*

Penny was irked beyond belief. She glared a hole through Luke, then down at her tiny pea-shooter. "I think it's about time you gave me a real gun." She extended the P380 to Luke and beckoned him to swap it out.

"Not 'til you learn to shoot properly."

"I can shoot," Penny argued.

"A bow, *maybe*, and based on the elk guts that I'm still picking out of my teeth, you ain't as good as you think."

"But," Penny blurted, "what about Mesa?"

"I know you aren't even talkin' about that drifter you took down."

Penny scoffed. "The dude was charging me."

"Dude was in a motorized wheelchair," Luke rolled his eyes.

"Still pulled off the double-tap," Penny claimed with authority.

"Need I remind you that two to the wheels and one to the head does not constitute a double-tap, young lady."

"Don't young lady me!" Penny shouted. "I want a real gun, Luke."

"Real guns mean real responsibility. And you... You still have much to learn, my young Padawan." Luke lifted his pack from the ground. He headed toward the body shop and left Penny standing in his wake, perplexed.

"What the fuck is a Padawan?"

The inside of Jake's Auto Shop was a hoarder's wet dream. Stacks of trash, newspaper, crates, buckets and bins piled ten high, floor to ceiling. Luke dug through the receptionist station. He scavenged through boxes, drawers, and anything else in sight. Luke ducked down and rummaged through the bottom drawer only to emerge with a mangled tire-pressure gauge. "Any luck?" he called out to Penny, who stood on a chair in the customer lounge. She dumpster-dived through a set of shelves that once held Styrofoam cups, sweeteners, and individual-sized creamers. She tossed a stack of coffee filters and hopped down from the chair. She paraded around the lobby, picking up and discarding empty boxes until she came across one that wasn't entirely barren.

"What do ya got?" Luke inquired. He saw the hopeful spark in Penny's eyes.

"What the hell are these? Ewww. Disgusting," Penny surfaced and held a dangling pair of gigantic Truck Nuts, the ultimate in trailer hitch testicles. "Is this what you're looking for?" she sarcastically asked Luke as she tossed them his way.

"Real funny," Luke snatched the nuts out of mid-air with a smirk, then tossed them aside. They plunked off the ceramic flooring and bounded down a hall. Elvis took off in hot pursuit. "What we really to find is a battery with a decent charge."

"Yeah, good luck with that," Penny said as she turned her back to Luke and made a path to the front door.

"Hey," Luke said as Penny stopped and pivoted on her back heel. She twisted around toward Luke and cocked her head sideways with a most sinister grin.

"Yes?" she crooned.

"Where do you think you're going?"

Penny motioned across the parking lot with her head. Luke followed her signal, which led out the door and straight for–

"Oh, just going to Target. Gonna do some light shopping," Penny said.

Luke put his hands on his hips like a disgruntled elderly customer at a grocery store after the manager wouldn't accept her coupons. "Not alone, you're not," Luke said as Penny scoffed. "We talked about this."

"You talked," Penny said. "I tuned you out. And besides…" Penny clapped her hand against her outer thigh as Elvis stirred. "I'm not going alone. Elvis is coming with me."

"Elvis? I–Nope. Still don't like it."

"And I don't like hanging out in hardware stores and garages all day. I'm a girl, Luke. Girls need things that you can't get in places like this."

"What on earth do you need that you can't wait ten minutes for?"

"What'd you call me earlier? A paddle wand? Maybe you're the paddle wand with much to learn."

"Padawan, not paddle wand. It's an apprentice for a Jedi Knight."

"Nerd alert. You ever stop to think I may need feminine products?"

"Again?" Luke asked in disbelief.

"It's called that time of the *month* for a reason, you genius."

Luke stood, dumbfounded and utterly corrected. "Right, well, but–I–Yeah, I still need you to wait for me."

"I'd rather find these sorts of things on my own if you don't mind." Penny turned her back once more. "Besides, you gave me a gun, remember?" She sauntered away. "This big powerful gun that's going to protect us should anything bad happen." The nametags and metal rings on Elvis's collar jingled as he paraded toward Penny. He turned a corner and slid to a halt at her side, oversized truck nuts firmly embedded in his teeth as drool oozed down the side. "Put those down, dumbass. You look ridiculous."

Ω

A sliver of sunlight sliced through the clouds and filtered into the ravaged and ransacked market, silhouetting Penny and Elvis as they tore a path through the train of familiar red shopping carts.

Penny scoped out her surroundings. It was eerily quiet, although she didn't expect much else. Most places Penny and Luke looted were empty and repeatedly picked over. The essentials: food, water, gas (both for a car and propane), weapons, ammo, and first aid supplies, were, at best, few and far between. They would often find clothes and shoes, which, if the right size, came in handy, but their efforts were mostly for naught.

Penny passed a cash register to her left, which was busted open. What looked to be the carcass of a possum was surround by mixed-denomination bills and coins which littered the checkout conveyor belt. Penny laughed. The scene resembled a demented late-night poker game or, better yet, a marsupial strip club. Penny rifled through the money and picked out several bills. She looked down at an expectant Elvis and said, "Figures. I find three hundred bucks, and I'm wishing it was toilet paper." She shoved the wad of bills into her pocket. "Beggars can't be choosers."

Elvis whimpered.

"Let's keep moving." Penny tucked her P380 into her beltline and navigated further into the store. She thought to herself how odd it was that the store grew brighter, rather than darker, the further the pair traversed from the outside doors and windows. That was until she looked upward and saw that a police helicopter had crashed through the roof of the building. It hung upside-down, held fast by steel trusses. The artificial ceiling had burnt away around it and allowed light to pour in through a gap in the ceiling like a wave exploding through a rocky shore. Penny winced, having a clear view of the chopper cockpit. Through the twisted wreckage, she saw a charred skeletal torso. Penny was no stranger to tragedy and death, especially given her circumstances. Still, the way the pilot dangled, the way the edges of his bones turned an ashy white, made her feel uneasy. Nausea clawed at her throat as her stomach contracted violently like a tumble dryer.

"Was he alive when he burned to death? Did he feel it? The heat. Did the smoke fill his lungs or cloud his eyes? Did he think of his family? Did he have a family to think about? Did he have a name, or do names even mean anything anymore?" These thoughts and others shifted through Penny's skull, like animation slides, before she was distracted. A winter moth flitted across her face and averted her attention like a magical daydream. The insect danced away, its silken wings of taupe and white fluttered as it moved further from Penny's sight.

Ω

Luke tromped through the snow and circled the back of the strip mall. Colossal snowflakes began to fall even faster and filled in Luke's footprints in the crisp snow almost as soon as he lifted his feet. The wind screeched amidst the groaning tree branches. He winced and shielded his face from pellets of snow and ice. He reached a roll-up garage door that sat beneath a splintered and crumbled sign that read 'Brooklyn Tire Supply.' Luke hunched over and shoveled snow from the base of the door. He shimmied and wedged his gloved hand between the rubber base and the frozen ground until he attained a formidable grip. Luke tried to hoist the door open and upward with a jerk, but it didn't budge. He grunted and jerked and repeatedly tried to pull with more power and aggravation. Luke stood and kicked at the door as if that would magically work. He looked to his left and then did a double-take. On the side of the garage door, a padlock dangled, unlocked in its latch. He smirked, crossed to the padlock, and yanked it free from its resting place. He turned and chucked it into the tree line behind him. Luke bent back down and hoisted the garage door open. It squeaked and squealed as it rolled upward, on its tracks, until it bounced to a halt.

Luke lowered his hood, wiped frozen snot from beneath his nose, and stepped inside. He looked over the store, which was a shell of its former self. The interior was once rustic and full of brickwork. Yet the bricks now crumbled and disintegrated beneath years of weathering and decay. He moved further into the garage; his footsteps echoed on the floor—the stillness of it all sent a shiver down his spine. Luke often shuddered at the sights he and Penny encountered. Towns and cities, buildings, and skyscrapers used to be beacons of their time; now, they were reduced to rubble, frame, and ash. The insides hammered down upon by every snowfall and every rain that came through. Even the air inside these buildings smelled stale, like a rotting memory.

He gazed over the inventory that remained untouched. Rusted and bent tire rims rested within their displays. A few eye-popping posters of SUVs traversing the wilderness hung, barely affixed to the walls as thumbtacks held their frayed edges in place. He kicked debris and cardboard aside as he moved from the garage to the storeroom when a sign of hope caught his eye. Luke rushed to the corner of the room. *"This is too good to be true,"* he thought. He combed through the picked-over interior and emerged with a pair of all-season tires. Their tread was in nearly perfect condition. He ran his fingers over the jagged rubber grooves and sighed with ecstasy as he felt the thick tread. Luke spun the tire around in his arms and continued to inspect its integrity, and just then, his joy faded. The scowl that Luke typically wore like a badge of honor was back in its rightful place. A deep slash tore through the underside of the tires and directly through Luke's reason for hope. "Why?" Luke questioned all of the Gods in the heavens simultaneously as he heaved the tire across the room. "Why are you doing this?"

Luke threw an adult-sized tantrum as he kicked and fired anything in his path as he stormed toward the store's front doors. Luke inhaled and exhaled like a bull about to charge. His nostrils flared, and his eyes were full of rage. He swiped at the register countertop and tossed trinkets, papers, and a cordless phone against a nearby wall when glass shattered and drew his gaze. He stared down at a broken picture frame surrounded by fragments of glass. Luke stepped to the wreckage, stooped over, and eyed a photograph of a family of four. He stared down at the family: the mother, father, and a daughter no older than twelve. The mom coddled a baby boy in a light blue blanket that matched her eyes. Luke stood frozen, unable to move, unable to think. He was, however, able to cry. A few lonely tears seeped from the corners of his eyes. The tears slid down his rugged face and pattered rhythmically against the picture.

CHAPTER 11
THE BARE NECESSITIES OF LIFE

Penny scrambled through clothing displays and store aisles in chase of the winter moth. Without knowing why Penny was running, Elvis remained right on her heels. His tongue hung out as his head bobbed up and down.

Penny hurdled a bent and broken baby crib and high-stepped through plus-sized dresses that littered the floor. She was gaining on the invasive insect. What ran through Penny's head at that moment is a mystery. She didn't know why she wanted to catch the moth. She doesn't know what caused her to give chase. She just knew that she had to see where it was going.

Within an instant, Penny was in striking distance. Like a child trying to catch a firefly in a jar, Penny reached out for the moth. As she lunged, she narrowly missed her attempt to enclose the moth in the palms of her hands. The moth swooped upward and landed on the top of a full-length mirror that shone beneath

159

a ray of sunlight. Penny stared in awe as the moth flexed its furry wings. She stared at it, and it seemed to stare right back at her, that is until Elvis barked.

"Shhhh," Penny warned and looked up only to see the moth flutter away toward the hole in the roof. "Look what you did," she scolded Elvis. He dropped to the ground and rested his head on his massive paws. Penny shook her head in disappointment, then slowly raised her eyes to the mirror. Penny examined herself with Elvis at her side. She realized it had been months, maybe a year, since she'd gotten a good look at herself, not counting a quick glimpse in the visor mirror in whatever car they'd stolen last. Penny gasped as she hardly recognized herself. She pulled her hair back from her face and studied the person who stood reflected before her. Penny wasn't a little girl anymore, nor was she a full-grown woman. Still, she saw beauty despite her years in survival mode. Penny traced a scar on her face–the car accident. Then, the scar on her neck–a knife wound from a drifter in Mesa, no, not the one in the wheelchair. Lastly, Penny parted her hair near a cowlick on her parietal ridge. A sliver of skin, round and pink, bubbled up in a circular shape, like a birthmark or a burn. Penny stared, frozen, eyes fixated for a moment until she shook off a memory.

She looked down and picked at the dirt and blood caked beneath her fingernails. They were long, too long, especially for a pitcher. "You'll never throw a drop-ball with these nails," she said to herself while Elvis looked on. "I was good too. Not to brag, of course." Penny crouched down and propped her elbows against her knees, staring back at herself in the mirror. She started to think of her life, what she'd done, how she got here. Penny's eyes misted as she thought of her mother. What she wouldn't give to know that Jess was alive and safe. Her face then pinched in anger when she thought of all the everyday things the attacks took from her: games, dates, dances, texting, a high school crush, parties, college. The list went on. When the attacks started, Penny never imagined a life like this. She told herself it was temporary. The military would intervene. Someone would save them. But days turned to weeks. Weeks turned to months. And months… months led her to this very moment: squatting in a rundown department store, chasing moths, and talking to a dog.

Penny stood and turned her back to the mirror and looked down at her companion. Elvis sprang up on all fours. He shook himself off and sent dirt, dust, and dander airborne. Penny sneezed and frightened her pet. He rubbed up against her side like a cat, like Reggie used to. She reached down and petted him lovingly. Elvis purred in delight. *"Reggie? Is that you? Did you reincarnate like they taught us in my World Religion class? Are you somehow this random dog we found? And what if finding Elvis wasn't by chance? What if this is fate?"* Penny's thoughts raced as she navigated eternal life questions. Penny was fixated, locked deep in deliberation until she heard it—A stream of piping hot urine splash against her boot. "ELVIS!" Penny screeched and hopped away from the canine, who had decided to use her leg as a makeshift fire hydrant. "Gross." Penny tried to shake her leg dry, but her pants were soaked and sopping wet. Elvis lowered his head and started to sniff his urine. "Get your head outta that," Penny ordered. "C'mon. Let's go find something new for me to wear since ya ruined these."

Penny and Elvis ransacked what remained of the store. They started in the pharmacy. Like everywhere else, medicine was picked clean, down the allergy pills and kids vitamins. She found a near-flawless North Face jacket tucked in between items in a toppled clearance rack. Penny set her gear on the floor, took off her old, worn coat, slung it over the rack's metallic rail, and picked up the North Face merch. She tried it on, extending her arms and measuring the sleeves. It fit like a dream. Content and without thinking, Penny kept moving. She picked up her tactical gear but forgot her coat hanging on the rack. She found a toothbrush-toothpaste combo wedged between shelving units as she and Elvis walked toward the clothing aisle, passing a cosmetic counter on her left. She stopped and stared long and hard at a makeup kit that rest beside a brushed nickel bathroom mirror. Penny's eyes squinted with doubt, and her face scrunched as though she held an internal debate. She looked into the mirror and glared at the bags under her eyes and her pale skin. She thought she looked like a vampire who hadn't slept in decades.

"You know what, Elvis…Screw it. I'm doing this." Penny snatched up the makeup. She snatched up eyeshadow. She even took lip gloss. Penny had an overwhelming desire to feel beautiful. For the first time in maybe forever, Penny needed to be beautiful. She dropped the rest of her tactical gear and made her way to an adjacent set of shelves, where she plucked a hairbrush from its display. She shuffled down the endless tan rows of shelves and took anything and everything not already claimed by looters or other survivors. Penny then snagged a tacky pair of hoop earrings, bracelets, and necklaces. She even nabbed a handful of hair extensions and the only box of hair dye left on the shelf. *"This is what the Grinch must have felt like while ransacking the Whos,"* she thought.

With a renewed sense of purpose, Penny sprinted to junior's clothing. Typically Luke had led the shopping sprees, and they'd only hunt for camo and tactical gear. Boots, blacks, greens, thermals, and so on. But not today. Today, Penny was dead set on a post-societal makeover. She rifled through jeans, leggings, and sweaters, then stopped as she laid her hands on the unexpected. "You know what? Why not?" Penny shrugged and exclaimed with a glimmer, a sparkle, in her eyes.

Penny spent the next twenty minutes cleaning herself up. She scrubbed her teeth through what felt like sandpaper-like layers of film. She used snow and a loofa to wax dirt from her pores. And finally, she ripped and tore through knots of her hair with her wet brush. Elvis waited patiently outside of the changing room stall and stared at Penny's lower legs and feet. His eyes were transfixed on her every move as she tied a bow in what looked to be lace-up heels.

"You ready?"

Elvis stood up and barked.

Penny looked down at the locked stall, about to unlatch when she wondered why she even locked it at all. Habit? Sense of security? She didn't know but locked it was, nonetheless. "No judging, OK?" Penny said. Elvis tilted his gaze to the side as he awaited Penny's arrival. "Here goes nothing."

Penny unlatched the door and swung it open slowly. She stepped out into the open. Penny's transformation was nothing short of miraculous. She looked Cinderella-esque. Her black suede booties hugged her ankles tight, but that was just the beginning. Penny had picked out a burgundy form-fitting flare dress with lace sleeves; the base hovered a good six inches above her knees. A V-cut on the back showed an amount of skin that Luke was sure to loathe.

"Well? What do you think?" Penny asked as she held the edge of the dress and spun for Elvis. For the first time in maybe her entire life, Penny actually felt pretty. She felt grown up. And she almost forgot her situation. Penny almost forgot about all the dangers that constantly orbited her and Luke's universe. Almost.

The sound of metal crashed down and startled both Penny and Elvis. Elvis stood at attention, and his fur bristled. He spun toward the entrance to the changing room and slowly inched toward the unknown. His head was down, and his muscles flexed as he snarled; his teeth looked like chiseled ivory.

"Luke?" Penny called out as another clamor rang out. Whatever that sound was seemed to move in their direction. Penny reached down for her gun, then realized she was in the dress. Frantically, she searched for her coat, then saw the North Face jacket and realized she left her coat behind. "Crap."

Elvis let out a throaty growl. His paws now centimeters from the entrance. Penny looked nervous. She glanced for a weapon, but her options were limited: a wet floor sign or a mannequin head. Penny grabbed the sign and braced herself. She held fast with bated breath, waiting, waiting, watching, as her muscles tensed. Then, without warning, an orange and white house cat bound into the room and hissed at Elvis. Elvis barked like a maniac as the cat swiped at his nose. Its claws penetrated the fur on the side of Elvis's face and drew blood. He whimpered like a coward with his tail between his legs and galloped from the changing room. The cat gave chase.

"Elvis," Penny cawed. She heard the hunt throughout the store as Elvis ran into displays, boxes, and more, as the cat meowed and kept its pursuit.

Penny sighed and shook her head. "Some guard dog you are." She re-entered the stall to collect her things. She sat down on the bench next to a stack of candy bars she'd looted. One by one, she picked up the candy and stuffed it into her bag. Penny picked up the last piece and gave it a once over. She knew she should probably have rationed it. Luke would have. But Luke wasn't here, and Penny was starving. She peeled back the dark brown wrapper and exposed a layer of milk chocolate. Her mouth watered, and her eyes grew as big as her stomach. She was about to sink her teeth into the candy bar when strange high-pitched breathing came from outside the stall door. "Elvis. I swear if you even–" Penny started to say but was interrupted as a tiny bear cub crawled under the stall on its belly.

Penny was startled at first. She pulled her knees tight against her chest and curled into a ball on the bench. But the more she looked over the cub, the more she started to relax. It wobbled to its feet and stood on its hind legs before her, no more than two feet tall. Its beady eyes and wet black nose looked like a stuffed animal she used to adore in Mrs. Donley's kindergarten room. Hindsight being what it was, Penny might have told you that relaxing for just a second around a black bear, even a baby, was a mistake; even so, hindsight's no use to any of us until it's too late. She leaned forward toward the bear and outstretched her hand to stroke the bear's spikey black fur when it screeched, then hightailed it back under the changing room wall and out of sight. "Hey!" Penny objected to the cub's retreat. She knelt on the floor and poked her head beneath the door to get a look. The cub was gone in a flash. The idle look on Penny's face was instantly gone as an ominous shadow blocked the light from outside. A deep grunt and snort echoed in the tiny chamber as booming footsteps approached. Penny's eyes widened as she caught a glimpse of something wholly unimaginable. She quickly realized baby bear hadn't strayed too far from Mama Bear.

Penny lunged to her feet and pushed the latch as far as it would go into the lock. She retreated deeper into the stall and dug into the depths of her bag. She scoured through clothes, supplies, and ammo and finally pulled out a switchblade. Penny backed onto the bench and lifted her legs off the floor. She triple-checked and made sure they were out of sight. The bear's footsteps moved closer, closer, still closer. It crunched debris in its path and pounded against the ground like Native American powwow drums. The beast stuck its nose beneath each stall as it passed and sniffed for its prey.

Penny knew all about bears. She'd studied them in school. Any other day, or any different situation, she'd be able to tell you how black bears were usually not aggressive toward humans. How they were ordinarily tolerant of people, and they often lived near human settlements. She'd also tell you that black bear attacks were one in a million. However, there was nothing usual or ordinary about Penny's current situation. She was too frightened to think, too terrified to react. This black bear was unusually aggressive and had undeniably shed its fears of humanity. She stuffed the candy bar away, deep within the bag. She failed to realize the animal caught the scent of her fear, not the two-hundred-calorie snack. The bear took three more long, calculated steps and stopped directly in front of Penny's stall. Penny held her breath and sealed her mouth shut with trembling hands. Sweat poured from her brow and dripped down to the floor while tears welled up in her eyes. There was a chilling silence.

Penny prayed to the Gods that whatever misdeed led to her current predicament would be forgiven. Penny prayed that the bear would sense she was no threat and decide to move on. She prayed for Luke to burst in and save her, as he'd done before, only this time she promised herself she would show her gratitude. Yet, Penny's prayers would go unanswered, for the bear stood on its hind legs and stared down over the stall door at her. It stood higher than any man Penny had ever encountered, easily at seven feet tall. Its body was a blend of black and a deep wood brown, while its face appeared painted with sprinklings of cinnamon and peanut. The animal had a deep scar between its hazel eyes that seemed to glow a silver hue in the soft light.

Penny trembled, tilted her head upward in slow motion, and locked eyes with the four-hundred-pound black bear who towered over her. The carnivore let out a blood-curdling roar and flashed its three-inch incisors—the bear's razor-sharp claws ripped wildly at the air.

"Holy shit, holy shit, holy shit!" Penny rattled off in a panic as the bear dropped down, charged the stall, and rammed its shoulder into the wall. The impact rattled the rafters and bent the metal supports that held the barrier in place. The bear roared again as Penny cupped her hands over her ears. It hacked and slashed at the door and shredded the particleboard. It would be clean through to Penny in seconds, and she knew she had to move fast. She fell to the floor, landing on her stomach, and started to shimmy and scoot backward, feet-first into the next stall. The bear lowered its shoulder and charged once more. It slammed into the door and sent the wood splintering off its hinges as it flew into the wall and screamed past Penny's head. Penny pulled with her legs and feet and pushed with her hands, forcing herself to safety. She got to her knees and collected herself when the bear bashed violently into the partition, shattering a hole in the wall. It stuck its razor-toothed muzzle through the gap, just inches away. Penny was face to face with the bear's razor-toothed muzzle. It showered her with hot breath and a spattering of saliva. Penny was sent onto her backside as the bear lunged again. The wall cracked in half and started to crumble to the ground. Penny spun around and dove headfirst toward the final stall in the row. A screw protruding from the stall's base dug into Penny's shoulder as she army-crawled beneath. She yelled out in distress but knew she didn't have time to stop.

Penny lunged backward, propped up onto her knees, and got to her feet as she slipped into the final stall that tucked into the corner of the room. She noticed that there were boxes stacked, ten-high, on the changing bench, and a smattering of mannequins piled, floor-to-ceiling; figures of all shapes, colors, and sizes. Some had clothes. Others were bare. Boys, girls, men, women, and even a few dog mannequins topped the mass grave of fiberglass and plastic humans. Penny's eyes darted up and down and left to right as she scanned the cold, dead mannequin faces who stared absently through Penny's soul. She was haunted by their looks. In a strange sense, Penny almost had the odd sensation that they'd been waiting for her. They were waiting to watch. An audience to witness her mauling.

"Owww!" Penny cried out. In her staring contest with the hoard of mannequins, she failed to realize she'd backed into the nearside wall of the stall. The bear hacked and slashed beneath the partition, claws outstretched, and had torn into the back of Penny's calf. She looked down and saw blood streak down her leg. It flowed like a river and stained the material of her boot. Penny kicked at the bear's paws and parried the attacks. She hobbled backward and pressed her back firmly against the mountain of mannequins. Penny's slowed her breathing as her calf burned and throbbed. She looked down at her bleeding calf and winced in pain. She watched the flashing claws and muzzle of the bear slowly start to back away.

Penny heard the bear rustle about in the next stall. It paced back and forth. Its roars subsided and turned into more of a grumble. The bear seemed to tire and grow frustrated with this game of cat and mouse. Penny felt a sense of calm wash over her like a blanket. Her heart rate lowered to a manageable level, far from the cardiac arrest that was pending. Penny's eyes surveyed her sides and the stall in front of her. The disturbing faces and bodies of the brood of mannequins now provided her a sense of security as she moved even deeper into them. Penny cautiously inched forward after what felt like an eternity. She dragged her hobbled leg behind her as blood continued to trickle down and drip to the floor, her new fancy shoes stained red.

She stopped in front of the stall and didn't dare look beneath. She refused to give the bear any further incentive to attack. She put her ear to the wall to listen. It was too quiet. So quiet that Penny heard her heartbeat. In the distance, she caught the sounds of birds; a murder of crows making a ruckus: a mixture of hoarse coos, caws, rattles, and clicks. For the first time in her life, Penny wished Luke were here. What she wouldn't give to have him by her side, cracking terrible dad jokes, telling his mind-numbing war stories, or even critiquing her every move. She wanted, no, she needed his support right about now. And while he rummaged through tires and dead car batteries, she was stuck here, wallowing in a sea of mannequins and regret. Just as quickly, her thoughts shifted to Elvis as she kept her ear trained to the wall. She cursed the cowardly canine under her breath. However, she knew he would have been nothing more than an appetizer for a black bear had he stayed and stood his ground like a loyal guardian. These thoughts and others raced through Penny's mind as she continued to listen quietly. It felt safe. It sounded safe, and that should have served as a warning. A millisecond later, the bear smashed into the stall and sent Penny bodysurfing on the partition onto the heap of mannequins. She landed with a thud as the mannequin parts were sent airborne like bowling pins. The bear let out a hellacious roar and started to climb up the mound, pinning Penny under the severed stall.

The bear stumbled and staggered on mannequin heads and arms until she reached Penny. It put the weight of its front paws on the partition and smashed Penny downward. Penny's vision was a blur, and she felt a piercing ring deep within her ears. She desperately scrambled to squirm free from beneath the broken wall. The bear sniffed and roared again as Penny cupped her ears to shield the sound; it was only growing more irate; this caused it to lose its balance as it swiped at anything that moved. A mannequin tumbled toward the bear, and she mercilessly decapitated it with one clean strike. Penny's life flashed before her eyes. "No," she said. I am not going out like this." She willed herself free and was able to wiggle beneath a mannequin. She wriggled around like a toddler in a ball pit. The bear saw Penny's leg snake between a couple of golfing mannequins that sported V-neck sweaters and visors. She bit down hard and narrowly missed Penny, tearing into plastic Tiger Woods's face. The bear whipped around wildly, mannequin head firmly between her teeth. She growled, gnashed, bit, and tore. The black bear tossed the mannequin head aside and sent it flying against the wall, splitting the nose in two. She looked down again and had a clear shot at Penny, who continued to squirm and pray for escape. As the bear lunged for a bite, its weight shifted and caused her to lose her balance. She tumbled down to the ground.

Penny looked back; the shift in momentum had broken her utterly free of the door and mannequins. She slid down the pile of body parts and scooted on her hands and knees. The bear was directly in front of Penny as it lumbered to its feet but faced the opposite direction. Penny rushed between the bear's hind legs and shimmied under the stall door that was somehow still locked shut and hung by a loose bolt. Penny got to her feet and sprinted toward the changing room exit. She looked back to see if the bear was following and ran into a shopping cart. Penny tumbled to the ground as a glass tabletop lamp flew into the air and crashed to the ground. Shards of porcelain flew in all directions. The bear roared again after it realized Penny had slipped past. Penny, now on her back, propped herself up on her elbows as the bear rumbled from the changing room stall. It showed its teeth as saliva dripped from its gums and splashed against the floor tiles like acid.

"Luke!" Penny squalled until her voice went hoarse. She prayed that he'd hear her.

Ω

Luke rummaged through a tool bin that was abandoned in the parking lot outside of the tire store. He tossed and fired broken wrenches and lug nuts in all directions. The metal clanked and crashed inside the drawers like symbols and snare drums. He grunted as his knee buckled when he tried to stand. "C'mon, old man," he taunted himself as he worked out the kinks. Luke exhaled and put his hands on his hips.

"Help me!" Penny screamed one more time in the distance. This time her voice didn't come from her mouth and lungs but the entirety of her soul. Luke snapped his head to the side after hearing his name fused with the wind, like a ghostly echo, and bolted out of sight.

Ω

Penny sprinted as fast as her heeled boots would take her. She knocked over racks, display shelves, shopping carts, and anything else in her path to slow her ferocious hunter. She high-stepped down the home goods aisle and hurdled pillows, towels, and clothes hampers. Penny looked over her shoulder and saw the bear gain speed. It burst through the promotional display of an animated film and sent Blu-rays into orbit as it carved a hole through the oversized characters' lower halves. The bear made up ground and fast. Penny cut on a dime, like she used to round third-base, and raced toward the front registers. She hopped atop a train of shopping carts and slid across them. The bear didn't bother. It lowered its shoulder like a linebacker and pummeled the carts aside.

"Penny?" Luke answered her desperate outcries as he charged across the massive empty parking lot as he sprinted toward the Target entrance. He pulled his .44 Mag from his belt and lowered his head, shifting into second gear as he rushed toward the unknown. He skidded to a screeching halt as Penny exploded through the front doors like a bat-out-of-hell. She blew past Luke in a flash. "What the?" Luke asked, watching Penny truck through the lot with no real sense of direction, only that she was running away from the store. Luke whipped back around and saw the bear rumble after her, its massive paws planted in the snow. "Holy fu—" Luke uttered. In a panic, Luke backpedaled, raised his hand cannon, and squinted his eyes, taking aim at the bear through the tumbling snow. Luke fired and hit the bear on its shoulder. The bear flinched but kept coming. Luke fired again and stumbled. Off-balance, Luke fell onto his backside, with his legs spread open in a V-shape. That shot also hit the bear, this time in the chest, but did little to slow the hairy locomotive. Luke squinted and aimed a third time. The bear closed fast. Luke squeezed the trigger and the gun fired with a bang; this time, he struck the bear directly between her eyes. The bear toppled over forward in a cloud of red mist and slapped the snowy pavement. Her momentum carried her directly toward Luke. The bear skid to a halt mere inches from his crotch. Luke's eyes slowly opened. He looked down to see the bear's massive head nearly in his lap. Steam rose from the warm blood that pooled beneath him.

Penny arrived at Luke's side. She looked down in disbelief.

"That's a big fuckin' bear," Luke said.

Penny nodded and helped Luke to his feet. He patted himself down and made sure that all vital organs and man parts were still intact. Luke turned to Penny, who leered back at him expectantly. "What?" Luke asked as he traced her gaze to his gun. "Oh, right." He reached around his back, pulled a .9mm from his beltline, and handed it to her. "Guess you earned it."

"Thanks." Penny accepted the gift with trembling hands.

Luke looked down at the bear again, then back at Penny, and noticed her outfit.

"Where are your clothes?"

"Don't even start."

"What? I was just—"

Before Luke finished his thought, Elvis rushed in between him and Penny. His hair stood upright on his back. Elvis growled over the dead beast with his teeth on full display and his ears pinned back.

"You've got to be kidding me," Penny said. Elvis took a menacing step forward, almost daring the bear to stand until the bear's body twitched. Elvis yipped as Luke and Penny jumped back.

Ω

Luke and Penny trudged up the snowy terrain of the hillside and left the plaza in their wake. Luke had a car battery slung over his shoulder, tied with a rope, as Penny lugged her pack, unable to pry her eyes off her new shiny weapon.

"Be careful with that," Luke demanded.

"I know, I know," Penny answered as she tucked it away in her bag. Penny, Luke, and Elvis dug and clawed upward as the hill's incline grew steep and the snow slippery. "So, how much further?" Penny asked, completely out of breath.

"About two hundred feet less than the last time you asked."

Luke powered ahead and reached the top of the hill. Penny looked up at him and shielded her face from snow pellets as they smacked her like frozen torpedoes.

"Son-of-a-bitch." Luke stopped in his tracks and dropped the battery in a powdery pile of snow.

"What is it?" Penny asked as she too crested the hill, only to see their Mercedes stripped of all four tires, the trunk and hood were both open, and the insides were picked clean. Someone had stolen everything inside and all of the car's working parts.

Penny spit like a ballplayer, grimaced, and said, "Well, that sucks."

CHAPTER 12
THE HAMMER AND THE NAIL

Over the span of the next few days, Penny, Luke, and Elvis trekked through the snowy terrain of downtown Denver, dwarfed by the skyscrapers that loomed large overhead. They scoured through each car, passenger van, box truck, and any other vehicle they came across. Penny rooted around in glove boxes, seat cushions, and door pockets and even checked the visors for spare keys. Luke tried to hotwire cars while Elvis sat idly by. If the past two years had taught them anything, it taught them patience. After a dozen failures, they'd often stumble across a prime candidate when they'd least expected it. They'd stolen police cruisers, soccer-mom mini-vans, and even the ice-cream truck Penny loved to ridicule Luke over. They'd appropriated smart cars that didn't seem too intelligent and even *borrowed* a couple of mopeds that came through in a pinch. Car batteries would often die, or the cars themselves would run out of gas with no nearby stations or options to siphon. On rare occasions, more extreme situations would cause them to abandon their mode of transportation. Drifters, gangs, hordes of psychopaths, and cannibals would cause Penny and Luke to improvise. And by improvise, that meant to run, hide, or find another way of travel.

In this case, none of the above were true. Penny and Luke weren't running from a pack of meat-eating humans or gangs of wild animals; technically, they weren't running at all. Instead, they walked. Like so many times before, they just walked. And slowly at that. They navigated suburbs, rural hillsides, and shopping centers on foot.

They sought shelter in the most unlikely places, from gas stations to hospitals. From one-bedroom apartments to luxurious mansions, mansions that Penny ofttimes wished they'd never depart. Yet, leave, they must. They had no choice. Penny's mother was out there somewhere in the cold, dark world. No amount of plush king bedding, goose feather pillows, infinite supplies of food, wine, or other material goods would keep them from their mission. Much of their time in post-eradication America involved walking, sleeping, eating, and more walking. And nearly all of it was time spent alone, which now meant the three of them. This solitude was intentional on Luke's part.

Luke based half of his philosophy on his sniper training; stealth was vital. He found the other half of his philosophy in a 20th-century film entitled 'The Usual Suspects' that claimed, *"One cannot be betrayed if one has no people."* Luke always said he was too old to make new friends. Outside of Walnut and the occasional run-in with a former military buddy, Luke neither had nor wanted new people hanging around. On occasion, Penny and Luke would stumble across a person or family in need. Luke was typically hesitant to intervene, opting to take a more omniscient approach. His training emphasized protecting others, yet the mission always came first. Penny, on the other hand, was quick to risk their safety for the safety of others. Despite seeing all she had already seen, all of the tragedy, horror, and suffering, she still had the invincibility of youth coursing through her veins.

Sometimes, Penny and Luke were themselves the family in need. In one instance, by sheer luck, they'd been rescued by Walnut. Penny was abducted by a gaggle of misfits while on a supply run fifty miles from their home. Luke had tracked her location to an abandoned church when he, too, was blindsided and taken prisoner.

While the villains argued what they were going to do with the pair (the options being slavery, skinned alive, or fed to farm pigs) like Mr. Bilbo's trolls, Walnut unexpectedly crashed the party at thirty miles per hour in a Volkswagen bus.

Penny and Luke looked at each other in disbelief and wondered which of the two had managed to call Walnut for help. Truth be told, neither did. Walnut was settling an old grudge at the most random and opportune time. The former pastor at that exact church had won Walnut's custom-built ham radio in a rigged poker game. So, Walnut was there to collect and settle an old debt. Little did he know he'd also splatter a couple of lowlifes on his windshield, like bugs, and save his friends in the process.

Walnut did recover his old ham radio, after all. He also found a pair of custom-made walkies that had a one-hundred-mile range. He split them up like a best friend pendant, keeping one for himself and giving the other to Luke. Walnut instructed Luke to reach out once per day, at eight in the morning on channel twelve. Of course, Penny loved this exchange. She razzed Luke about it for days on end and asked questions like how long Luke and Walnut had been dating, if she could be in the wedding party, and where they planned to honeymoon.

This encounter was neither the first nor the last time Penny and Luke ran into less than hospitable society members. Most of these meetings were one-offs—random twists of fate that pit them against other desperate souls. Otherwise, decent folk that searched out and competed for the essentials. Though, in other cases, the folk weren't so decent in the slightest. For instance, they once encountered a couple of cannibals who fed their neighbors' flesh to their three tiny children. Penny had watched plenty of horror films and shows, and the idea of cannibalism seemed so extreme to her, almost unfathomable. But now, in this screwed up existence, she could almost understand the temptation and the hunger.

Yet, worst of all were the countless brushes with death that revolved around the Prophet and his Flock. When the world veered into the gutters, the desperate needed somewhere to turn, someone to turn to, and the Prophet provided. Penny and Luke's most recent interaction with the Prophet's Flock took place just outside of Offutt Air Force Base, south of Omaha. Luke picked up a distress call from the base and hoped they would find sanctuary from Luke's former men-at-arms. Instead, what they found was a trap.

The Flock had overtaken the base and used its emergency communication system to lure in new followers (slaves). When the pair approached the base, they were face to face with an entire platoon of the Flock's members. The Flock had wrangled up dozens and dozens of innocents inside a church, and as always, Penny wanted to rush in, intervene, and save the day. However, cooler heads prevailed, and some keen observation quickly swayed her rash judgment. Luke had pointed out that they were outnumbered, at least one-hundred to one, and far outgunned as well.

You see, one last thing to know about the Flock is that they're incredibly resourceful. Not only did they have the manpower, the railroads, and demented belief system, but most importantly, they had an arsenal of firepower and were not to be trifled with. Rumor had it that the Prophet had summoned a new kind of evil in his command. This new evil went by several names, and the nomenclature would vary depending on who told the story. Stories that spread across the land like wildfire. Some called them fiends, while others called them stalkers. Penny and Luke simply knew them as 'The Howlers'. The way folks told the story, Howlers were a brand of science gone mad. Prisoners experimented on by the government, injected with DNA altering drugs, and outfitted with high-end tech. These super soldiers had one purpose: to inflict pain. They had a particular thirst for blood and violence. Walnut theorized the howlers were to be used by our government to root out the president's opponents in the country's autonomous zones. Though, with the attack on our mainland, they never had their chance.

Through one of his confidential informants, Walnut heard the Prophet had freed the Howlers. They have remained his most fearsome, ruthless, savage, and loyal minions ever since their creation.

It had been two months, three days, and seven hours since they last met the Flock. Penny knew as much because she kept a record of everyone and everything they'd encountered in a journal that used to belong to her mother, which Penny stowed away in her bag after a return visit to their home in Sutton. Penny stared down at the pages. She flipped between illustrations, maps, and other random ramblings. At the same time, she balanced on the top row of icy metal bleachers that overlooked a high school football field. A track encircled the gridiron, and the snow-covered the faded midfield logo.

"Will you get down from there? You're gonna fall and break your neck," Luke called out from a field below with Elvis at his side. Despite fighting the good fight and saying no to a pet for years (both pre and post-apocalypse), Luke had quickly warmed to the handsome yet craven German shepherd.

"I will not," Penny replied as Luke turned his attention to a pamphlet map he held in his gloved hands. "Where we headed, anyway?" Penny asked as she tight-roped the bleacher to the end of the row, then performed a pirouette on the edge of the metal seat. She nearly fell as her boot slipped, and she angled backward. She outstretched her arm and grasped the metal rail behind her to prevent her from falling twenty feet into a bed of boulders. Penny quickly spun around, thankful to see that Luke was so focused on the map that he didn't notice her slip.

"Thinkin' we'll cut through Countryside Mall, see if it's picked clean."

"Cool," Penny said as she hopped down the bleachers; her boots clanked against the snowy metal of each step. "You think the pretzel stand's still open?"

"I highly doubt that."

Penny trudged through the field and arrived at Luke's side. She peeked at the map for a moment, then took in the sights that surrounded her. It wasn't too different than the softball fields in Sutton. Scoreboards, concession stands, ghosts of fans that would never return. Even being as far removed from that world as they were, Penny still missed it. There were sleepless nights that she longed for it. For the rush. The roar of the crowd. The cheers of her teammates and coaches. The exhilaration of dominating opponents. "I woulda been a senior this year," Penny said as she looked over at Luke.

"Mmm-hmm," he replied, barely taking notice.

"Woulda had a prom too. Probably would have gone to some football games in a place just like this."

"Yep," Luke said, his focus still mainly on the map.

"Woulda applied to colleges. Thinking probably an Ivy League."

"Sounds good."

Penny, irked by Luke's lack of attention, carried on, "Woulda dated a guy or two…"

Luke nodded as he folded the map into a rectangle.

"Maybe even a girl?"

"What'd you say?" Luke perked up after he tucked the map in his pocket and spun toward Penny. That got his attention.

Penny walked away from him as a smirk crossed her face and said, "Nothin'."

The three of them walked on in silence for close to another hour. Penny was surprisingly good at playing the quiet game. Sure, there were times when she just wanted to blurt things out, to break up the monotony, but she knew that would come with consequences. The last thing Penny wanted to do was get Luke started on one of his war stories. Tragedies that typically ended up with his troop were outmanned and outgunned. Ultimately some poor private would lose an arm, leg, or finger. That was until Luke would swoop in on his helicopter and save them from the Taliban, Nazis, North Koreans, or whoever Penny forgot to remember. Even worse than that, Penny didn't want to listen to him share another story about him and Jess dating ever again. The thought of them holding hands with sweaty palms again was enough to make her want to crawl in a hole and die.

Luke stopped abruptly and whipped out the map again.

"We good?" Penny asked.

"Yeah, just seeing how much longer we have to go before you ask how much longer again."

"I   didn't   even   say   anything."

"Yet," Luke said, as he ran his finger down the outline of a street, then stopped and pointed. "'Bout another mile, and we're there."

"And how long before we find this guy? The one your friend says knows who took Mom. If he's still there," Penny asked with a hint of doubt and sarcasm.

"Couple days, as the crow flies."

"And if there aren't any crows?"

Luke ignored her jest, tucked the map away once more, and carried on. This time, however, the quiet game wasn't going to be an option. He looked back, gave Penny a once over, sizing her up or judging her.

Penny always felt like Luke assessed her more than their current situation. He assessed her posture, the way she carried her gear, how she wore her gloves—you name it, he assessed it. "What now?" she asked, afraid of what was coming.

"Gun?" Luke said.

Penny patted her beltline.

"Safety?" Luke asked.

"It's on," Penny answered.

"And mine?"

"Your gun or your safety?" Penny looked thoroughly confused.

"Both."

Penny exhaled, rolled her eyes, and said, "Gun's on your right hip. Well, the Mag, I mean, the .22's on your ankle."

"And the safety?"

"Mag doesn't have one. And you forgot to put on the .22's when we were at the store."

"I did not," Luke snapped back.

"You sure about that?"

Luke leered at Penny, then slowly bent over to check the safety in his ankle holster. At the same time, Penny flanked Luke, bent down quick as a wink, and packed a tight snowball. Doubled over, Luke said, "My safety is on, what you rambling abou—" but before he finished his sentence, Penny pelted his backside with a snowball. "What the?" Luke jolted upright like a rocket taking flight. He shot Penny a dirty look and swiped the snow from his pants. "You little, why–I was–I coulda... Dammit, Penny."

"Don't even act like it hurt."

Luke's face turned beet red in embarrassment, and Luke didn't do embarrassed, so he reacted the only way he knew how. "You drop down right now and give me twenty."

"Yes, drill sergeant, sir," Penny saluted and mocked, yet stook her ground.

"I'm serious," Luke commanded. And he was. "Drop down and give me twenty."

"I'm not dropping anything. I'm not one of your simps that you can just order around."

"Simp?" Luke asked. "What's a simp?"

"Now, who's the padawan?"

Steam boiled out of Luke's ears. "You listen to me right now, young lady. You owe me an apology."

"An apology? For what exactly?"

"For actin' like a child. What you did was–"

"Hilarious?" Penny shot back.

"Irresponsible. What if my safety was off? Huh? And I accidentally pulled the trigger?"

"Then you'd be right. That *would* be irresponsible. Of you for forgetting the safety."

"This isn't a joke."

"Whatever," Penny said as she crossed her arms and stormed off.

"Don't you walk away from me," Luke bellowed as Penny strode out of sight.

"C'mon, Elvis," Penny called out without as much as a glance back.

Elvis looked up at Luke, then back to Penny, and again to Luke. The dilemma played out across the dog's face.

"Go on," Luke permitted him, and Elvis hurried away.

The mile that remained seemed like an eternity to Penny. Luke was a distant shadow in her rearview, but her emotions began to spill over. She felt... angry. Penny didn't know why, but Luke's rejection of her horseplay infuriated her more than it should have. She clenched her gloved fist and wanted to scream. She wanted to pick up a dozen snowballs and pelt the old man right in the face until his eyes bled. She wanted to rain fire down upon him and leave his ashes smoldering. Yet, amidst the snowy and fiery thoughts of violence that flashed through her brain, Penny didn't realize she'd stopped walking and was face to face with Luke.

"Something on your mind?" Luke did not overlook Penny's flared nostrils or the rage that built within as her chest rose and fell with each breath.

"No," Penny barked back.

"Fine. Then I got something," Luke approached Penny and pointed to a spot just beneath her diaphragm. "You stab a perp, here, and you see black blood; what organ did you hit?"

"Are you serious right now?" Penny asked.

"What did you hit?" Luke said.

"I'm not playing this game, Luke."

"I'll say it again, what organ?" Luke said with a drill sergeant's tone.

"Liver, OK, asshole. It's the liver."

"Puncture the abdominal aorta," Luke slid his hand to the left, "how long 'til he bleeds out?"

"Do not touch me," Penny said, swatting Luke's hand away.

"I said, how long 'til he—"

"Twenty-seconds," Penny shot back. She took a step away from Luke. Her eyes filled with anger. Her teeth grit. She was about to lose control.

"At two-hundred-yards, a hollow-point round will—"

"Hey. Captain Price," Penny shouted as Luke's face washed with a shocked expression, more stunned than aggravated. "You mind backing off the Call of Duty throttle for two-goddamn-seconds?"

"This stuff's important."

"To you, maybe. And in any other situation, I'd think you mean for me too, but you don't."

Luke raised his hand and pointed his finger, about to speak.

"No, I'm not done," Penny interrupted and continued, "All day, all night, all it is, is military this, military that, speaking in codes and riddles. Tango, whiskey, foxtrot, delta, there's a bogey on my six… Whatever the hell all that means.

"Get to the point, huh."

"You're a hammer, Luke. And to a hammer, everything looks like a nail."

"Now who's speaking in riddles," Luke said.

Penny continued, "Then, I hit you with *one* fuckin' snowball, and you lose your shit." Luke raised his hand again, but again Penny interrupted, "And no… I will not watch my language." Luke's hand slowly descended. "Do you ever think we can talk like normal people? Have a normal conversation? Stop being a goddamn hammer? Just for once?"

"Why?" Luke said before thinking.

"Why?" Penny was even more enraged. She paced back and forth and tore through the snow until her feet dug into the mud below. "Why?" Her words hung in the air. "Maybe 'cause I'm not like you, OK? Maybe because to me, everything isn't about the mission. Everything isn't kill or be killed; take that hill; charge that platoon. It is NOT that black and white." Without realizing it, Penny's hand was in Luke's face as they stood chest to chest. She stared up at Luke and continued, "Maybe it's because I still think about how the world used to be, how it could be again. I don't know. You pick a reason." Penny grabbed Luke by the inside of his coat, just below the collar, and pulled him close. Her eyes changed. The rage dissipated and slowly morphed into tears. "Or maybe it's because I've been thinking about mom." Penny loosened her grip and spun away. "What if she is gone?"

Luke reached out and put a hand on Penny's shoulder. She rejected him and pulled away. "She's not gone."

"So you say. But what if she is?" Penny took a step in the opposite direction. She sensed Luke reach out to comfort her again, and she wanted no part of it. "Every night, my dream's the same—the same as every day before. We find a guy who saw mom with some other guy or some group of people who had a tan Ford Bronco. Then we find that guy wasn't our man, and it turns out he didn't even own a Ford Bronco. Or worse, he did, but it was purple. Remember that guy?" Penny huffed and rolled her eyes.

"Then we start over at square one, tracking down a car from nineteen-eighty-something, that for all we know is in a junkyard or buried under two feet of snow. I mean, look at us. We're on what? Car number five in what's goin' on two years? And cars aside, on our good days... On the good days, we find more bodies, like the nurse or the teacher in that school, and we think it's mom. But it never is." Penny turned at looked deep into Luke's soul. Her eyes now overflowed with tears like someone turned on the faucet. "And you wanna know the worst part? The worst part is that sometimes I don't even remember what she looks like. And sometimes, I wish it was her we found, so I wouldn't have my heart shattered every goddamn time we don't." Penny struggled with these thoughts for quite some time now; only she hadn't dared tell Luke. It seemed, for months and months on end, that they'd merely gone through the motions. Penny wondered if they were honest with themselves. She worried they were living out a dream to avoid the harsh reality. Avoid the fact that the odds of finding her mom at all, in any condition, dead or alive, were slim to non-excitant. Sure, they tracked leads, and early on, some of them felt promising. But lately; lately, it all felt so hopeless.

"So you wanna quit?, then" Luke asked. "That what you're telling me?" His tone surprised Penny. She expected defiance and rage. She expected the military man with bulging and boiling veins. But this Luke, this Luke sounded defeated. "Fine. You can quit. Here. Take it." Luke dug around in his bag and pulled a walkie from it. He tossed it to her and said, "Call Walnut. See if he answers you. You can stay with him. Or hell, find your own place, I don't care." Now Luke turned his back on Penny and stared out at the winter sky. "But I'll be damned if I let one of your dreams or a nightmare, or any other shit keeps me from what I know to be true. What I know in my heart." Luke spun back and faced Penny. Tears welled in his eyes. "Your mother's alive, Pen. I promise you that. I can see her

189

when I close my eyes. I'm sorry that you can't." He stepped closer. "I can feel her when I sleep." Still, he stepped closer. "And 'til I have her in my arms, I keep moving, or I die trying. I have no other options. But you… You do you."

Penny and Luke stood, frozen, rooted in the snow. Neither broke eye contact nor said a word for what felt like an hour. Finally, Penny turned her head to the side and whispered.

"What was that?" Luke asked, not sure if he heard Penny or the wind.

"I said," Penny gulped, "I don't wanna quit."

Penny rested her head in the palm of her gloved hand. "I'm just scared. I'm sorry, Luke."

Penny felt the cold embrace of winter wrap around her like a sheet of ice, but only for a moment, for seconds later, something happened that that Penny did not expect. Luke wrapped his massive arms around her. She pulled in close and sobbed into his chest as they held each other tight.

"I got you," Luke said for only the second time in the two years they'd been fighting. He hadn't held her in his arms since the day of the attack when earth and stone crumbled around them as they hid underground. Suddenly, Luke felt an odd sensation burn in his heart. He felt, for the very first time, like Penny's dad.

Ω

The following day, Penny woke inside Countryside Mall's loading dock. Tangible darkness bathed the vast space. Elvis snored at her feet while Luke appeared to be asleep. In two years, Penny could count the times she'd woke first on just one hand. She thought he must have been some sort of cyborg, always watching, never dreaming. But today was different. The dying embers of the night's fire faded and flickered, reflecting off of Luke's calloused face. Smoke swirled around him like an enchantment, somehow protecting him while he slept. She looked down at his hands. They were clenched together and trembled. His nails were long, dirty, and muck, mud, and blood covered his palms. His body twitched and shook like a rattlesnake. Initially, Penny thought he must have been shivering from the cold, so she removed her blanket, stood, and tiptoed over to Luke. With a gentle touch, she laid the blanket down over him and tucked it ever so carefully around his shoulders and under his chin. Penny expected this slight touch to wake him, but it didn't. Before she stood, Penny heard a faint sound; Luke's voice. His whispers were too quiet to make out what was said, so she leaned in closer, closer, and still closer until she felt the heat of his morning breath on her ear.

"No, please God, no… Jess…" Luke mumbled.

"Luke… Hey, Luke," Penny said as she softly shook Luke, trying to wake him. "You're having a nightmare."

Luke rolled over onto his other side, pulling Penny's blanket with him. Penny sat down beside Luke, pulled her knees tight against her chest, and stared out a gaping hole in the rolling door to the loading dock. She was so tired but knew she wouldn't be able to fall back asleep. Her eyes were bloodshot, and the skin around them swelled with fatigue like she had been stung by a bee. She continued to watch Luke sleep. To see this man, this machine, so broken, even in his dreams, changed the way she looked at him. He had always seemed so much larger than life, invincible, the perfect soldier. Yet, at this moment, she witnessed an unexpected fragility. When Penny thought about this, she smiled, not in a joking or mocking sort-of way. It was the same way Penny smiled when she saw two older people dance at a wedding or when she watched her three-year-old neighbor pull his baby sister in a tag-along wagon. Luke was human, and she liked knowing he had this side to him.

Penny squinted as a light suddenly blinded her. She turned her attention from Luke, stood, and made her way to the hole in the door. Penny peered out at the sky and saw a sparkling sunrise, a radiant golden glow that shimmered off the snow. It was the first time she'd witnessed the sun coming to life in nearly a month. It rose like a flower opening, sharing the gift of life and light with our world. It enveloped the landscape like fire scorching the edges of a diamond. Penny glanced down at her clothes and thought back to the day before, when she was dressed like a beauty queen. Now, she just looked homeless. There were more stains on her pants than drops of rain during a thunderstorm. She quietly marched over to her gear, stooped down, picked a bundle of clothes from her bag, wrinkled but mostly stain-free, and disappeared around the corner.

By the time Penny returned, Luke had awoken and propped himself up against the loading dock wall while Elvis licked at a dry black stain on the ground.

"You just gonna let him do that?" Penny asked.

"He ain't hurtin' nothin. Probably just dead rat guts or whatnot."

Penny said as she feigned throwing up in her mouth and said, "Long as he's lickin' your face and not mine."

Luke glanced up and noticed Penny was outfitted in clean tactical gear again; boots, pants, jacket, gloves, and the works. "Decided against the blue dress and glass slippers, I see?"

She spun around to show off her war-riddled clothes. "Yeah, it didn't quite fit the end of days theme I was goin' for."

"It looked nice on you, though." Luke avoided eye contact. Compliments, especially towards Penny and feminine hygiene, didn't come easy.

"That's kinda sweet. Surprisingly." Penny blushed.

"I mean," he interrupted, "it was too short. Like, way too short. And I probably woulda thrown a jacket on if I was you. You were showin' way too much of this," Luke gestured *breasts* with his hands and cupped them beneath his chest, "but you know, aside from that, it was real nice."

"…And you ruined the moment."

Luke laughed as he got to his feet. He collected his supplies, lugged his pack over his tired shoulders, and stomped out the morning fire. "You ready to hit the mall?

"I don't think that's even a question you ever have to ask a girl. Especially a teenager."

"Fair enough," Luke said as he attempted to kick in a door that led to the ginormous mall that had been partially barred shut. It left a space big enough for them to squeeze through. Elvis squirmed his way inside the opening like one of those show dogs that weaved between poles at a competition. Penny slid her right leg through and turned sideways, and eventually disappeared into the other side.

CHAPTER 13
THE MASSACRE AT
COUNTRYSIDE MALL

The interior of Countryside Mall was massive. It stood four towering stories tall. The bottom floor, where Penny, Luke, and Elvis had entered, housed an old video game arcade. Most arcades went the way of the Dodo in the early 2000s, yet this one still stood. The next two levels included your typical mall variety stores: Lotions; candles; half-priced tee-shirts and ripped jeans; a Lululemon pop-up-shop with four-hundred-dollar pairs of spandex; a food court with bourbon chicken and a Cinnabon; a handful of department stores on the edge of extinction; and even a pharmaceutical drug store. The top floor was a dedicated movie theater, one of only three in the entire state after the Covid pandemics of 2019, 2022, and 2026 wreaked havoc on the entertainment industry. Luke walked past the old arcades and looked over them with a sense of sadness. He stared longingly like a soldier saluting a field of headstones of his fallen comrades. Thick brown dust had settled on the machines. Some of the arcades were smashed and toppled as looters and rioters must have had their way, breaking the machines for nothing but kicks and a few tokens.

"Luke," Penny said in a solemn tone.

Luke stopped and looked at Penny; instinctually, he clutched at his gun.

Penny noticed his reaction and said, "It's not that. Nothing's wrong, I mean, I. Well, about yesterday, I…"

"What is it?" said Luke.

"What I'm trying to say is about how I acted yesterday. Not the snowball part; that was funny, but the rest. About mom. I just wanted to say, I'm really, really–"

"Forget it." Luke started to walk again. "It's fine. We're fine."

Penny continued and followed Luke through the maze of antique arcades. She wanted to believe him, but there was an overwhelming sense of unease building. A pang of nagging guilt stabbed her right in her gut. *"Was I giving up on mom? Taking the easy way out? And for Luke, seeing him like that in his sleep, calling out for my mom. How could I be so insensitive to his feelings? His needs? How could I be so selfish?"*

Penny let out a suppressed sigh. She needed a distraction to combat her guilt, so she stopped directly in front of a Terminator 2 pinball machine as Luke marched on without noticing. *"That'll do,"* she thought as she stared in amazement at the artwork—cybernetic machines stomped on piles of dust, ash, and skulls as they waged war on humanity. This version of the apocalypse would have been much more exciting. The buildings on the pinball game's backdrop looked eerily similar to most they'd encountered, with their skeletal metal frames, piles of rubble, brick, and debris.

Penny's eyes followed the body of the machine. She stared down at the bells and whistles, the bumpers, ramps, and the traps. Out of nowhere, Penny started to mash the buttons on the sides of the cabinet. She sent the game's flippers into a chaotic fit and made a knocking noise that caused Elvis to run to her side. He jumped up and rested his paws against the cabinet glass and watched the flippers flap like wings of a bird. Penny slid her right hand down the machine and gripped the plunger. She slowly tugged the plunger knob back until she stretched its coil to the max. Penny looked over at Elvis and said, "Ready?"

He barked. Penny released the knob, and the plunger smacked back against the machine with a bang and boing. Again and again, Penny pulled on the plunger to Elvis's delight.

Eventually, Luke realized Penny had stopped following him, so he backtracked, emerged at Penny's side, and said, "Havin' fun?"

"I wish it worked," said Penny. She stopped flipping and plunging and turned to Luke. "Did they have these when you were growing up? Or was that after your time?"

"How old do you think I am?" Penny started to count on her fingers. "Don't answer that," Luke snapped, "smart ass."

Luke and Penny carried on down a row of pinball machines until they reached an intersection. Luke scanned both directions like a professional tracker. To his left, a row of 'Pop-a-shot' basketball machines, and to his right, a—

"Skeeball," Luke beamed as his eyes lit up with a schoolboy's glee. He walked toward the long wooden ramps with a skip in his step. Paint flecked off the score display, and years of neglect had warped the ramp, but to Luke, the machine remained flawlessly flawed, perfect in his eyes. Luke hunched over and pulled a chipped and dented wooden ball from the ball return. "Seventh grade," Luke gushed as he stared at the ball with a nostalgic glint.

"What about it?" Penny asked.

"Can't tell you how many quarters I spent on this," Luke turned to Penny said. "Used to make it rain."

"Please, do not say that ever again, I beg of you."

Luke had a look on his face, a strange look. He shared a smile that Penny had never noticed before, not even with her mother. It was nice, she thought, seeing him lose the commando act, if only for a moment. Yet, what happened next was far more peculiar as Penny returned a smile, just as strange. Suddenly, their faces seemed to glow in an unusual moment of silence. Penny and Luke just stood. They stood and smiled; neither knew the reason why the other was doing so. The longer this went on, the more awkward it became for both of them.

"So, seventh grade?" Penny repeated, breaking the silence.

"Rolled me a perfect game, twice. It's all in the wrist."

"Well, that explains why you were so good in seventh grade, then. Lots of wrist stamina, I imagine,"

Penny laughed to herself and drew a stern look from Luke.

"Watch-n-learn, rookie," Luke said as he turned and eyed the ramp. He cracked and popped the joints in his neck as he ran his palms over the skeeball. Luke wound up and rolled the ball up the ramp with a slight heave and near-perfect form. It climbed higher and higher as it reached the top of the ramp, where the ball appeared orbit-bound... Until it wasn't. Luke's velocity was comical at best. The ball failed to crest the small ramp, and its momentum carried it backward. The ball rolled pathetically back toward him and bounced on the floor until it landed at his feet. Luke picked the ball up and stared it at accusingly as if it were the ball's fault. "Guess I'm a little rusty," he said as he rolled his shoulders and stretched out.

Penny, never failing to seize an opportunity to show Luke up, swaggered over to Luke's side and held out her hand. "Gimme."

"Excuse me?"

"It's my turn," Penny demanded as she snatched the ball from his hand like a professional pickpocketer. She stared at him commandingly and said, "Do you mind?" Penny motioned for Luke to give her space and move aside.

Luke grunted and reluctantly did as she asked. "*Besides*," he thought, "what *was the worst that could happen? She'd probably break the machine or send the ball into the gutter. Then he'd show her.*" His next roll would be a winner. He plotted strategically and knew full well he'd get a fifty-pointer next time. All he needed was for Penny to fail miserably and to learn a little humility.

Penny lined up her shot and took in the angles like a billiards player. She mockingly popped her neck, winked at Luke, wound up, and rolled. The ball turned over in a flurry as it wobbled up the ramp with pace. It careened off the bumper and hit the ball hop, the take-off point. The ball soared through the air in slow motion. Luke and Penny's eyes widened as the ball banked off the top right corner of the cage. It kissed the inside edge of the one-hundred-point cup and fell in the hole. "One hundred points. Is that good?" Penny chastised. Luke grunted again, made an about-face, and headed for the arcade exit. Penny was quick on his heels, trailing after him. "Was it? Good, I mean? Did I win?"

Luke wasn't giving in. He wasn't going to allow Penny any satisfaction in besting him. He carried his wounded pride along in his wake.

"I must be a baller if I beat the champ," Penny gloated. "Hold on. Does that mean, like, I'm *the* champ now?"

"Keep showin' off," Luke said.

"Oh, I plan to," Penny boasted as the trio exited the stairwell and entered the second-floor rotunda.

Ghosts of commerce surrounded them, with there being more spider webs on the shelving than products. Penny passed in front of Luke, now being the one with a spring in her step, and drew his evil eye.

"Before you go on and get too far ahead, I think we should–" Luke was interrupted by a crash. It sounded like a swat team ramming through a door. Then, another crash as glass shattered.

Luke and Penny ran from the center of the concourse toward the commotion. They weaved in and out of toppled kiosks until he reached the mall's main intersection. Luke skid to a halt alongside a Rack Room Shoe store. He peeked around the corner.

Penny craned her neck around him and tried to get a look while Elvis stood like a statue on her heels.

"Get back," Luke ordered.

"I wanna see," Penny said as she stared down the long, coal-black corridor. A scream rang out and echoed in the cavernous mall, followed by footsteps that clamored toward them.

Luke ducked back in the corner of the store, inspected the area, and scouted out their options. Most other stores were either barred up or too exposed for cover.

"Should we head back? The way we came?" Penny asked.

Luke considered it until another bang came from behind them. It sounded like they were being surrounded. Luke's mind raced. "Inside." The shoe store had plenty of cover and was dark enough they could disappear, at least he hoped.

Penny, Luke, and Elvis ducked inside the store without a sound. They crouched behind a set of shelving lined with scattered, empty shoe boxes and a couple of loose size fourteens. Penny did her best to calm Elvis, who panted a mile-a-minute. She rubbed the tiny spikes of hair between his eyes and brushed his furry back. He seemed to be put at ease by Penny's touch as he laid down beside her. Penny listened intently. She heard the footsteps grow nearer from all directions; the empty caverns of Countryside Mall made it challenging to discern the footsteps of twenty people from two. All Penny knew was the loud pattering of feet on the tile floor was got closer with each step.

"Help me. Somebody, please," a woman pleaded—Elvis and Penny both shot upward. Penny slid a box to the side, which gave her ample room to peek over the shoe rack. Out of nowhere and in a flash, a woman ripped past the storefront. Penny didn't get a great look, but it appeared the woman was malnourished, wore tattered clothing, and ran for her life. "Ahh!" the woman cried out again and pedaled back into Penny's view.

A percussion of footsteps approached, this time from the other side. Within seconds, and only twenty feet away, three men surrounded the woman. They all wore blue jeans with flannel shirts beneath leather biker vests, only they weren't actual bikers. They were bullies and cowards who were generally only tough when they had numbers. Truth be told, an actual biker gang would have mopped the floor with them and burned their vests in a bonfire until nothing remained except the patch stitched onto the breast: a lightning bolt that split a skull in two. The leader was short, Napoleon short, and his long hair flowed like a river of black. His beard was patchy, and his goatee stretched beneath his Adam's apple. The man's teeth were stained brown and yellow, and his lips were cracked, chapped, and covered in ungodly sores.

"Poachers," Luke whispered as he too peered through a crease in the shoe rack.

The poachers were a ruthless band of thugs who traveled in packs and preyed on the weak, and they'd claimed dominion over parts of the country. They were small-scale and no threat to the Prophet and his Flock, but concerning to Penny and Luke nonetheless.

"Hush now, sweetie, we ain't gonna bite... Not too hard, at least." The lead poacher said as he stalked the woman like cornered prey. She scrambled toward an emergency exit door and yanked at the handle, unable to open it.

The woman pounded on the door with her open palm and pleaded for a miracle. "Please. Please don't do this," she begged.

"Here, kitty, kitty, kitty," the man said as he chuckled like a perverted hillbilly. He towed a sledgehammer on the ground behind him. The sound was like nails on a chalkboard, only more blunt and terrifying.

The other two men, wearing similar clothes to their leader, fanned out and trapped the woman in place, giving her nowhere to run or hide. They were of similar build, both muscular and tall; their biceps stretched the fabric of their wrinkled and faded shirts. One man had a scar over his right eye and held a large blade in his left hand, while the other cradled a sawed-off shotgun in his arms like he was swaddling an infant.

Penny crouched back down behind the shelving and started to dig in Luke's bag. She pulled out weapons and ammo.

"Where you goin'?" Luke asked, although it was pretty obvious.

"I'm not just going to sit here and do nothing if that's what you mean. Besides," said Penny as she found her weapon of choice, the .9mm, "there's only three of 'em."

"There's never only three of 'em." Luke grabbed ahold of Penny's forearm. "You know this."

Penny yanked upward and tried to pull away from Luke's grip, but before she broke free, a sickening thud came from the concourse. Luke and Penny peered upward and saw the door behind the woman burst open and ram into her back. The woman slammed to the ground, face down, as blood covered the back of her head. Five additional poachers stepped out of the doorway and stood over her: two small men, identical twins, both with pasty white skin and long hair as red as a fire engine, and two women with short black hair and ebony skin, all of which wore baggy clothes, leather vests, and reeked of drugs and desperation. Lastly, a behemoth of a man flanked them in the shadows of the doorway. The behemoth stepped forward into the light, accentuating his unsettling physical features. And if that weren't enough, five more Poachers followed closely behind. The giant man's eyes were crooked, and the left side of his face seemed to droop. He had very few teeth left in his rotting mouth. He looked diabolical but also a little on the slow side, mentally speaking. He resembled a more demented version of Sloth from the Goonies.

The man gripped a machete tight and wrung the handle in between his sausage-like fingers. The monster groaned orgasmically. He bent down over the woman and flipped her onto her back. Her eyes opened slowly, and she began to focus on the creature that towered over her. The man's giant paws muffled the woman's cries. He dropped to his knees and straddled her as he looked her over like a piece of prime rib. Drool seeped from the corner of his mouth and dripped onto her blouse. The woman kicked and screamed and pleaded and prayed, afraid of what was to come next. The poachers clearly got off on this as they laughed in unison and cheered the monster on. The beast set his machete down at his feet and slowly ran his hand up the woman's side. He gently brushed against the side of her chest and placed his fingers over the woman's throat. For a moment, it looked as if he would strangle her or crush her windpipe with a single squeeze, like choking the pulp from an orange. Instead, the man tore a pearl necklace from around the woman's neck and stuffed it into his pocket. The man cackled joyously in ecstasy.

"Hey. What the hell do you think you're doing?" the lead poacher snapped.

"Pret-ty string. My pret-ty string," the monster uttered monosyllabically.

"Unh-uh," the leader said, "you know the rules, Iggy. All essentials go to the boss."

"Iggy?" Penny whispered to herself. She thought, *"What an unusual name for such an unusually odd-looking character."*

Luke pulled Penny from her train of thought, tugged at her arm in an attempt to urge her to be quiet. He motioned downward and looked at her knuckles as they tremored against the shelves.

Penny held her right hand as tight as possible with her left in hopes it would stop her quaking. This moment brought back a flash of memories from her birth father, Roach. His hands would tremble like this, either from nerves or withdrawals, and typically took place when he cut lines of cocaine or mixed a new batch of meth. Roach had the fixation of inhaling a pack of menthols to calm himself. Penny only had scoldings from Luke and a judgy eye from a German shepherd that smelled of old socks and beef jerky.

"Not e-ssen-tial. Iggy's," Iggy snapped back as he held his catcher's mitt-sized hands against his chest. He shielded the pearls from his leader.

Infuriated, the leader backhanded Iggy across the mouth. The leader towered over Iggy, reached down into his chest pocket, and snatched the jewels. Iggy fell to the side, whimpered, and clutched his apple-red, swollen face.

"Valuables, food, and weapons. They all go to the boss. Don't you make me tell you again," the leader warned. "Understand me, boy?"

"Iggy under-stand," Iggy said as he nodded.

"Get to your feet, you pathetic mongoloid."

Iggy did as he was told, to the amazement of Penny. How was it possible for someone so big and so strong to look so feeble compared to a man that stood no taller than five-foot-two? "*A cowardly giant,*" she thought.

The lead poacher circled the woman like a lion that stalked a wounded gazelle.

"But these shoes," the minuscule marauder lauded, "these shoes would look divine on my Sarah-Belle. Don't you agree?"

The companions and Iggy nodded in approval. The leader crouched down at the woman's feet and started to pull at her shoelaces, comically frustrating him with her double-knots. The woman, more alert than before, began to fight back. She squirmed in a failed effort to wiggle away, then kicked the leader square in the jaw. The act did little to help her chances. All she did was bloody his bottom lip and severely piss him off.

"Hold her down, ya morons," the leader demanded. His lackeys did as he asked like obedient little lap dogs. "Gimme the blade, Iggy," he commanded. Iggy kicked his machete across the floor to his leader; the metal scraped against the broken tiles. "You don't wanna give 'em up? Fine. Then I'll take 'em," the leader said as he licked his leathery lips and smiled.

Penny's breathing slowed as she gnashed her teeth together. Her once trembling hands were as stoic as a statue, and her eyes narrowed as she turned to Luke. "I don't care what you say," she said in a hushed voice. "I can't sit here and watch this.

Penny slowly rose to her feet as the leader rolled up the woman's pant legs and rolled down her socks. He sized the woman up and lined up her ankles with the blade. Penny didn't believe her eyes. He was going to cut her feet off just to get a pair of shoes. And Penny, Penny wasn't about to let it happen. She slowly cocked her gun and flipped the safety off.

"We can't get involved," Luke hissed as he grabbed ahold of Penny's wrist.

"And if that was me?"

"But it ain't," Luke said as he attempted to pull Penny back down behind cover, "and besides, there's thirteen of them and two of us."

"Three of us," said Penny, staring at Elvis, "and we're ending this, now.

The leader raised his machete high in the air, eager to claim the shoes for his wife at any cost. Penny took a half-step out from behind the shoe rack and aimed. Her hands slightly trembled as she focused her sights directly between the man's eyes. The man's arm began to descend as Penny's finger started to squeeze the trigger, but before either struck, a series of spine-chilling howls echoed through the concourse. The unnerving sounds were deep and guttural. The noise bounced off the walls and windows and beckoned everyone's undivided attention.

"Howlers," Iggy gulped. "Howlers, Howlers, Howlers," he stammered and clamored backward, straight into the wall. His eyes raced and scanned his surroundings in complete horror.

Another howl came from the stairwell from which Iggy and the rest of the crew arrived. In an instant, the sadistic sounds enclosed around them.

Penny ducked down behind the counter, covered her ears, and closed her eyes. It was evident Penny was familiar with the Howlers and their handiwork. She loathed the sounds, and worse, the horror that came after. The ferocity that pumped through her veins was draining by the second. She rocked back in forth and muttered under her breath, almost as if she was speaking in tongues.

Luke, too, was conscious of the trauma the Howlers inflicted. He knew they struck fast and without forgiveness, and worst of all, didn't discriminate. They were actual monsters in every sense of the word, and in the last two years, the Prophet unleashed them on the innocent and guilty alike.

Luke unfurled his weapon and chambered a round; then, he slid a wrinkled and faded wallet-sized photo from his chest pocket. The laminate protective layer peeled from the corners. It was a picture of him and Jess on their anniversary. He looked at the image of himself and Jess standing on a pier, blanketed by a sparkling sunset and foam-crested waves of the ocean.

"Give me the strength," he said as he kissed the picture and tucked it away in his pocket.

The poachers locked and loaded and scanned every millimeter of visible space for the impending doom that cannonballed toward them like ghosts in the darkness. One of the many bearded poachers raised his pistol in a flash and fired a flurry of rounds wildly toward the ceiling.

"Where are they? You see 'em?" the leader asked as he desperately twisted in a semi-circle like he was trying to spin a hula-hoop.

Shadows weaved in and out of sight as they tore past. Windows shattered as howls rang out, and poachers begged for their lives in torturous misery. The leader spun three-hundred and sixty degrees and toppled over, tripping over his feet. He looked up, and his mouth opened wide in fear. Another shadow whizzed by his head and ripped across an open doorway as the howls grew louder and louder, closer and closer. It was a claustrophobic nightmare.

Iggy pulled a mallet from his back pocket and beat it against his meaty palms. "Arghhh," he growled at the shadows and swung wildly at nothing, nothing but the air.

"Iggy!" the leader shouted. "Look out." Iggy turned to him, scared and confused. "Iggy!" the leader called again and watched as Iggy was pulled out of sight by a black mass that moved faster than light. Iggy vanished in a flash, his screams dopplered away and echoed in the distance.

Luke rested his head against the rack. He looked over at Penny, who held her hands firmly against her ears. She was shielding the symphony of screams that resonated from the concourse. The Howlers tore the Poachers limb from limb, one at a time. Luke heard their skin stretch and their bones snap. Gunfire rang out in a flurry, but as the seconds passed, the time in between blasts had lengthened. The shower of bullets turned to a trickle, and soon the shots had ceased. Luke looked down at Elvis, who whimpered and covered his muzzle with his paws. Luke reached down and brushed his head. He hoped to calm the canine. He hoped and prayed that Elvis wouldn't give away their position.

Within seconds, the leader of the poachers was alone in the middle of the concourse. Blackness surrounded him as clouds covered the only light that shined into the building. He fired a shot blindly to one side, then the other, as he whipped left, right, left, and right again.

Penny slowly pulled her hands from her head only to hear tormenting silence swiftly replaced by a bedeviling scream. She clamped her hands back over her ears like a pair of noise-canceling headphones as the lead poacher cried out in agony. His screams pinballed off the walls and windows as he was torn apart from the inside out.

As the man's cries died out, the silence returned. The now seemingly unoccupied mall sounded more like an abandoned church or library than the once-bustling center of commerce. Luke tapped Penny on the shoulder and signaled to her that the screams had ceased. He was quick to shush her, not wishing to fall into a false sense of security. While it was quiet, he wasn't sure it was clear.

Penny turned slightly to her side and angled herself in a position to peek through a tiny sliver in the shoe rack. Through the partially obstructed view, she made out a vile, red river of blood that stained everything. As her eyes surveyed, the sound of footsteps approached. Click. Click. Click. A lean, twisted shadow moved closer with each step, and labored breathing followed. Each inhale sounded like an asthmatic cackle. Penny ducked down and made herself small. She looked to Luke, who again readied his gun as he took a long, deep, quiet breath. *"Would that be his last?"* Penny wondered. *"Was this how it ended?"* Click. Click. Cackle. Click.

The Howler inched closer. Penny looked upward as her bottom lip quivered. Two hands slammed down on the rack above her. The skin was charred and black and rotten. The fingernails were long and sharp, like bones chiseled with a rock. The breaths grew louder. Each was more profound than the one before. The wheezing was upon them, cackling, crackling more and more. Penny looked back to Luke, who nodded. She knew what this meant. She nodded back, reached into her beltline, and readied her gun against her chest. Luke started a countdown and put three fingers up, then two, then one—

Suddenly, another howl came from further down the concourse, summoning the rest of the Howlers to follow. The shadow disappeared in a flash, and the deafening silence returned once more.

Penny and Luke exhaled simultaneously. Penny had nearly forgotten Elvis was with them until she saw him stand out of the corner of her eye. She yelled in fear and quickly covered her mouth.

"Relax," Luke suggested at a whisper as he got to his feet cautiously. "Just the dog."

"Relax? Really? That's your advice?"

They waited for some time before they vacated their position. Luke wasn't optimistic the Howlers had left the mall, and Penny was unable to move a muscle. So they sat, frozen until Luke was confident the coast was clear. He was the first to rise to his feet. He stretched out his legs and crept toward the concourse. Penny stood next and followed close behind.

"Ho-ly Shit," Luke exclaimed as he stared out into the mall hallway.

"What now?" Penny exclaimed. She trailed Luke so closely that all she saw was the back of his shirt. Luke winced and shook his head. Penny peeked around Luke's torso and caught a glimpse. Instantly, Penny fought the urge to vomit as she stared out at pure carnage. It was a retail slaughterhouse. Blood coated the walls, shredded flesh speckled the linoleum, and intestines dangled from an overhead light fixture like a cannibal's mistletoe. Penny averted her eyes. She was no stranger to bloodshed and death, but this was gratuitous. Even the most savage beasts would deem this unthinkable. An unease manifested deep within the pit of Penny's stomach. Moments earlier, Penny was prepared to end the Poachers' existence, to steal their very last breath and watch them suffer. But now, Penny almost felt sorry for them. The woman the poachers were about to kill or mangle for her sneakers was torn apart like a Thanksgiving turkey. Her arms legs ripped from their sockets, and her head was missing entirely.

"Luke," Penny said as she stepped over a severed hand.

Luke stooped over what remained of Iggy's body. He lifted his chin, turned to Penny, and answered, "What is it?"

"I wanna go now."

A pleasant surprise awaited Penny, Luke, and Elvis as they exited the mall's south entrance.

"Will you look at that?" Luke said. "What do you think?" A grin stretched across his face as he smirked and twisted strands of facial hair just above his lip.

"Guess the Poachers won't be needing this

anymore," Penny said as she stared out at a garbage truck that was triple parked across the handicap spaces. The truck sputtered and spat a hypnotic spiral of black exhaust into the sky. The Poachers' symbol was spray-painted onto the rumbling beast's side over a coat of neon green paint. They'd found their ride.

CHAPTER 14
THE PIT STOP

The garbage truck's engine gurgled as the vehicle barreled down a two-lane highway. With one of its headlights shattered, a single beam of light illuminated the yellow dashed line that divided the freeway like a sixty-thousand-pound cyclops piercing the pavement. Luke focused on the road and gazed out at the vast darkness as he faded between consciousness and highway hypnosis. He stretched in his seat and glanced across the bench at Penny while Elvis slept between them. A dim, yellow, overhead light shined down upon Penny like a halo. "Can't believe you're still writing in that diay."

"Diary?" Penny asked as she whipped her head in Luke's direction. Diaries were for children and teens with a crush. For Luke to insinuate she used *a diary* was nothing less than insulting. "I'm journaling if you must know."

"I stand corrected." Luke threw his arms up, admitting defeat.

Penny turned her attention back to the book. It had a Carolina-blue leather cover with a slight tear on its top left corner, with Jess's monogram etched into the body; its gold hue still shimmered if the light hit it just right.

"Whatcha workin' on?" Luke asked as he looked over Penny's work.

"More of the same," Penny said as she held up a page. Detailed pencil drawings of people littered the page with descriptions and captions beneath. At the center of one of the pages was a sketch of Iggy. The likeness was remarkable, down to a chipped front tooth and cinderblock-sized hands. Around the picture of Iggy was a woman with a black robe and dark hair, a man with a top hat and a large cross that dangled from his neck, and a set of conjoined twin girls that stood atop a hillside, wearing a summer dress.

"You're a really good drawer," Luke said, as he admired the sketch.

"Artist," Penny replied in a harsh tone.

"Huh?"

"Drawers are four-year-olds with sippy cups. I'm an artist."

"Fair enough. How many you got in there?"

"What, drawings?" Penny said sarcastically as she sniggered. "Half the book so far. Most of the folks we've come across." Penny thumbed through various pages, each filled with people, places, and moments from the past two years. "Got the Poachers, Settlers, the Flock, the Believers, and a whole chapter on the Howlers even though we barely got a glimpse of 'em."

"Thank God they never get a glimpse of us," Luke said.

"Not that we know of," Penny corrected.

"What about us," Luke redirected. "In your book. What group do we fall under? What's our name? The Crusaders? The Chosen? The Warriors? My money's on Crusaders, just like Indiana Jones."

"Who?"

"How did you get to be seventeen without knowing about Star Wars or Indiana Jones," Luke said. "My daddy made me watch 'em when I was still in diapers.

"Guess my dad had other plans for me."

Luke instantly felt ashamed. "I'm sorry, Pen, I didn't mean to–"

"It's fine. And besides. After he left, softball and the apocalypse kinda took up all my time."

"Yeah, guess you're right. Maybe after we find your mom and the world gets back to normal, we'll have ourselves a movie night."

Penny looked out the window, lost in thought and regret. She never had a daddy-daughter movie night like so many other things missing from her childhood. What she wouldn't have given to sit in pajamas with a giant bowl of movie theater popcorn in her lap as she watched the classics with a loving father. Her eyes focused on a blue road sign with pink and green graffiti symbols covering most of it.

"Looks like there's a couple of gas stations at the next exit," Penny said. "We should check it out."

"You got it, boss," said Luke as he flipped on the blinker and merged into the exit lane.

"Why'd you do that?"

"Do what?"

"That." Penny pointed down at the blinker. "Why do you even use it?"

"Habit, I guess," Luke flipped the blinker switch back down to its neutral position. "And just because there ain't no cops doesn't mean we shouldn't follow the rules."

"Says the guy driving a dump truck at ninety-five in a sixty."

Luke laughed as he turned through an intersection. "It's a waste management vehicle. Not a dump truck."

"So you're an expert on utility vehicles now?"

"Not utility vehicles. Not entirely. You're looking at class seven or eight heavy-duty machinery.

"Semantics," Penny said.

"Do you even know what that means? *Semantics*?"

"Do you?" Penny shot back.

"So, uh, anyway," Luke avoided the rebuttal like the plague, "you uh, you never answered my question earlier."

"Which one?" Penny pondered.

"Our clan? Our group name? What is it?"

"Isn't that obvious?" said Penny as she looked down to her side at Elvis, then back up at Luke. "We're the Damned," she said as she flipped the pages to the back cover and held the journal up for Luke to see. Sketched onto the inside back cover itself was a hyper-realist portrayal of Luke's grimacing face and one of Penny standing tall atop a hillside wearing her gas mask. Between the two of them was a symbol Penny had created: a scale built upon a crucifix, half in darkness and half in light. The side in darkness was weighed down, pulled toward flames with hands reaching out of the fire.

Two miles of somber silence later, Luke pulled into an abandoned Pickman's Convenience Store parking lot on the corner of Eighth and Hartford. Four gas pumps stood in a row, with another two gutted and rusted down to skeletal copper pumps, valves, and motors.

Penny hopped down from the passenger side of the truck and scrunched her nose in disapproval. "The first thing I'm looking for is an air freshener."

"Told you bringing Elvis was a bad idea," Luke grumbled.

"We're driving around in *actual* garbage, and you blame the dog?" Penny jabbed. She turned, half-expecting to see Elvis at her side, but he wasn't there. "Elvis?" A whimper came from the bed of the truck. Penny looked up and saw the dog rock back and forth as his head bobbed in and out of the open doorway. "Just jump," Penny said to an unsure Elvis. He continued to rock comically, almost daring to leap but chickened out. "You big baby." Penny marched over to the side of the truck, reached up, and grabbed Elvis around his waist and shoulders. She slowly lowered him to the ground as his front and back legs stiffened in fear until he was placed gently on the parking lot surface. "C'mon, boy."

Penny led Elvis toward the convenience store entrance, where Luke waited with a bolt action rifle in his right hand. He put his left hand on the door to keep Penny from entering just yet. "You know the drill," he said as he peeked through the chipped and faded vinyl lettering and decals on the dainty glass door.

"Stay quiet. Look for anything we can use. Then get out before anybody knows we were here," Penny rattled off nonchalantly as Luke quietly opened the door for her. "I know what I'm doing, Luke." She slid through the opening and disappeared into the store with Elvis on her heels.

"Nothin' personal," Luke said as he watched them move deeper inside the store, then turned to face the street. Luke spoke the truth: this wasn't personal at all. For Luke, life in the military had injected routine, drill, and practice into his bloodstream. When shit got real, all soldiers were able to count on were their training, instincts, and reactions. In times of high stress, the nerves that connect the inner ears and the brain shut down, resulting in what's known as auditory exclusion. During the heat of battle, soldier's instincts would naturally betray the collective and look out solely for the individual. This betrayal spelled trouble for the troops and had the potential to lead to the deaths of hundreds, if not thousands, in wartime. Luke and superiors who came generations before him knew this. This knowledge is why he and many before him relied heavily on routine, repetition, and barking the same orders to Penny day in and day out. For one day, Penny's adrenaline would rush through her body like a tsunami. Her hearing would disappear, her eyesight would turn to blurred tunnel-vision, and all she'd have to fall back on would be Luke's drills.

Inside the moonlit convenience store, Penny and Elvis moved up and down the aisles past toppled over shelves, empty boxes, egg cartons, and cigarette packages that peppered the floor. Penny hopped atop the checkout counter and slid across the glass that still made a home for lottery scratchers and cheap souvenirs.

Penny turned back to see Elvis lick rotten curds of milk coagulated inside a ripped carton just in front of the dairy cooler. "Oh, no, no, don't do that," said Penny. Elvis paid her no attention as he swallowed a thick clot of expired milk with a gulp. "You're disgusting."

Outside, Luke readied his weapon and kept watch like the Queen's guards at Buckingham Palace. The darkness and silence that encroached around him were palpable until the rumbling engine and dim parking lights of an old station wagon clunked down the road in Luke's direction. Luke cracked the door open a hair, stuck his head inside, and called out, "Might wanna hurry it up in there."

"Roger, Roger," Penny replied sarcastically.

"I'm serious. May have some company," Luke said as he turned his attention back toward the station wagon. Its tires were low on air as it clunked along, and its bumper was partially detached and scraped against the ground, sparks shooting up in its wake. Luke watched as the vehicle squealed to a halt beneath the filling station sign. The signage proudly displayed 'buy-one-get-one Mike and Ike's candy' and 'two-dollar tacos from the food bar'. Beneath the food sale sign sat the ever-affordable six-ninety-nine price for a gallon of unleaded gas. The driver's side door of the station wagon whined as it swung open on its rusty hinges. An older man climbed out, stretched his long thin legs, and popped his back. He carried a shotgun on his hip as he turned and curiously clocked Luke from across the street. The man was bald with a scraggly salt and pepper beard that stretched thin across his dark brown skin. He was wearied, yet there was an absolute vigilance in his eyes, despite the purple bags that rest beneath them. His clothes were stretched and stained with soot and dirt, and he wore a long jagged scar beside his left eye that rested just above a cluster of caramel-colored freckles.

There was tension in the air that Luke could cut with a knife. Luke felt it, and it was evident the thin man did as well. They stared at each other, motionless, for an eternal nanosecond until Luke saw the man's unsteady hand raised just above the hood of his car. It hovered there for a moment until the man pounded against the roof three times; the resounding thuds echoed in the night.

Luke slid his finger around the trigger guard, rested it on the base of the trigger, and tapped the metal as he watched the action unfold across the street. A million scenarios raced through his thoughts. He kept his icy stare on the man, just yards away. Luke shifted his focus between him and the car's tinted windows as he thought about what may lie inside. Luke started to lower the muzzle as the back doors of the wagon flung open simultaneously. He took a deep breath and, like a sheriff of the Wild West, prepared himself for a duel as he brought the butt of his rifle upward and tucked it square against his shoulder. Luke squinted and focused, ready for anything that may come his way. Soldiers, cannibals, wild dogs, he'd seen it all. But he wasn't quite prepared for what happened next as two children jumped out of the back seat of the station wagon and dashed toward the store.

"Make it quick, Wesley" the man grumbled in a scratchy voice as he spit onto the sidewalk.

"Ok, daddy," a boy of no more than ten quipped. He had an innocent and adorable face with round cheeks and big brown eyes, and he wore a pair of baggy carpenter jeans with a red hoodie.

"Look out for your brother," the man hollered to the second child, a girl. Her long black curls bounced off her shoulders as she ran after the boy. She was certainly older than her brother—probably Penny's age. She had a woman's body with a youthful face and captivating hazel eyes. The girl disappeared inside the gas station for an instant, apparently to run reconnaissance, then popped back out and held the door open for the little man. The father slowly backpedaled toward the gas station entrance. He stood guard at the door, and under no circumstances did he break eye contact with Luke.

Meanwhile, Penny had picked through most of the aisles, cabinets, shelves, and drawers in the convenience store's showroom and now rummaged her way through the storage room. She perched herself over a pile of small cardboard boxes that scattered across the storage room floor. Most of the packages had fruit snacks or granola bar labels stamped on them. Most of the boxes acted as a microcosm of the search for Penny's mother: they were empty. Penny tossed aside empty package after empty package until she unearthed one tiny cardboard square that surely must have had a reward buried deep inside.

Penny dangled the box upside down and rattled it like a child shaking a present on Christmas morning. She picked up a small flashlight that sat by her side and put it between her clenched teeth. The beam flickered and cut through the darkness. It illuminated the folded flaps of what Penny hoped would be edible goodness. Her stomach growled in anticipation as she unfolded the first flap, pulling it from the depths of the box. Penny's jubilant fingers raced and grabbed hold of the second flap and yanked it outward. She took both remaining ends of the opening in her hands and swung them open. She tilted her head sideways and angled the flashlight into the package. Her smile widened as she prepared to claim her prize—she longed for some jerky or other meat product that hadn't expired or recently bled on her clothes. Suddenly the beam of light reflected off two small orbs inside. Eyes. A rat's eyes. Before Penny could blink, a frightened, cornered rat leaped out of the box and landed on Penny's chest.

Penny screamed like a banshee and fell onto her backside. She swung and swatted wildly into the air as she hoped to scare the rat from her jacket, not daring to touch the little monster. Penny, Jess, and Penny's grandmother, whom she barely knew, were all scared of rats.

The rat hissed as it unfurled its sizeable front teeth. They looked like two tiny wooden stakes. Penny screamed out again and chugged backward across the floor. She reached and clawed for anything to repel the rodent. Penny slammed into a magazine rack that toppled over and landed at her side with a clang. A trucker magazine landed at her side. The cover had a fully decked-out monster truck, outfitted with decals and accessories. Standing in the truck bed were three scantily-clad women dressed in less clothing than the truck itself. Penny grabbed the magazine, rolled it up like a police baton, and swung wildly at the rat until it scurried away into the blackness.

"Everything alright in there?" Luke's voice probed as he peeked into the store through a crack in the front door.

"It's fine. I'm fine." Penny brought her knees to her chest and dusted herself off. The bells on the door chimed as Luke let it close.

The space surrounding Penny looked as if a tornado had made its way through just as Elvis strolled in and stood at Penny's side, surveying the aftermath. He stared at Penny with his tongue dangling from his mouth.

"Don't even look at me."

Elvis cocked his head and slapped his tongue against Penny's cheek like a warm and wet prickled glove. She wiped the saliva from her skin and leaned against him, resting her head against the scruff of his neck. Penny took comfort in his companionship until a scent crept into her nostrils. She sniffed and immediately recoiled as Elvis's stench made her nose wrinkle up. "You do stink," Penny said as she reached into her jacket pocket. "Guess it's a good thing I found this. Elvis perked up as he heard plastic crinkle from within Penny's coat. "Let's not get too excited," she said as she pulled out a pine tree air freshener, still in its wrapper, "you can't eat it."

At the same time, Luke and the man across the street remained locked in a stalemate. Both kept their eyes trained on the other until the siblings emerged from the gas station with an overflowing cardboard box. Luke wondered what they found, and he hoped Penny would be so lucky. The kids sprinted to their father and showed him their prizes. The man smiled approvingly, enthusiastically rubbed the boy's head, and patted his daughter on her shoulder. Luke watched as the boy dove back into their vehicle and closed the door behind him. The father whispered in his daughter's ear. She turned and looked across the street at Luke curiously, and at her father's direction, the girl crossed to the trunk of the wagon and opened the hatch. She resurfaced with a small, red plastic gas can with a black spout. She handed it to her father and ducked inside the car. The man lowered his gun to his side and shuffled over to the street corner. He set the container on the sidewalk and made his way to his driver's side door. The man hunched down and stooped inside the wagon and grabbed the door handle. He paused before pulling it shut. The man looked back at Luke and nodded before he shut his door and drove away into the night.

Luke sighed a deep breath of relief. Goose prickles covered his arms. He didn't believe his eyes, and he couldn't recall the last time someone showed such humanity and generosity. "Wait 'til I tell Penny about this," he said as he strode across the street.

Oblivious to Luke's run-in with fellow survivors, Penny stood in front of a grease-stained unisex bathroom door. The bathroom sign dangled vertically from a single hook that barely clung to the door, and the dull brass doorknob was coated in grime and mildew. She looked down to the floor and cringed as cockroaches scurried back and forth beneath the door. Elvis's eyes darted side to side as he followed the insects' movements.

"Guess it's too much to ask for this to be clean, huh." Penny slid her hand into her sleeve and reached out. She grasped the doorknob with a repulsed look on her face and twisted the handle. Penny pushed the door open with her boot as she nervously parted her squinted eyes as the door creaked open. What Penny saw was nothing short of a miracle. She shined her light into the restroom, checked the sink, the toilet, the corners, and finally, the window that was cracked open. It *was* clean. Not spotless, but mostly untouched. Unlike most public restrooms Penny had encountered recently, this one appeared to be unused. There were no urine splashes on the toilet seat or feces in the sink—no graffiti on the walls or phone numbers left to call for a good time. Instead, Penny saw clean tiles, porcelain, and even a clear reflection in the mirror. *"Maybe only germaphobic girls used this bathroom,"* she thought. That would be about the only reason Penny could think of that would account for its cleanliness. She took a step inside, and before closing the door behind her, Penny looked down at her companion. "Watch the door, okay." Elvis laid down at her feet and yawned and rested his head on his paws. "No one likes a smart-ass," Penny quipped.

The further Penny moved into the gas station restroom, the more amazed she was at its condition. Aside from the bugs, it was immaculate. Floor to ceiling tiles looked as if they'd been recently scrubbed. An artificial fairy castle cactus stood on the windowsill, topped with tangerine-colored blooms. Even the drain in the middle of the floor was free of dirt, hair, and debris. A broom closet was tucked away on the side opposite the toilet and sink. Before Penny sat to take care of her business, she recalled the necessary steps etched into her subconscious by her drill sergeant, Luke Dixon.

"Check the corners," Penny said to herself as she scanned every right angle in the room. "Plan your escape," Penny remarked while sizing up the window. "Look for any doors and hiding places, yadda, yadda, yadda," she mumbled as she stepped over to a broom closet opposite the toilet. Penny twisted and yanked on the handle, but the door appeared to be locked. "Good enough." Penny marched back to the pristine sink and set her flashlight, and sidearm down on the outer edge of the bowl-shaped basin. The light blasted the gun's grip and hammer and cast a shadow over the closet door. Penny hummed to drown out the splashing toilet water while she tapped her toes on the tile floor. She fiddled with her breast pocket and pulled out a small bag of trail mix. She tossed a roasted peanut into her mouth and crunched away at its stale exterior.

Penny held the packaging up in front of her face and read the nutritional facts with poignant curiosity. "Three servings?" Penny scoffed at the recommendation. "What a joke," she said as she dumped a handful of mix into her mouth. She bit down on a cocktail of nuts, chocolate, and pretzels, chewing so loudly that she just barely caught wind of a strange noise that seemed to emanate from the closet. Her jaw popped as her chewing slowed. "Hello?" Penny called out as she tucked the trail mix back into her pocket. "Elvis. That you?" she hoped beyond hope. A bumping sound came from inside the closet as the door rattled against its hinges. "Elvis," Penny cawed once more as her voice quaked. "Please don't be rats."

The closet door handle rattled as Penny thought she saw an eye peek through the crack between the door and the wall. Definitely not rats. She screamed and stood, pulling her pants over her waist as she fumbled for her flashlight and weapon. Penny's head twisted from corner to corner, floor to ceiling, as she saw the immaculate room in a whole new light. Someone lived here, she thought. Someone was in the closet. Someone... "Watched me go to the bathroom?" Penny said aloud as she trained her sights on the door. "Come out here, now. Freakin' weirdo."

Penny crossed to the closet, her flashlight in one hand, her gun in the other. She cautiously raised the pocket-sized light torch and placed the metal between teeth. Penny inched closer and closer. She moved her hand toward the closet knob and gripped the handle. She twisted, prepared to yank the door open. "Last warning. I'll shoot the shit out of you if you don't–"

Boom! The door burst open. A tall, heavy-set man of about fifty charged out. He, unlike the bathroom, was filthy. His head was shaved and covered in brown goo. He wore stained coveralls and had a long greasy beard caked with a dry substance that resembled bird poop.

Penny tripped over her own feet and fell backward to the tile. Her gun was jarred loose from her hands and slid across the floor. The man broke toward the bathroom entrance and bolted the door shut. He turned back toward Penny and breathed heavily. He looked down and saw the gun resting between his feet. A thick green mucus seeped from the corners of his mouth and dangled six inches below his beard—the murky goo bounced up and down like a yoyo on a string. Penny clambered backward, pushing herself with her feet and hands toward the closet from whence the man came. Her hands scoured around the depths of the space. She searched for anything to use as a weapon. Penny panicked and prayed for a wrench, a knife, or an axe, as anything blunt or sharp would do. Instead, Penny found herself armed with a plunger. She swung wildly as the man approached. He grunted like a wild animal and stalked her with each step. She aimed her flashlight at the man's eyes, which seemed to stun him ever so slightly. For a brief moment, Penny got a better look at the man. His face was pale, and it was clear that he had avoided sunlight for many, many months. His tongue was covered in boils and scabbed-over sores and flopped around his toothless mouth like a dying fish slapping against the barren river banks.

The man shielded his eyes with the back of his hand. He rushed toward Penny once again, with heavy unbalanced footsteps. "Luke," she tried to scream, but the man put his hand over her mouth and muffled her cries. She swung the plunger wildly to fight him off. *"If only this were her softball bat. If only this man's head was a softball."* If only she hadn't dropped her gun. Then it hit her. *"My gun,"* she thought. She had to reach it. The man dove down at Penny and tried to mount her. Instinctively, she rolled onto her side and scampered toward the sidearm. She reached for the weapons, arm outstretched, but she was pulled back by the man. Penny turned and looked at him. He had a stranglehold on her ankle and was much stronger than she was. He tugged on her leg and drew her nearer and nearer, like a deep-sea fisherman reeling in a marlin. Penny freed her other leg from beneath the man's weight and kicked him square in the mouth, knocking him back and loosening his grip. She bound to her feet and limped toward the .9 mm that lie in the corner of the room. She stood over it and doubled over to pick it up. Just as her fingertips kissed the granulate-black adhesive grip, the man roared and jumped onto her back.

Penny lunged forward and nearly lost her balance, then she pushed off the wall with all her might. With the man riding her like a cowboy on a rodeo bull, Penny backed into the sink. The man's back plowed into the porcelain and his head smashed against the mirror. This action drew Elvis's attention as the dog could be heard barking and pawing at the bathroom door. Penny gripped the plunger tight in her hands and jabbed it backward, smacking the filthy rubber cup against the man's face. "Luke!" she screamed out once more.

Luke leaned against a brick wall. He used his knife to pick food between his teeth when he finally heard Penny's cries. Luke tossed the blade to the ground and grabbed his rifle, which butted up against the doorway. He rushed inside to the sound of shattering glass from deep within the store. "Tell me where you are," Luke ordered.

"Get off of me," Penny yelled as Luke hurdled a shelf and reached the bathroom to find Elvis casually licking his paws.

"Get outta the damn way." Luke gave Elvis a nudge with his boot. Luke grabbed the handle and pushed and pulled, but the door wouldn't budge. Luke inhaled deep, took a step back, and lowered his shoulder. He plowed through the door like it was a tackling dummy. The wood door exploded off of its hinges and splintered into a billion tiny pieces.

"Penny," Luke said as he looked down to see the gangly man on top of her, riding her with the plunger stuck to the top of his head; its handle bounced back and forth. The man was pawing at her coat, scratching at her chest with his blackened fingernails.

Luke took one step toward the man and delivered a boot to his chest. He sent the man flying into the wall, sucking the wind right out of his lungs.

The man's head bounced off the tile as he desperately gasped for air; his deflated lungs collapsed. Luke rolled the man onto his back and straddled him with the muzzle of his rifle planted between the man's crossed eyes. "Say goodnight, asshole."

"Luke, wait!" Penny shouted.

Luke's trigger finger slowly pulled back, about to end this man's life.

"Please, no," Penny said once more with gentle sincerity.

"What?" Luke released his grip on the trigger and looked back at Penny.

"Look at him."

"I've seen enough."

"No. You haven't. Just look." Penny pointed at the man's face.

Luke surged with adrenaline but did as Penny asked. He pulled the barrel back, revealing a red mark from the muzzle imprinted on the man's forehead. His eyes navigated down the man's face. Luke observed the man, his fingers in his mouth, and Penny's bag of trail mix in his hands.

"He's hungry," Penny said as she pulled the smattering of crumbs from her breast pocket. "He just wanted my food."

Luke cooled off a hair and took a step back away from the man. The man shuffled his way into the corner and hid his face as blood poured from his nose down into his beard. He turned the bag of trail mix upside down and dumped the remainder into his mouth. The man chewed in ecstasy, and the rest of the world ceased to exist as he sucked the salt from the peanuts and gnashed them to a mushy pulp with his gums.

Luke helped Penny to her feet and said, "Let's get out of here."

Penny nodded and blew past Elvis, who sat at attention. "You really are useless; you know that?" Elvis's tongue dropped out of his mouth and dangled, and his tail wagged with joy as he followed Penny out of the store.

Luke reached the threshold of the restroom and looked back at the man. He pitied him. The man had reminded Luke of the countless droves of displaced souls he had encountered during wartime: children, the elderly, the weak, the starving. Luke knew this man wouldn't survive long, and he also knew there wasn't much he could do to delay the inevitable. True pity would have seen Luke pull the trigger. But for Penny's sake, he stayed his hand. Her sympathy was a light of hope, an orange and gold blossom across a dark sky. Luke reached into his pants pocket as these thoughts rifled through his brain and pulled a wrapped candy bar from its depths. He tore the wrapper down the middle.

"That girl saved your life." Luke snapped the candy in half. "Penny Wells just saved your life." Luke tossed the broken chocolate to the man who lunged for it and caught it in his sticky palms. "You'd do right to remember that," Luke said as he disappeared out the door.

CHAPTER 15
THE STUDENT DRIVER

Luke swerved in and out of rundown cars, trucks, and buses that blocked their path on the highway. Maneuvering a motorcycle in this vehicle graveyard would be difficult enough, and it was exponentially more treacherous in a garbage truck. Eventually, Luke fishtailed past a jackknifed semi and pulled into a slice of an open road as they headed straight toward a small abandoned town. He glanced over at Penny. Her eyes wide open as she stared out her window. "Hey," he said as he nudged her on the shoulder. She slightly turned in his direction and looked at him out of the corner of her eye. "Smells better in here." Luke hoped to provoke a reaction as he tugged the elastic string of the tree-shaped air freshener that Penny swiped from Pickman's. It bounced up and down like a seesaw and smacked against the bottom of the rearview mirror.

"Not really," Penny said.

Luke took a whiff of the air. "You're right. Still smells somethin' awful." Luke laughed and continued, "It's like when someone douses a room with a bucket of air freshener after they take a massive–"

"Can we not talk about this," Penny said as she turned her attention elsewhere. She tried to disappear, hoping that Luke would just drop all forms of communication, but Luke, like Penny, was stubborn.

"Look, I get it if you don't wanna talk, but–"

"I feel so useless," Penny exploded out of the blue. "Like all the damn time."

"*Apparently, she did want to talk about it,*" Luke thought. "Don't say that, Penny."

"Why not? It's true. That family in Osage. All those people in the church. The lady at the mall. The hungry guy at the gas station that watched me pee. I let them down."

"The hungry guy that what?" Luke slammed on the brakes.

"I'm just sayin'; I wish we could do more for people."

"Hold up," said Luke. He played back Penny's words in his mind. "The guy watched you pee?"

"I'm serious, Luke."

"So am I. I'm seriously gonna turn this truck around." Luke shuddered and beat his fists against the steering wheel. "And to think I gave that pedophile half of my candy bar."

"You're missing my point," Penny said. "No one cares about your damn candy bar. I mean, look at us. We just spent the last two years looking for one person–"

"Not just one person. Your mother. My wi—"

"I know who she is. You don't have to keep reminding me." Penny turned to Luke and stared straight at him with fire behind her eyes. "And in the meantime, we come across all these people who need help. We *can* help them. We *should* help them. But we don't. And why? Because we gotta keep moving. We gotta follow the leads."

"What we gotta do is survive," Luke said as he placed his hand on Penny's knee. She rolled her eyes and looked away. "As much as we'd want to, we can't save every stranger we come across."

"But we could try."

"And we'd be dead if we did."

"You don't know that," Penny snapped.

Luke took a deep breath and shut the truck engine off. He took the keys from the ignition to stop them from jingling and shifted his entire body in Penny's direction. The two sat in silence as he waited for her to look his way.

"What?" Penny asked, annoyed.

"Look at me," Luke said. "C'mon. Look at me," he asked again as he grabbed Penny by the shoulder and twisted her around in her seat. She shook her head, shrugged, and opened her arms, begging him just to spit it out. Luke continued, "I know this ain't easy. But what we're living in right now, this hell, this was my life for fifteen years. Day in and day out, I didn't know if I'd ever have the chance to see home again. I buried brave men and women in villages that didn't have a name and weren't on any maps, ten-thousand miles from their families. So when I tell you that we don't have a choice. We don't. And when I tell you that watching someone die, no matter how hard, is the only way for us to make it out alive. It's the only way."

"That's not fair."

Luke lifted Penny's chin and wiped a tear from her cheek. "No. It ain't fair at all."

Penny sniffled and wiped the rest of the tears from her face. She usually hated herself for allowing Luke to see her cry, but it wasn't so awful this time.

"You know what? I got something that'll cheer you up."

"You found a magic lamp with two wishes left?"

"Not quite." Luke held the truck keys out over Penny's clenched fists. "Here. You drive us the rest of the way."

"You serious?"

"As a heart attack," Luke said.

"But, you wouldn't even let me drive the Prius."

"And now I'm letting you take this big boy for a spin." Luke slapped his palm against the dash.

He and Penny both cracked smiles. Luke opened his door, walked around the truck, and entered on the passenger side as Penny hurried across to the driver's seat and danced past a bewildered Elvis. She fastened her seatbelt and gripped the oversized steering wheel. Penny beamed with excitement as she stared out the murky windshield. Dogtooth-brick storefronts lined both sides of the street: a bank, Huynh's Bistro, the law offices of Bischof, Crone, Haynes & Lasman, Turnipseed's Organic Market, and a Griffith's Sporting Goods. Luke wondered which establishment Penny would drive through first.

"You ready?" he asked as he eyeballed the runway. Second thoughts flashed through his mind in instant regret. Penny didn't reply; instead, she slipped the keys in the ignition, cranked it over, and revved the engine. "Now, what you wanna do is—"

"I got this," Penny interrupted. She slapped the gearshift into drive, and the trash truck blasted down the street like it was shot out of a cannon. The momentum pulled the vehicle left. They hopped the curb and wiped out a newspaper stand.

"Watch out for the—"

Penny plunked a stop sign.

"Nevermind," Luke said.

"This is easy!" Penny exclaimed as a smile stretched from ear to ear.

"Do me a favor and slow down a bit." Luke gripped the door handle until his knuckles were as white as bed sheets. Rather than hit the brakes, Penny slammed on the gas. "The other pedal. Hit the other pedal!" Luke shouted as they were headed right for a decorative concrete fountain that rested in the middle of a roundabout.

Penny looked down at her feet, lifted her leg, and stomped on the brake pedal. The truck squealed to a halt. Luke's face planted into the dash and was slingshot back against his seat. He rubbed his nose and stared at Penny as a trace of blood seeped onto his finger. Penny and Elvis looked to each other, then at Luke.

"You really should wear your seatbelt," Penny said with a smile. Luke growled under his breath then smiled back as a trickle of blood stained his teeth.

An hour later, Penny seemed to be getting the hang of the whole driving thing. There may or may not have been a dozen new dents and dings on the front of the truck; she lost count. She sped in a relatively straight line as they passed ski resorts, Hoosier Ridge, and the gravel peaks of Mount Lincoln, Colorado; the eighth-highest summit of the Rocky Mountains. Dark red and black clouds formed overhead, and lighting brewed in the charged atmosphere.

Luke rummaged through the glove box. He tossed napkins, q-tips, and other garbage aside.

"Whatcha lookin' for?" Penny spun in his direction.

"You keep your eyes on the road," Luke said. I can't find the map." He continued to scour.

"On top of the visor. Put it there after we left the gas station."

Luke pulled the visor down, and the map, along with a half-dozen other items, fell in his lap.

"What's this?" Luke chuckled as he flipped through one, two, five, and ten-dollar lottery scratchers. "You stole scratch-offs?"

"Stole's a little harsh, don't ya think? Besides, the guy that watched me pee wasn't gonna use 'em."

"Will you quit bringing that up." Luke shivered and cringed.

Penny motioned to the lottery tickets, pulled a hair clip from her hair, and tossed it to Luke. "Scratch 'em." He snagged the clip out of the air. "But if we win, I get it ninety percent."

"That ain't exactly fair. Ten percent? Seein' as how I've been doing all the heavy lifting, I figure I should get at least sixty," Luke said.

"Who said you got the ten percent? I was donating that. I just planned on buying you a new truck."

"Ain't nothin' wrong with my truck," Luke stated with authority as he began to scratch. "Nothin', nothin', and more nothin'. That figures"

"What about the big one?" Penny asked. She gawked at the ten-dollar gold and black scratch-off in

Luke's lap. The label boasted the chance to win $200,000 in cold-hard cash.

"I'll save that one for you," Luke rolled the window down and tossed the losing tickets into the breeze.

"Rebel," Penny gasped. "I hear littering's like a gateway drug. Pretty soon, you'll be jaywalking, or worse."

"Let 'em write me a citation," Luke said. He unfolded the map and smoothed over tears and creases in the wrinkled paper. He scanned the highways, rivers, and roads and slid his finger along a path in the mountains.

"We there yet?" Penny asked with a sarcastic smile.

"Should be by mornin'. You ready for this?"

"If what your 'source' says is true," Penny used air quotes, "I've been ready for this for two years." The smile faded from her face. "Who is it, by the way?"

"My source? Or the people they say have your mom?"

"Both," Penny shot back demandingly.

"You know I can't give up my informants. Be against the code and all."

"Fuck the code," Penny said. Luke craned his neck with intensity and glared a hole through her that had the potential to pierce the earth's core. "Sorry."

"Nah. You're right. Fuck the code," Luke said as he lightened up a shade. "I forget you ain't a kid no more."

"Does that mean I get to use the AK?"

"Not a chance."

Penny applied pressure to the brakes as she careened around a lookout. The twists and turns of the mountain path had a two-foot shoulder with long, thin posts that served as markers for the drop-off. On the other side of the posts was nothing more than death by plummeting.

"Good turn," Luke commented approvingly.

"Thanks, boss. So, who's the source?"

Luke covered his mouth and coughed a name.

"I didn't catch that," Penny said.

Luke coughed again; this time, the name was more prevalent. "Walnut."

"Oh, hell no," Penny sat upright and tightened her grip on the wheel. "You did not just say Walnut is your source."

"I mean—"

"You remember what happened last time we followed Walnut? Hell, the last *three* times we followed Walnut? I almost died."

"This time, it'll be different," Luke said. "Walnut promised."

"Oh, so I'm not gonna get kidnapped by a bunch of cannibals."

"Let's hope not. I really don't like the idea of you being the main course of a family bar-b-que."

"Oh, doesn't that makes me feel all nice and fuckin' fuzzy?"

"Look, just cause I said I could lighten up on your cursin', doesn't mean I want you talkin' like a pirate."

"Fine. Just can't believe we're driving straight through the Rockies based on one of Walnut's conspiracy theories." Penny exhaled with enough pressure to fill a tire. "And who did ol' Walnut say took her this time? Elvis?"

Elvis perked up on the bench seat.

"No, he wouldn't say."

"Wouldn't or didn't?" Penny asked. She thought Luke's answer was strange, for Luke was never one to mince words. Most times, Luke used as few as humanly possible.

"Wanna listen to the radio?" Luke asked.

"You mean the depressing recordings from dead people's broadcasts?" Now Penny's suspicions were at an all-time high, as Luke avoided her question altogether and besides, he hated flipping through the walkie channels. "Sure," she said with a hint of mistrust behind her tone. A tone that Luke caught wind of but didn't acknowledge.

Luke pulled the high-range walkie that he got from Walnut from his bag and flipped it on. He twisted the dial and scanned through channels, battling white noise with every crank of the knob, until finally, a static-filled station faintly broadcast. A man with a high-pitched voice spoke a mile-a-minute in a foreign language.

"That one Chinese?" asked Penny.

"Korean," answered Luke. He twisted the dial again until they heard another voice.

"Russian?"

Luke nodded.

"What's he saying?"

Luke listened intently for a moment. His Russian was fuzzy, but he was able to pick out words here and there. "Lady Liberty is dead. America is dead. Anyone who tries to escape…"

"Is dead?" Penny filled in the blanks. "Do you think we're still trapped? Behind the wall, I mean?"

Luke listened for another minute, then replied, "He seems to think so."

241

"I don't like it," Penny said. "Try another channel." Luke did as directed, flipping a half-dozen more times until a Spanish-speaking woman came over the air with relatively good reception. "There. Leave it."

Luke set the walkie on the dash, leaned back, and kicked his feet up. The group drove in silence for a few miles and enjoyed a strange sense of calm in the woman's voice. Penny didn't know what she was saying. Luke, on the other hand, did. He knew hers was a call of distress, a recording the woman must have sent out months back, maybe more; a call for help. But Luke didn't dare tell Penny. She carried the weight of the world on her shoulders, and he didn't dare add to it. Instead, he closed his eyes and started to doze to the woman's voice and the purr of the engine.

"Hey, Luke," Penny interrupted.

"Yeah?" Luke opened one eye.

"You think in Mexico all they play is American stations?" Penny laughed until she snorted. Luke chuckled. Her joke wasn't that funny; in fact, he wasn't even sure why she laughed so hard in the first place but hearing her happiness lit a warm fire in the hearth of his heart. He closed his eyes again.

"Just don't hit anything else, okay, baby girl?"

"Baby girl?" Penny was taken aback.

"Sorry, Freudian slip, I guess. I only meant–"

"No. It's fine. Baby girl is just fine." Penny gripped the wheel tight. Her eyes welled with tears when she said, "Mom called me that all the time." Penny did everything in her power to keep from transforming into a bumbling fool. She barely contained her tears as a smile crossed her face as wide as the ocean blue. No ugly crying, she told herself.

"Wake me when we get to exit ten." Luke rolled onto his side and nestled his head against the seat cushion, almost instantly falling into a deep sleep.

Ω

Luke was no stranger to nightmares. Most times, when he closed his eyes to sleep, ghosts of his past would visit unannounced. His victims often haunted him and begged the question, 'Why? Why did you kill me?' And most times, Luke had the same answer. 'It was my job,' he'd say. Or 'I was just doing my duty for my country.' Other nights when Luke drifted off into dreamland, things would be more pleasant. He'd see Jess, but not as things were today. He'd recount their first date at the drive-in movie theatre, or he'd relive their first kiss. Those dreams were often too short and few and far between. Then, there were nights like tonight when Luke would slip into the twilight and dream about his time on the road with Penny. Things that occurred, things he feared, and things he hoped would never come to pass. Tonight's nightmare matinee was a work of fiction, a work of fiction that had haunted Luke for longer than he'd care to admit.

The summer sun scorched down as heat radiated off of the desert floor. Vultures ravaged animal carcasses that plagued the landscape. Cars, scraps of metal, and ladders were burned, mangled, and stacked against the one and only Freedom Wall that divided our border with those surrounding us; in this instance, Mexico. Beneath the twisted metal was a pile of bodies stacked against it like a human snowdrift.

Penny and Luke sped across barren earth in their Benz as they chased a low-riding pickup truck. The truck screamed across the desert with a low-life gangbanger in the bed that hung on for dear life. The man wore a stained white tank top, and tattoos covered every inch of his skin, even his face. Penny sat in the back seat of the Benz and peeked over the headrest with a pair of binoculars.

"He's heading for the gate." Penny's head began to rise above the seat again.

"I told you to get down!" Luke demanded.

"He's got a gun!" Through the binoculars, Penny watched the gangbanger pull a Glock from his waist and fire his gun. The muzzle flare startled her as she ducked behind the seat. Bullets strafed the hood and windshield. Luke grasped the steering wheel with his right hand, leaned out the open window, and returned fire. "We can't let them get away."

"I know that." Luke stopped firing and glanced over his shoulder to see Penny peek over the seat again. "Didn't I tell you to get down?"

The lowrider made a hard right turn and zipped straight toward a fifty-foot-tall gate in the wall. It was monstrous and looked to be a twin of the gate used to hold back Jurassic Park's dinosaurs. Twin-gunners stood atop a guard platform and handled .50 caliber machine guns. Since the erection of the wall, the military strategically stationed soldiers to keep intruders out of the country. However, after the attack, forces to our north and south took control and prevented our escape. These guards hadn't seen action in some time and had their fingers on the triggers, just waiting for a reason.

The truck slowed as it approached the gate and the gangbanger in the back hopped out. The man waved a white flag at the guard. "Ayudame, soy Mexicano, ayudame."

The gunner was either too far away to hear his pleas or didn't care as he unloaded a torrent of lead into the man and the truck behind him, shredding the gangbanger into a cloud of red mist.

"No!" Penny yelled out as she witnessed the massacre and watched as bullets pulverized the truck.

"Jess!" Luke yelled. He slammed his foot down on the brake pedal and jumped out as the car skid to a halt. Penny charged out after him as the two ran toward the lowrider.

Fire and smoke from the engine block billowed as Luke reached the truck. He opened the passenger side door and pulled Jess from the wreckage. Bullet wounds littered her face and body like Bonnie and Clyde and soaked her clothes in blood. Luke held her in his arms and sobbed as he screamed at the heavens.

He slowly turned and saw Penny standing behind him. To his surprise, she shed no tears. Instead, the look on her face was the same look she had when Vernon Weathersby took her cat Reggie from her at the age of nine.

"Penny, I'm—I'm so sorry."

"Shhhh." Penny reached into her beltline and pulled a pistol from 'round her back. She rested her arm at her side and tapped her index finger against the trigger.

"What are you doing?" Luke stared at Penny with tears in his eyes as he cradled Jess in his arms.

"I don't need you anymore, Luke." Penny lifted the gun, aimed directly between Luke's eyes, and pulled the trigger.

PART THREE

FULL CIRCLE

CHAPTER 16
THE RECKONING

"Luke," Penny grabbed Luke by the arm and shook him. Luke tossed and turned in his sleep until Penny practically slammed his head against the window. "Luke, wake up." His eyes snapped open as he woke. Luke had the incredible gift of appearing wide awake mere seconds after he'd opened his eyes. "We're here."

Luke stretched his arms and legs. It took him a moment to shake off his nightmare. The thought of Penny eventually moving on and leaving him behind was weighing on his subconscious more than he'd ever admit. He looked outside, then wiped a porthole through the fogged-over glass of the passenger window. A sign just outside his door read 'Holiday Village Mobile Home Park – 2 Miles'. "How long was I out?" he asked.

"About five hours," Penny answered. She looked at him with pity and concern. "What was it this time?"

"Talkin' in my sleep again, huh?" As brilliant of a poker face that Luke had, his nightmares always gave him away.

"Yep. Most of it was gibberish. But you kept saying, 'you need me, you need me.' Kinda sounded like a sex dream, so I panicked and tried to wake you up, but you just wouldn't."

Luke sighed heavily and laughed. "You're actually funny; you know that?"

"I've been told."

"Yeah? By who?"

"Elvis," Penny said.

Luke smiled again. But his happiness was deeper than getting a rise out of Penny's humor. He was relieved that he didn't have to disclose more about his dream, this reoccurring nightmare of his. The one where Penny decides she'd be better off without him. Maybe he was afraid of losing her. Or perhaps, he knew he needed her more than she needed him.

"Wanna talk about it?" Penny asked. "Seems like you maybe wanna talk about it."

"Hell no, I don't wanna talk about it."

"Fair enough." Penny adjusted in her seat and scanned the gravel road before them. It was a one-lane path covered in dirt and grey rock. Heavy trees lined both sides, and fog made it impossible to see more than ten feet in front of their faces.

"Take us up the road about another mile. We'll be on foot from there," Luke said.

As Penny drove them up the bumpy road, she took note of how silent it had gotten once again. A hush fell over the group that was so deathly still that Penny heard Elvis's stomach growl. The last time things had been this way was the last time they thought they'd located Penny's mother. The more she thought about it, the more Penny realized this must be what people call the calm before the storm. She looked over at Luke and watched him for a moment as he sat muted and motionless. The wheels in his brain must have been moving one-million-miles-per-second as he likely planned their every move from this moment on, like a chess grandmaster.

Penny knew that even if she spoke to him, he wouldn't hear a word she said. It reminded her of softball for some reason. There were times that she would be pitching and miss a call from the coach, or times where she was at bat and swung for the fences, despite the sign to bunt. She called it the zone. A place in her mind that she went to escape. Like the mind castle she used to run to when her birth father, Roach, decided to beat her. Penny was deaf to the world while in the zone. Her eardrums filled with a low buzzing sound, and the only thing she was capable of hearing was herself. Sometimes it frightened Penny how much she and Luke were alike. She tried so hard for so long to pretend it wasn't true, but time for pretending had long since ended. A thousand what-ifs ran through Penny's brain. *"What if I didn't give him such a hard time? What if I would have accepted him sooner? Would things have turned out differently? Would my mother have left her job as a nurse and caretaker if Luke and I were closer, like father and daughter should be? Would Mom have gone to my last softball game instead of staying with Novalee? Was all of this my fault?"*

"Hey," Luke grunted. "You hear me?"

She hadn't. Luke had been talking, and Penny didn't hear a single syllable that came from his mouth. "Sorry," she apologized. "Was in my head."

She looked around and realized she'd pulled to the side of the gravel road and had stopped driving.

Luke opened his door and stood on the step rails of the garbage truck. He scanned the area with sharp, piercing eyes and ducked back inside. "This'll do just fine.

Luke dug around in the weapons bag and stacked ammo three boxes high, and removed handgun attachments at will. Penny fidgeted with her necklace and wrung her hands together in anticipation.

"I hate this part so much," Penny said.

"It's not gonna be like last time," Luke assured.

"What do you mean?"

"I mean that I have a feeling that this it. This is the right place. I'm going in first. I'm going in alone."

"Bullshit. I'm comin' too," Penny snapped.

"Like hell you are. This ain't up for debate. We don't know how many people they have. We don't know if the place is rigged with traps. We don't even know if they're still here." Luke pulled a hunting knife from the bag and slid it into his ankle sheath. "You stay with the truck and the guns." Luke twisted a suppressor on a barrel of a pistol. He reached down to the ground and picked up a tactical vest. Luke filled the pockets with ammo, blades, and other accessories. He tossed a black jacket on over the vest and looked up at Penny. "If you don't see my signal or if I'm not back in twenty minutes, you run."

"What?"

"You heard me. You take the guns. You take the truck. You take the damn dog, and you get as far away from here as you can." Luke zipped the bag shut and held it out for Penny. He pulled a flare out of his back pocket and clutched it tight. "I'll pop it when it's clear.

You got me?" Luke took a long slow breath as he eyed Penny over as if it were the last time he would see her. He reached out and placed his soot-stained callous hand on her cheek and held her face with such compassion that Penny started to tear up.

"I got you." Penny took the bag as Luke broke the embrace and took off toward the tree line.

Luke moved through the dense woods effortlessly and graceful, like a deer. He hurdled downed trees and weaved in and out of branches and bushes with ease. Luke sprinted toward a small gap between two gigantic Douglas fir trees, each easily fifteen feet in circumference. When he reached the opening, he pulled a small pair of binoculars from his jacket pocket and crouched down low for a look. The view through the binoculars was blurred and out of focus. Luke twisted the center focus wheel and put his eyes back on the ocular lenses' soft rubber padding. He surveyed the landscape and scouted a cluster of fabricated houses in what was otherwise the middle of nowhere. In front of the single-wide trailers sat rusted swing sets, discarded toys, stacks of discarded tires, fire pits, and a bathtub Madonna. The trailer court was the kind of place where Christmas lights stayed up all year round; a true Walmart wonderland. The low-hanging mist told Luke that God had abandoned this squatter's paradise a long time ago, even before the attacks.

A few guards patrolled the area. Luke counted a half dozen but knew there were likely more inside the homes. They were protecting something, but Luke wasn't sure of what precisely at first glance. Drugs, weapons, *Jess?* He could only pray that she was here and still alive. Luke got a better look at the men patrolling the perimeter; they were more of a makeshift redneck-militia than a private army, but they were armed to the teeth nonetheless. They wore a mix of camo, hunting gear, and cut-off shirts. Luke processed the men, the trailers, and their equipment and came to a quick conclusion they were what Penny called Renegades. At first glance, he thought this may have been a Poacher camp, but Poachers littered everything in sight with their insignia, which was nowhere to be found. And it definitely wasn't the Prophet, or his Flock, for their numbers would have been a multiple of one-hundred.

Luke slid in the shadows beside a rundown SUV and saw a tetherball pole behind one of the trailers. But instead of ball and string attached, two women in their fifties and a girl, no more than twelve, were chained to the pole, cold and badly beaten. The women's skin had turned a dark shade of purple from the frost, and they wore shredded white linen dresses that were soiled in dirt and blood from shoulder to thigh. The girl wore a winter coat over a denim skirt and looked to be otherwise unharmed; physically speaking. Luke wanted to free them but fought the urge. He knew they'd have to wait. If they saw Luke now, they may scream and give him away. If Jess was here and if they had any hope of living, Luke would have to come back for them.

Ω

Penny sat restlessly in the truck. She pulled an old stopwatch from her coat and stared at the hands that moved at a snail's pace while sliming its way through molasses. Seconds seemed like minutes and minutes like hours. Furiously impatient, Penny shoved the stopwatch back in the coat and groaned. She reached up and pulled down the visor. The last of the lottery scratchers fluttered down into her lap like a feather descending in a light breeze. Penny shrugged and grabbed a corroded dime from the truck's cup holder. She scratched the silver coating away, and her eyes grew wide. "Fifty bucks." Then, the realization hit her like a Mack truck, completely sucking the wind from her sails. "Lotta good this'll do."

She gripped the ticket on each end and began to tear but stopped before the edge was serrated. She stared at the ticket and knew that giving up on this meant giving up on things going back to normal in some small way, a sacrifice that Penny did not wish to make. In her heart, she knew that it was silly and childish to have such hope, but she kept the ticket nonetheless. Penny opened the glove box and tossed the scratch-off ticket inside. She tucked it neatly away behind a stack of napkins and some plastic spoons and forks. Penny closed the box and sunk back into her seat until a putrid smell snaked its way into her nose. She immediately looked at Elvis accusingly. "That you?" she asked before turning toward the back of the truck.

The answer seemed too obvious. The trash truck was bound to smell like rot and filth, but this smell was overpowering. So overpowering, Penny no longer smelled the pine-scented air freshener. "Let's take a look," Penny suggested as she climbed out of the truck with Elvis on her heels.

Penny marched around the back of the truck and stood before the compressor. She pressed all the buttons and levers in hopes of raising the gate, but each attempt failed. "Must be a fuse," she guessed and stared at Elvis as he stared right back blankly. Penny took a long stride upward and started to climb the back of the truck.

Ω

Luke moved from tree to tree and car to car, with stealth and precision. There was little wasted movement on his part as he stalked the guards. He reached the broken window of the first of the trailers and peered inside. The home was mostly empty, with ravaged furniture strewn across the rooms. A swarm of slithering maggots surrounded filthy dinner plates piled high in the kitchen. Luke ducked back down and listened hard as the first guard walked along a worn path until he reached a rope swing. The guard sat, pulled the last cigarette out of a soft pack of menthols, flipped it into his mouth, and caught it between his lips. He crinkled the package, tossed it to the ground, and sparked his Zippo lighter against his pants. The man raised the lighter to the cigarette and started to puff. An orange glow manifested at the end of the toxic cancer stick. The man inhaled, taking a deep drag off the cigarette. It seemed to soothe his lungs, if only for a moment. The man leaned his head back and looked to the sky. He puckered his lips and set himself to blow a smoke ring, but instead, he coughed. All that came out of his mouth was a spurt of blood, followed by the shimmering metal of Luke's blade as it pierced the back of the man's skull and exited through his open mouth. Luke retracted the knife, covered the man's gurgling cries with his gloved hand, and carted his body out of sight.

Ω

Penny had nearly mounted the beast as she planted her right foot in a groove near the top of the truck. Oddly, this reminded her of the rock climbing course she'd taken over the summer between seventh and eighth grade. When Penny reached the green trash mobile summit, she peered down with her eyes half-open and half-closed. The smell was even worse from up here; it was so bad that she wanted to vomit. Penny looked down and saw a black tarp tied to the four corners of the top of the truck. "Figures," she said as she scooted along the top rail and reached the first corner. The knot was a bowline knot and one that Luke had taught her to tie a few years back. This prior training made undoing it much simpler. Penny looked ahead to the next corner and saw several chunks of metal standing upright in her way. Scooting wasn't going to be an option.

Penny got to her feet and began to tightrope the length of the truck. She stepped over one of the shards, and when she planted her foot, she slipped on an oily black substance. Penny's arms flailed as she nearly lost her balance and fell headfirst to the ground below. "Oh crap," she said with a sigh as she regained her composure and carried on. Penny knew the kind of grief Luke would give her if she broke her ankle in general, or how much worse it'd be if she did it while dumpster diving. After a few cautious steps, Penny reached the next corner. She undid the knot and carried on to the third, then the fourth. Penny became increasingly vigilant and surefooted with each step.

Once Penny dismantled all four knots, she took hold of the tarp's edge and reeled it toward her into a tube shape. The tarp peeled back and exposed the truck's green edges, gears, and springs. Next came pipes, boxes, and large chunks of broken tables and chairs. Then, a shimmering glint of light caught Penny's eyes; a diamond. But as the tarp inched closer and revealed more of the truck's contents, Penny realized the diamond was attached to a hand. The hand was attached to an arm. And the arm was attached to an elderly woman whose skin was rotten to the bone. Penny pulled the tarp with haste and heaved it over the side, exposing dozens of corpses. Flies buzzed in and out of orifices while worms oozed from eye sockets and nostrils. From young to old, male to female, and everything in between. The poachers kept their victims in the truck; a mobile burial ground used to transport their essential goods to their leader. Some were missing limbs, some savagely beaten, and all of their dead eyes stared blankly at Penny.

Penny gagged and climbed down as fast as her arms and legs would carry her. She reached the ground, doubled over, and vomited, her breakfast splattered against the cold earth. After her stomach emptied and she dry-heaved a few times, Penny wiped puke from the corner of her lips and sat back against the truck tire and tried to catch her breath. *"Why do you always have to look,"* she asked herself.

Elvis pranced into view and sat at Penny's side. He sniffed the air for a moment, then drew closer and sniffed the corners of her lips; his cold black nose tickled Penny's cheeks. She pushed him away. Elvis sniffed again, then spotted Penny's discarded breakfast. Slowly, he inched his paws closer and closer and tilted his muzzle toward the steaming bile. His tongue outstretched like a frog trying to snag a fly.

"You are so nasty," Penny said as she grabbed Elvis by the collar. "Remind me again why I let you hang out with us?" She reigned him in and kicked rock and dirt and buried the vomit. She got to her feet and stared out into the forested abyss. "This is taking too long."

Ω

Luke heaved a fifth body atop the pile of guards between towering stacks of tires and trash on the backside of a trailer and wiped coagulating blood from his blade against his pants. It had been years since Luke had to use stealth to this end—ten years to be exact. He took out the trailer park guards the same way he'd taken down members of the Russian militia on a mission to extract a diplomat's kidnapped daughter. And unlike the Russian soldiers, and all members of the federal security service, these amateurs stood zero chance.

Luke put his head down and bolted through the shadows toward a grey trailer. He climbed the wooden staircase without a sound, pulled the screen door open, and entered. As Luke stepped foot inside the trailer, he scanned the living room and kitchen for guards. He spotted a woman's jacket on the back of a chair at the breakfast table. Instinctively, he scoured through the pockets. The breast pockets held a liter, a pack of cigarettes, and a St. Anthony charm.

He reached into the side pocket and pulled a necklace out. Luke lowered the chain through a space between his thumb and palm. He watched as a silver dove pendant slid down the chain and dangled in the air. "Jess," he whispered as he stared longingly at the charm, engraved with their wedding date.

Luke thought back to a day several years earlier. He and Jess sat on a blanket that covered the tall grass in a local park.

Ω

They stared out at a lake with a fountain in the center and watched two girls and their grandfather try to catch a fish.

"Can we just say here forever?" Jess had asked.

"Who's gonna pick up Penny from practice?" Luke said.

"Seeing as how you're the official soccer mom now, I thought you would," Jess chuckled.

Luke's jaw dropped from this then beardless face. "That all I am to you? A chauffeur?"

"Don't sell yourself short; you do make a good omelet."

"I guess that means you don't want this," Luke asked as he pulled a box from behind his back.

Jess snatched the box from him and opened it. "It's beautiful," she said, and she stared lovingly at the same silver chain and dove pendant that he now held in his hand.

Ω

"She's here," Luke stuffed the necklace into his pocket and tiptoed down a dark, musty hallway that led toward the bedrooms. He pulled his silenced pistol from his waist and maneuvered effortlessly into a child's room. Twin bunk beds lined one side of the room with an art desk on the adjacent side. Superhero posters with torn edges clung to the wall as pet stains soiled the thick carpet. Luke backed out into the hallway and crept toward the master suite.   He pushed the door open with his foot but took a sharp step back when the door whined unexpectedly. A man stood at the edge of the bedroom and looked out the window. He'd just awoken as he pulled his jeans up around his waist and tucked his t-shirt into them. Tattoos covered every inch of his arms, including one of a mermaid. The man was a literal giant, easily six-foot-ten and four-hundred pounds. About as big as Iggy, but only more muscular. His massive frame blocked most of the light that tried to enter the room.

"That you, Sam?" asked the man in a deep country voice.

"Sorry. Sam's a little busy."

The man spun and saw Luke in the doorway with his pistol at the ready.

"Whoa, buddy. Don't shoot." The man held both hands out at his side. "I don't know who you are, but whatever it is you want, you can take it.".

"I'm looking for my wife. Maybe you've seen her? Pretty. Blonde hair. Name's Jess. Luke eyed the man curiously as if he'd seen him before.

"There ain't nobody named Jess here. Please, just take what you want and leave."

"You sure about that?" asked Luke. "Because this was hers." He held the dove pendant in front of his face.

"I don't know what you're goin' on about, mister. I got that for my girl on her birthday." The man took a step in Luke's direction.

"Don't do that," Luke said. "Don't you take another step."

Luke knew there was something off about this guy. Not only was he built like a supersoldier, but he was way too calm for this situation. His meek act didn't fit his size, look, or profile. As the man took a small step back, Luke looked past him and what he saw rocked him to his core. Luke flashed back to the day of the attacks. The day Jess was taken. Outside the window sat the '84 Bronco that he and Penny had passed while they raced to Novalee's home to search for Jess. Luke's eyes widened in shock. "You took her," he said under his breath. The man watched as Luke's expression morphed, now chocked full of rage and fear. Luke's hand uncharacteristically shook. "You took my wife," Luke said.

"Think you got a case of mistaken identity, sir," said the man as he sidestepped toward the bed.

"Where is she?" Luke asked.

"Buddy, I'm telling you. You got me mixed up with someone else. I live here with my wife, my brothers, and their families. This is my wife's room. Sophia. Not Jess."

The man took another slight step to his left and slowly lowered his arm.

"I'm not gonna tell you again. Stop moving and put your hands up."

"She's out getting breakfast," the man continued calmly. "Here, let me show you a picture of her." The man reached atop the headboard cubbies and dug through ads, magazines, and photographs.

"I will shoot you where you stand," Luke barked.

"Naw, brother, it's cool. Just wanna show you her picture—"

In a flash, the man pulled a hatchet from beneath a magazine. He roared and lunged toward Luke as his hand choked the black tape grip of the miniature axe. Luke unloaded three rounds into the man, the first hit him in the chest, the second on the shoulder, and the third grazed his arm, which did nothing more than agitate the monster. Within half a heartbeat, the man was on top of Luke. He swung viciously and tried to decapitate Luke with a single blow, but Luke ducked under his attack as the hatchet plunged into the door frame. The man yanked at the hatchet to dislodge the weapon when Luke delivered an uppercut to his ribs that sent the man staggering backward. Luke fired another shot from the gun but missed as the man grabbed Luke's hand at the last minute. Luke continued to pound away at the man's kidneys as they jostled for control of the weapon. The man slammed Luke's arms into the wall and jarred the silenced pistol free of Luke's grip. Luke watched as it fell out of reach, behind a dresser.

The man bled from multiple holes in his arm, waist, and torso; yet seemed entirely unaffected. He picked Luke up like a rag doll and threw him across the room, slamming him into the drywall. Luke staggered to his feet: He knew this wasn't going to be easy. He'd fought men of this magnitude before and taken them down. One thing about giants was that they typically made more noise when they fell. And a commotion was exactly what Luke was trying to avoid. Luckily for Luke, the man had yet to call for any help.

The man lowered his shoulder and charged Luke like a human battering ram. Luke strafed left at the last moment and sent the man headlong into a closet. The door splintered in two.

Luke reached into the closet and grabbed a leather belt that dangled from a wire hook. He straddled the mountain of a man and wrapped the belt around his twenty-inch neck. Luke pulled the straps back tight and strangled the man. The man rose to his feet and carried Luke on his back. His veins and eyes bulged as he stumbled backward. The man clutched at his throat and gasped for air as Luke pulled the leather belt until the material began to crack. "Where's my wife?" Luke grunted through clenched teeth. "Where is she?"

Without warning, the man bent over, and with all the strength he had left, threw himself backward, and slammed Luke against the wall. Again and again, over and over, the man pounded Luke into the plywood until the wall exploded and the pair smashed into the kids' room.

Luke lost his grip on the belt and fell to the ground. Somehow the man didn't seem to lose momentum or strength. He cracked his neck and smiled as he saw an aluminum bat that rested against the door frame.

"She called out for you almost every night." The man hammered down thunderous strikes. "Your girl was a fighter." Luke rolled to his side as a blow narrowly missed his head. With each swing and a miss, the man broke holes in the floor. "Made it more fun when we *took* her."

"You bastard!" Luke screamed, hopped to his feet, and ran straight at the man. Luke let his rage overtake his strategy, and the man was quick to pounce. The man wound up, swung, and smacked Luke square in the ribs. Luke crumpled to the ground. The man unleashed wicked blows repeatedly, as Luke deflected shot after shot with his forearms, but it started to take a toll.

Luke weakened, and the man hadn't even broken a sweat. He lifted the bat overhead and hammered down, only this time Luke caught the bat in mid-strike. But rather than jostle over control, as they did with the gun, the man released his grip and pulverized Luke's skull with his fist. Luke was sent face-first into the ground. His vision was blurred as the man grabbed him by the head and lifted him to his knees. "Say goodnight," the man said as he picked up the belt that Luke had tried to choke him with only moments before. The man stalked Luke and walked a deliberate semi-circle around him. He bent down and wrapped the belt around Luke's neck. The man squeezed with all his might until his muscles practically tore through his shirt. Luke's face started to turn purple, and his eyes began to swell. Luke raised his arms and tried to claw at the man's face, but he was too weak. The world started to turn black. Images flashed before his eyes. Jess. Penny. His mother and father. His world would end in a shitty trailer park in the middle of nowhere.

"C'mon. Why don't you be a good little boy and die already?" The man bellowed as he leaned back in a final attempt to snap Luke's neck clean from his body.

"You first," Penny's voice echoed from behind. Before the man spun around, Penny swung the man's hatchet down onto this head and split his skull in two like a piece of firewood. Blood streamed down the man's forehead like the Shoshone Rapids, and he dropped dead instantly.

"Luke." Penny slid to his side and tore the belt from his neck. Luke gasped for air and collapsed to the ground. Penny helped him sit upright as she peeled the belt from his skin. The leather wound so tight that it had almost singed onto his flesh. "You're okay."

"Water," Luke said faintly with a dry, scratchy voice.

Penny nodded and sprinted into the kitchen, swung open the fridge, dug through its dark belly. Seconds later, she hoisted an old ceramic jug from inside and ran the jug back into the kids' room. She popped a cork from its top and handed it over to Luke. He took a long pull on the jug and immediately gagged, coughed, and spit out a brownish-colored liquid.

"This is moonshine," Luke forcefully handed the jug back to Penny, who smelled the opening and scrunched her nose.

"Didn't exactly have a label on it." Penny lifted the jug to her lips, about to take a sip.

"What do you think you're doin'?" Luke asked.

"I just wanted to try it." Penny set the jug aside. "I'll see if I can find anything else." She disappeared out of sight for a moment. When she returned, she had a small plastic water bottle about a quarter of the way full. "You're not gonna like it," she said. Floating atop the water inside was a cigarette butt and strings of brown tobacco filler. Penny untwisted the cap and handed it to Luke. "But this is all I found."

Luke gulped, but even gulping ended in excruciating pain. His throat felt like a million ants were shredding it with razor blades for feet.

"Bottoms up," Penny said.

Luke took a deep breath and pursed his mouth. He drank the water until the cigarette butt reached the tips of his lips, then he tossed it aside. "Ahhh," Luke grunted as the water inched down his throat.

Penny stood over the dead man in the doorway; only now did she realize the gravity of what she'd done. The stress weighed on her as her knees weekend, and she braced herself against the doorframe. "Holy shit. I killed him."

Luke looked at her, then the man. "You did what you had to do."

"He's super fuckin' dead," Penny gasped. She walked around the man's body and carefully stepped over a stream of blood that seeped into the floorboard. "Look how big he is."

Luke struggled to his feet. "You done good, kid." He pulled the hatchet from the man's head and wiped the blood against a comforter on the bunk bed. "But I thought I told you to wait for my signal?"

"Good thing I didn't. Besides. The truck's full of dead people. It turns out we weren't smelling Elvis."

"The truck's what?" Luke did a double-take.

"Oh, and I won fifty bucks on that scratcher," Penny said with a smile. "What about you? Besides getting your ass kicked, you find anything?"

Luke pulled the dove pendant from his pocket and held it up in front of Penny's face. Her eyes widened.

"Isn't that?"

"I found it in the kitchen."

"Then that means," Penny said.

Luke nodded to confirm her hypothesis. "And the Bronco."

"*The* bronco?" Penny said.

Luke shook his head yes and pointed toward the master bedroom window. "It's right out there. He limped out of the room, holding his side.

"Walnut, you beautiful sonovabitch, you found her," Penny whispered.

Once outside, Luke struggled to catch his breath and leaned against the edge of the trailer. With his back to the siding, he scooted downward and sat on the cold ground. "There's one more patrol at that trailer across the way. Two men. Both of 'em got M13s. Figurin' they're watchin' over something pretty important."

"Mom," Penny said. A hint of optimism sparkled in her eyes.

"I hope so," Luke said. "Here's what's gonna happen. I'm gonna flank the hombre on the right. Then you cause a distraction. Throw a rock or—"

"Throw a rock? Really? That's your plan? Did a nine-year-old help you come up with it?"

Luke wheezed as he tried to catch a breath and finish his thought, but breathing was torturous.

"Hey," Luke uttered as Penny grabbed his silenced pistol from his beltline.

"Look at you. You can barely stand, let alone walk. Hell, you can barely talk or think for that matter."

"Penny," Luke took another labored breath. "Whatever you're about to do…" Luke shook his head. "Don't."

"No time to argue, Luke. You need me right now." Penny tucked the silenced weapon behind her back. "Let me show you what I can do." Penny stood and made a beeline for the two guards.

Luke will never forget what came to pass. Penny ran at the men and waved her arms wildly. She stumbled purposely, skid to her knees, and, "Please. Help me."

The men looked at each other cautiously, then walked toward Penny with weapons drawn. One of the men was tall with black hair, a black mustache, and looked Hispanic and resembled a walking toothpick. The other man was Asian and about Penny's height.

He looked like an eggplant with thick legs and scrawny arms.

"Please. They're coming."

"Who's coming?" the Asian man asked.

Penny grabbed the hem of his jeans and pretended to sob. "Poachers. Three of them. They have a truck a mile from here. You have to help me."

Penny lunged upward, grabbed the man's jacket, and continued to plead. "I'll do anything for you. *Anything*, I swear. Just protect me."

Luke was astonished at Penny's act. She was completely convincing. Though, that didn't stop him from hating every second of this plan. He only wished he could hear the entire exchange. Still, a generator just outside the trailer kicked on and overpowered the conversation. He strained with every ounce of concentration, but it was no use. Instead, Luke helplessly watched as he pulled a second handgun from an ankle holster. But this one didn't have a suppressing device, and Luke knew he would only use it if there were no other choice. For if Penny's plan failed and Luke fired, anyone and everyone within a mile would hear the shot.

"Anything, huh?" the Hispanic man said with a tempted voice as he looked down at Penny in all her vulnerability. He swung his M13 behind his back. It was evident to him that Penny was no threat.

"I have money. For both of you," Penny said as the Hispanic man moved closer and stood next to his friend.

"And what are we gonna do with money, sweetheart?" the Asian man said. His face pinched like he had sucked on a lemon for too long as a child. "Maybe we can put her with the others?" He looked at Penny and said, "Don't worry, it's safe there. You like tetherball?"

"Or—I can think of other ways you can repay us," the Hispanic man twisted his black mustache.

"Whatever you want. Whatever you need. I'll give it to you. Just help me."

The Hispanic man extended his hand and said, "C'mon darlin'. Let me show you my place. Then you can give it to me." He laughed as he looked at his partner and nudged him. Both men wore stupid grins and were missing several teeth.

"Thank you," Penny replied as she pulled the pistol from her back and fired two shots. The fist hit the Hispanic man between the eyes and dropped him instantly. The second hit the Asian man in the face. The bullet ripped through his cheek and exited near his eyebrow. Blood poured from his mouth, and his eyes went sideways as he fell to his knees.

Penny stood and hovered over the man as he bled. He looked up at her and pleaded. He gurgled blood and teeth from his mouth. The man looked as though he was about to beg for his life, but Penny hated beggars. And she hated perverts, rapists, and men like this more than anything, so she ended the man before he uttered a word.

Luke limped to Penny's side. He stared down at the wake of her carnage. "Don't you ever do anything that foolish again."

"Let me know if you wanna start keepin' score." Penny handed Luke his pistol back. "I'm counting the big guy as three."

"Don't get cocky." Luke shook his head, and they walked up the stairs to the final mobile home in the dirt courtyard together.

Luke entered first and swept the immediate vicinity. Penny drew her gun and carefully moved through the living room. The trailer's layout was reversed compared to the last. Luke cleared the first of three bedrooms to the right as Penny crept toward the kitchen and dining area. Luke turned and made eye contact with her as if to ask if she saw anything. Penny shook no and continued. She peeked in a laundry area that was full of cobwebs.

Luke checked the second bedroom that appeared to have belonged to an elderly couple. Paintings of Mary and Joseph hung over twin beds separated by a nightstand topped with a framed scripture passage that read:

> ***"'But the ones who endure to the end will be saved' - Matthew 24:13"***

Hundreds of photographs hung around the ten-by-ten room. Children throughout the years. Grandchildren. Family vacations. Weddings. A line of girls decked out in white dresses and veils on their first communion. Luke slid closet doors open as moths flew out at him. The closet smelled of mold and was full of old suits and floral print dresses.

Penny searched through the kitchen drawers and cabinets as she looked for weapons, ammo, or a sign of her mother. The place seemed deserted. She moved to the sink and stared down at bowls of rotten food. She twisted the blinds and stared out the window. Her jaw dropped as she saw the two women and the young girl chained to the tether pole. She had to tell Luke.

Luke made his way into the third bedroom. The room was stripped bare with nothing on the walls or in the drawers or closet. A door on the far side of the bedroom was closed and steam funneled from beneath the cracks. Buckets, pitchers, and pots were strewn across the floor, some with small amounts of water still in them. Luke took a few long, silent strides toward the door and put his ear against it to listen.

"*Dark and dusty, painted on the sky, misty taste of moonshine, teardrop in my eye,*" a man's voice inside the adjoined bathroom sang John Denver's '*Country Roads*' in a gruff southern accent.

Luke heard a light splash from within and knew the man must have been taking a bath, which would explain the generator and all the moist containers in the room. He wondered if the man had Jess inside with him. Terrible thoughts spiraled into the worst possible scenario. The only thing Luke could do to quell the chaos in his brain was to enter and pull the bandaid right off.

Luke gripped the door handle, turned, and stepped inside the bathroom with his gun ready for whatever came next. A man was chest-deep in murky water in an oversized resin corner bathtub with his head rested on the ledge and a washcloth covering his face. Steam escaped the room through the open door and filled the air as fog blanketed the picture window and bathroom mirror.

The man's arms were outstretched and rested on the tub's edges and were covered in prison ink. His left bicep had a piece of yellow tubing wrapped around, and a meth needle sat empty at his side. He had a spiderweb tattoo that spread across his entire hand— the same tattoo as the man who had taken Jess two years ago. He continued to sing off-key. "*Drivin' down the road, I get a feelin' that I should have been home yesterday, yesterday.*"

Luke tiptoed around him and checked for any sign of his wife, but she wasn't there, only the man.

"*Country roads, take me home. To the place,*" the man stopped abruptly as the floorboard creaked when Luke planted his right foot down beside the tub.

"Dammit, Addison, didn't I tell you to knock?"

Luke's knees started to shake, and they almost gave out. He turned to his side, grabbed a metal folding chair that rested against the wall, unfolded it, and sat directly behind the man. He extended the gun and placed it on the back of the man's head. The cold metal in Luke's palm seemed to make his skin the same cobalt grey color as if his blood pumped into the weapon itself, and it became an extension of Luke's arm.

"Turn and face me." Luke pressed the barrel of the gun into the man's skin until it began to leave an imprint. The man didn't budge. "I'm not askin' again."

"Take it easy, take it easy," the man answered; his voice came across as more annoyed than frightened. He slowly peeled the washcloth away. The dirt from his face left a pattern on the towel that resembled Christ's likeness on the Shroud of Turin. "Mind handing me a smoke. They're just on the counter."

"Go to hell." With more violence and might, Luke pressed harder and twisted.

"Alright, mister impatient. I gotta say, though.

I do find it pretty darn inconsiderate what you're doing. Coming into my home, ruining my high, and interrupting the first bath I've had in weeks. And at this point, I can only assume you killed my men.

Otherwise, you wouldn't be sitting here like a pervert, staring at my junk."

"Get… Up." Luke's hands trembled, full of wrath and rage.

"Thought you weren't gonna ask again," the man snickered, but his jollies didn't last long as Luke pistol-whipped the man and busted his head wide open. The man cursed, placed his hands firmly on the side of the tub, stood, and faced Luke as blood trickled down his forehead.

Luke's eyes ballooned as his mouth was agape. "You?" he questioned.

"Surprise," the man said as he held his arms out at his side like he waited for a warm embrace.

"Dad?" Penny said as Luke turned to see her in the doorway. She stood there, frozen, face to face with her stepfather, Luke, and her biological father, Clarence Ray Wells, aka Roach.

CHAPTER 17
THE HOMECOMING QUEEN

Elvis paced at the base of the trailer steps as Roach howled from inside the trailer, and his pain echoed into the misty morning air. Elvis climbed the stairs and pawed at the door, for once not running from the chaos. He whimpered, walked in a circle, and sat. He faced the door as Roach screamed out once more like a powder keg about to explode. Elvis spun his head to the side as a metal clank demanded his attention. He trotted along the frozen ground with high steps and a wagging tail until he reached the beat-to-hell Ford Bronco where Luke was cranking a bolt on the engine housing unit. He twisted a wrench with all the torque he could muster. Elvis sat and watched for a moment, then yawned and assumed his usual position, laying down, resting his nose on his paws.

Inside the trailer, Roach sat barefoot, bound to a folding chair with duct tape that clamped his wrists and ankles to the chair's metal legs. He was shirtless and wore a pair of dirt-stained blue jeans. The pants were riddled with rips and holes and not the intentional designer type that Penny's former classmates would have bought for a measly hundred dollars. His left eye swelled shut, and his cheek was split wide open as blood ran down his face. Scabs and scars from needles dotted the insides of Roach's arms. Apparently, the meth business was still doing quite well, and Roach was predictably a heavy consumer.

Like Elvis, Penny too paced. She wore footprints in a small red and black area rug that connected the kitchen to the dining area. She stopped moving and crouched in the corner. Penny had a tootsie pop between her purple-stained lips, and she stared at Roach with hatred in her eyes as she massaged her swollen knuckles. By the looks of Penny's hands, it was evident she'd taken out years of anger and revenge fantasy on Roach's mangled face.

"Look how big you grown," Roach boasted. "You still hit a ball three hundred feet?"

"Let me go get the bat, and we'll see if I can take your head off your shoulders."

Roach laughed a hearty laugh. "That guy out there. The walking Uncle Sam propaganda poster. You sleepin' with him? I mean, don't you think he's just a tiny bit too old for you? But I guess these days we ain't got much choice. Amirite?"

"Not that it's any of your business, but he's my step-dad."

"Oh, wow." Roach pursed his lips and nodded his head in approval.

"And he's a better dad than you could have ever been."

"Oh, now that hurts a little, darlin'."

Luke re-entered the trailer from outside with a ball-peen hammer in his hand and the bag slung around his shoulder. He let the screen door slam closed on Elvis before he entered.

"There he is. The few. The proud. The marine," Roach mocked.

"I cut the girls loose, gave 'em the Bronco," Luke said as he ignored Roach's chide. He dropped the bag and glanced down at Penny's knuckles. "Your hands alright?"

"Fine. Just getting warmed up," Penny answered.

Luke stood and wiped the sweat that pooled on his brow, then ripped off his jacket and pulled his sweatshirt over his head. Today was another grey t-shirt day, and that spelled trouble for Roach. Cuts and bruises, some old, some new, covered Luke's arms.

Roach looked up with his good eye and smirked. "For the record, big man. The girl hits harder than you."

"That so?" Luke shrugged and cracked Roach square in the face for safe measures and sent the junkie's head snapping backward like a Rock'em Socke'm robot. Roach popped his jaw and shook off the pain as he sprung forward in the seat. "It appears I stand corrected." He swirled his tongue around in his mouth and spat out a bloody molar.

Luke squatted in front of the beaten-down man and asked, "Why'd you take her?"

"I mean. She is *my* wife."

"Ex-wife," Luke grumbled.

"That's right. Almost forgot. Who knew they could serve you divorce papers while you took a shit in prison?" Roach laughed.

"Look, asshole. We've been tracking you for going on two years now."

"Not a very good tracker, I take it," ridiculed Roach.

"What I'm tryin' to say is, we're tired. Hungry. And frankly... The smell of the rot in your mouth makes me wanna puke." Luke swung the hammer around in a circular motion, like a baton-twirler, centimeters from Roach's crotch. "I'm only gonna ask you one more time; then I'm gonna rain down some truth on your tiny, pathetic balls—Where's Jessica?"

Roach sat motionlessly for a few seconds, then taunted Luke with a toothy grin. "In the words of Abraham Lincoln... Go fuck yourself."

"That's how you wanna play it?" Luke stood. "Fine by me." He circled Roach and continued to twirl the hammer. Roach flinched with each spin of the tool as it buzzed past with each whiff. "There are two-hundred and six bones in the human body. Did you know that?"

"Well, ain't that fascinating," Roach mocked.

Luke continued, "Twenty-seven in each hand." CRACK! Luke smashed the hammer against Roach's right hand. Roach bellowed in agony. "Twenty-six in your foot." THUD! Luke swung down with force and crushed the bridge of Roach's foot.

Roach blubbered, cried, and drooled as Luke continued to circle him.

"But here." Luke rested the hammer against Roach's crotch. "No bones, just tubes and cords and cells, and one swing of this hammer, and I can make them pop." Luke leaned in and whispered, "Literally explode."

"Stop," Roach mumbled. "I'll talk. Just stop."

"I knew you'd see things my way," Luke tucked the hammer into his pocket and stood in front of Roach with his arms crossed. "So. Where is she?"

Roach sighed and mumbled inaudibly.

"I'm sorry," Luke said, "didn't catch that."

"I said," Roach blinked his good eye, then opened it wide, took a long gasp, and continued, "Wait. What were we talking about again?" Roach rolled his head from shoulder to shoulder and cackled like a brood of hens.

"I've had about enough of this," Penny said.

"You tell 'em, Penny," Roach said as Penny leaped up and stormed over to an end table where Roach's blackened meth spoon sat beside a flickering candle.

"What are you doing?" asked Luke.

"Improvising," Penny said.

"Penny, I—" Luke began to protest.

"No," she interrupted. "We tried it your way. Now we try it mine." Penny reached down and pulled a pair of trauma shears from a bag on the ground.

Roach stared at the shears and followed Penny as she marched before him and held them in front of his curious eye."

"C'mon now, baby girl," Roach croaked, "don't do something you might regret.

"You don't get to call me that anymore." Penny tilted her head up and looked into Luke's eyes. Her knuckles were white from clenching down on the shears so hard. Her teeth grit. And her face was filled with a suppressed rage that was about to overflow and burn like acid. "Hold him still," she demanded.

Luke took his orders well for a commanding officer. He moved behind Roach with purpose and placed firm hands on Roach's shoulders. Luke didn't even flinch as he felt the sopping sweat that laid across Roach's skin like warm summer rain.

"Remember how I taught you?" Luke looked at Penny, not as a stepdaughter, not as a victim, but as a torturer in training.

"I know," Penny reassured him.

Roach began to struggle. He didn't like where this was going, not one bit. The veins on Luke's forearms bulged he shifted his grip from Roach's shoulders to his head. Roach tried to squirm, but Luke's arms felt like a vice grip.

"Hey, man, what the hell is she doing?"

"Quit moving so much," Luke said.

Penny bent down and came face to face with the man who helped to bring her into this world.

"Seven years," Penny muttered. "For seven years, I've prayed to God for this moment."

"God sure is one slow-ass movin' bitch, ain't she?" Roach mouthed off.

"All I wanted was five minutes alone with you. Five minutes to pay you back for all the things you've done. The name-calling. The abuse. The beatings."

"Them wasn't beatings," Roach sighed. That was discipline. I made you stronger. You and your momma both."

Penny backhanded Roach across the face. "I was weak! And you made me a victim. But never again." Penny pulled down Roach's eyelid with the pad of her thumb and said, "This is going to be very unpleasant." She slid the rusted spoon to the base of his eyeball. "But you've earned it."

"Whoa, whoa, whoa, wait," Roach shrieked. "Penny, wait."

"As long as I don't sever your optic nerve," Penny began to dig the spoon beneath the eye, slowly pushing inward, "you might still be able to see out of it."

"Ahh!" Roach screamed as he felt the spoon move deeper and deeper into his skull.

"There," Penny said as she stopped.

"There what?" pleaded Roach.

"Do me a favor, *Dad,*" Penny said to Roach sarcastically.

"Anything, just make it stop," he begged.

"Don't bleed all over my fuckin' floor," Penny repeated the words Roach had said to her on many occasions as a child. And damn, did it feel liberating. She smiled a wicked smile as she plucked his eye from its socket like a soft-boiled egg scooped from its shell.

Roach went ballistic as Luke released his grip. He bucked and panicked in his seat and nearly toppled over as his eye dangled like a prize from the bear claw machine. "Put it back. Put my fuckin' eye back in my head!" he cried.

"Shhh," whispered Penny as she slid one of Roach's meth-making latex gloves on over her fingers. She grabbed his eye and held it up to her face.

Roach stared at her with significantly impaired vision as if he were looking through a fish-eye webcam extracted with a meth spoon.

Penny tugged the eye taught and waved the shears in front of it, snipping and snapping and broadcasting her sinister intentions.

"Where." Penny snipped. "Is." She snipped again. "My. Mom?"

"Grand Junction, OK. She's in Grand Junction," Roach howled.

"Why Grand Junction? What's there?" Penny looked over at Luke, who moved to her side. His expression had changed dramatically. He'd gone from the skilled interrogator just moments ago to someone completely shell-shocked.

"Abandoned train depot," Roach whimpered.

"No," Luke grumbled as his eyes lit up like blazing cinders.

"I didn't want to, OK? You gotta believe me," Roach squirmed. "I owed him, and I didn't have nothin' else to trade. I tried with the girls out back, I did. But he wanted her."

"Who wanted her? Who did you owe?" Penny said.

"Do not say it," Luke said.

Penny held the shears closer to the optic nerve. "OWED WHO?!"

"The Prophet. He came here himself demanding payment. What was I supposed to do? Please, please put my eye back."

Luke stumbled backward and hit the wall with a thud. Penny's bottom lip quivered like a candle's flame in a stiff breeze.

"You're lying," Penny said wishfully, but the look on Roach's face told her everything she needed to know.

Luke slid downward and buried his head in his hands as the room fell dead silent.

Penny disappeared into her head. Into her mind palace. It was beyond words and thoughts how much she despised this man that sat before her. "*A man*," she thought. "*He wasn't a man. He was vermin. Lower than vermin.*" She was going to be sick. So close to seeing her mother, and Roach ruined her life yet again. She wanted to hurt him. Penny wanted him to suffer. An eye for an eye seemed so poetic, and she knew there was only one thing left for her to do.

SNIP!

CHAPTER 18
THE IRON HORSE

Grand Junction, Colorado, was named for its location at the Gunnison and Colorado rivers' junction. The small junction town was also a gateway to the monoliths, canyons, and Colorado National monument plateaus. Engineers constructed the train station in Grand Junction back in 1906, and millions of passengers rode the railway east to Chicago's windy city and as far west as Los Angeles and Seattle.

Over the past twelve months, the railway had taken on a different look. A makeover that resembled the slave trade of the transatlantic; only instead of Africans sent against their will to the Americas, women and children were carted off to devotees of the Flock, hordes of cannibals, cults, or the highest bidders. Rumor had it that the Prophet had managed to export some of his slaves to the very countries who held survivors hostage within the country and the freedom wall.

A snow-drift covered the rail station's sign, years of neglect staining the white brick. Broken stained-glass windows marred the façade as a still-functioning Amtrak locomotive had docked in the loading bay.

Hundreds of women and children, a tattered mess of frayed clothes and muck, were bound and shackled. They were offloaded and herded into groups by men dressed in hooded snow-gear with balaclavas and sub-zero respirators. They looked like post-apocalyptic Stormtroopers.

The train depot's engineer's office was transformed into a holding cell, crammed full of starving human cargo. In the corner of the room, one woman crouched against the wall and hovered over a child. The woman's long blonde hair covered her dirt-ridden face. She wore disheveled clothing like the rest, and her hands and feet were bound in chains; and purple, black, and yellow bruises were speckled across her face. The child was clearly in significant discomfort and had difficulty breathing; her skin had turned a putrid shade of blue.

"Slow... Easy... Try to relax," the woman said as she tucked loose strands of hair behind her ears. It was Jess. She was in terrible shape but alive.

A guard walked past, not paying the young girl a single ounce of attention.

"You have to help her," Jess called out.

The man stopped and looked at them. "What's the matter?"

"Paradoxical breathing."

"English," the man grunted.

"She's inhaling when she should be exhaling.

"So fix it," said the guard.

"She needs a respirator," Jess said.

At the same time, a second man walked by, the guard's superior. "Boss." The guard reached out and grabbed the man's wrist in passing. The boss had an AK47 strapped around his neck.

"Nurse Ratched here says the girl needs a respirator, or—"

"Or what?" the boss asked.

"Or her diaphragm is paralyzed, and she dies."

"Then she dies." The boss pulled away and barked out, "Prophet wants us gone in twenty minutes."

"Yessir," the guard said.

"His glory is exalted," the boss said.

"Above earth and sky," the guard replied.

The men performed a rehearsed handshake of which they interlocked arms like knights and slightly bowed their heads like samurai. They turned their backs to Jess and started to walk away.

"You can't do this," she yelled out. "She's just a child." Jess picked up a broken half of a brick and got to her feet. "You hear me, you cowards?" She fired the brick and plunked the guard on the back of the head. He fell to the ground like a sack of potatoes.

The boss lifted his AK and charged at Jess. "On your knees," he ordered. "Now!"

"You'd like that wouldn't you?"

He belted Jess with the back of his hand and said, "Now I see why your face is all bruised." The boss looked down at the girl, who wheezed with each breath in a sort of premature death rattle. He turned to Jess and said, "If you didn't belong to the Prophet, I'd put a bullet in your head right here."

"Lucky me," Jess said.

"Her, on the other hand." The boss unloaded a half-dozen rounds into the girl's chest. The girl coughed, spurted, and splattered blood everywhere until she gurgled and drowned on it. Jess fell to the ground and lifted the girl's head and watched as she died in her arms.

"No!" Jess pleaded. "Why!"

"See. Now she doesn't need a respirator."

Jess lay the girl's head down softly on the concrete floor. She picked up another brick, stood, and wound up to strike the man, but he was ready. This time, with the butt of his weapon, he hit her again and knocked her out cold.

CHAPTER 19
THE DECISION

Penny ran her fingers through her hair and roared out like a wild lioness as Luke wrapped duct tape around Roach's head. Blood leaked from his empty eye socket and a fresh puddle of urine pooled beneath his feet as he bucked like a wild stallion, screaming at the top of his lungs.

"I didn't have a choice! He woulda killed me!" Roach argued. "And you," Roach spit uncontrollably as he turned to Penny, "I can't believe you cut my fucking eyeball out.

"You sold my mother," Penny charged.

"Coulda been worse," Roach remarked.

Penny's anger stirred within like molten lava about to erupt. She raised the shears above her head and began to plummet downward when Luke grabbed her by the wrist.

"When did you sell her?" Luke asked as he took the shears from Penny. He motioned for her to step aside.

"Does it matter?" Roach said, foaming at the mouth as he started to cool.

"Answer the question," Luke commanded.

"Jesus, you are a persistent bastard," Roach said. "Two months ago. That help, detective?"

Luke seethed. Raw anger shot through him as he turned back to Penny. "I need you to step outside for a minute."

"What? Why?" Penny questioned in a frenzy.

A crazed look came over Luke. His fury started to swell. She knew he planned to do something awful, and he didn't want her to see him that way.

"You're gonna kill him?" she said.

Luke didn't deny it. "Please, Penny, just go outside."

Penny considered the gravity of this situation. She felt as if the honor of dismembering her father belonged to her. But she also knew that if she did it, there'd be no coming back. Killing strangers was one thing, but this was different. She placed her hand on Luke's arm, leaned in, and whispered, "Make him suffer." She crossed to her biological father, bent down, kissed his cheek, and said, "I hope there's a hell. And I hope you burn there."

Moments later, Penny walked down the trailer's rickety staircase. She put her hands on the back of her head and looked up at the sky. The sun peeked through the endless grey and shined down on her face. Somehow in this wasteland, Penny had found a moment of peace, despite Roach screaming and begging for his life in the distance.

Elvis came to Penny's side and licked Roach's blood from her pants. "Elvis," Penny chastised. She crouched down and petted the German shepherd's dense hair. She ran her hand through his wiry topcoat and massaged his neck. "You eat vomit, lick blood, are scared of cats, and you either take a nap or run away when I need you most... You're literally the worst dog ever. You know that?" Elvis whipped his head toward Penny's and licked the side of her face with his sandpaper tongue. "Gross." Penny wiped slobber, and God knows what else from her cheek when a crackling sound rang out. She bound upward and stared into the forest. The sound repeated again and again and burned into her eardrums like cicadas going through a wood chipper.

Elvis perked up and pinned his ears back. The scruff on the back of his neck stood upright, and he snarled.

"What is it?" Penny asked. She half expected Elvis to answer. She scanned the fog as clouds rolled over the face of the sun and blocked its light. The clicking noises reached a crescendo, then ceased, and silence fell over the earth.

A terrible feeling washed over Penny. Her skin turned pale, her stomach twisted in knots, and her heart raced and beat like a snare drum. And that was before the howls rang out.

"Oh, shit," Penny trembled. One after another, after another, the howls filled the air. The same sound she heard at the overpass and in the mall. And they were here.

Penny burst into the trailer to Luke's surprise as he froze with his knife to Roach's throat like he was about to slice. Roach had fresh cuts all over his body and was missing fingernails.

"I thought I told you to—"

"Listen," Penny interrupted, but they couldn't hear anything over Roach's whimpering. Penny smacked him across the mouth. "Will you shut the hell up?"

Roach's whines muted, and Luke listened hard. The howls grew nearer.

"They're coming," Penny cried.

"How many," Luke asked.

"Five, six, maybe ten. I don't know."

"We're sittin' ducks," Luke said.

"Cut me loose!" Roach demanded.

"Will you shut the hell up and let me think," said Luke as he considered his options. "We can make it."

"The garbage truck?" Penny asked as Luke knelt next to the bag. He nodded and pulled a shotgun out, a couple of handguns, and few clips of ammo. Aside from finding her mom, all Penny ever wanted was the chance to carry the big guns. But now that Luke placed the shotgun in her arms, a realization crept in like a shadow.

"What is it?" Luke noticed.

Penny gently laid the shotgun at his side. "I can't."

"What do you mean, you can't," Luke questioned.

"This won't work. The howlers are fast. You've seen them move." Penny reached into the bag and pulled out a handgun and a single knife, a six-inch blade, and sheath that tucked nicely into her beltline. "But I'm faster."

Penny fully expected Luke to argue and protest, but to her shock, he said, "Alright. I'll cover you."

Luke grabbed the shotgun, racked it, and chambered a round.

Another howl grew closer.

"Wait, guys. What about me?" Roach asked. Penny and Luke ignored him and moved to the door. Luke was locked and loaded while Penny stretched out her quad, ready to make a break for it, prepared to run faster than she'd ever run in her life. Even Elvis snarled and, for once, looked like he was ready for battle. "I can help."

"Oh, you're gonna help, alright," Luke said. "You're gonna stay here and draw the howlers in."

"You're using me as bait?"

"The worm attracts the fish," Penny said.

"The worm always fuckin' dies," Roach argued. "Seriously? Guys. Listen, I know I was a terrible person, alright. But I done my time. I rehabilitated."

"You kidnapped my mom and sold her into slavery two months ago, asshole," Penny reminded him.

"That's old news. This is a new day. Ain't you never heard about letting sleeping dogs lie?" Roach tugged at his restraints.

"No, but I have heard the one about letting my dog rip your throat out and use your windpipe as a chew toy?" Penny countered, hoping Elvis wouldn't give Roach a reason to call her bluff.

Luke stacked up aside the door and turned to Penny. "One," he counted.

"Two," Penny continued.

"I know how to get her back," Roach said with a flurry of desperation in his voice.

Luke turned back. "You'd say anything right now to get outta that chair."

"Yes, but that's not the point. The point is, I know how the Prophet operates. I know his routes.

"It's a railroad. I think we'll figure it out," Luke said.

"I know where he's gonna keep her.

"You're lying," Penny said.

"He's taking her to his compound; I know where it is, and I know the back way in."

"Bullshit," Luke said.

"How you think I got all these drugs?"

"You stole 'em," Luke hypothesized.

"Yeah. Stole it right out from under the Prophet's big fat nose. And get this. He keeps his drugs in the same place he keeps his stock."

"You mean his sex slaves. Like my mom?"

"Potato, Tomato, kid."

Penny spun to Luke and met his eyes. "He's lying. He has to be."

"If you don't cut me loose, you'll never find out."

"Then, why didn't you say somethin' sooner?" said Luke.

"I was about to, but those things outside kinda expedited my exit strategy."

Luke bit his lip and inhaled. He looked at Penny and said, "Your call, Pen."

Penny turned back to Roach. He batted his pathetic eye and mouthed the word, "*Please*." She pulled the knife from the sheath and stomped toward him. He winced as she cut the tape that anchored him to the chair.

Roach limped to the door and stood behind a watchful Luke. "Can I get one of them guns?"

Luke growled and grabbed Roach by the back of the neck and pushed him forward. "You stay in front of me the whole time." Luke reached around the meth head and gripped the door handle as yet another howl encroached. "Ready?" he asked Penny.

The front door blasted open as Penny and Elvis burst out first. Luke marched Roach down the stairs and gave him a gentle nudge forward with the double-barrel of a shotgun.

Penny sprinted through the side yards of trailers, ducked under a swing set, and leaped over a broken slide. Elvis zipped through obstacles and kept pace with Penny. As Penny ran, her eyes darted to the sides, keeping the forest at bay. Shadows moved in the distance and seemed to grow closer. She fired a few wild shots into the mist that hung around the trees like a Sherpa. Penny felt as if her feet barely touched the ground like she was running on clouds. She reached a ravine and carefully bound down an eroded bank that led to a frozen stream. Penny retraced her steps back to the truck and realized, "We're almost there," she told Elvis, who remained at her side.

Luke and Roach trailed behind. Roach's limp was a hindrance. Luke didn't know if this was due to his interrogation methods. He wondered if crushing the bridge of Roach's foot was a mistake or if the addict always had a limp. '*You're a hammer, Luke. And to you, everything's a nail.*' Luke recalled Penny's words, and she was never more spot on with her analysis. "Will you hurry up," Luke beckoned.

"Hurry up?" Roach challenged. "You broke my foot, and the girl fucked up my depth perception."

Whoosh. A black mass raced past their line of sight as another howl infiltrated Luke's ears. It was torturous, and if Luke had to guess, it was within fifty yards. Luke dropped to a knee and aimed. He scanned side to side down the sights of the shotgun and watched as shadows raced past them. He tried to lead them for a shot, but they were too fast and out of range.

"Twelve o'clock," Roach pointed straight ahead. A shadow darted toward them. Luke put pressure on the trigger, about to fire, when he was clawed across his face and plowed to the dirt.

Luke winced. It felt like a truck had run through him. He rose to his knees and twisted to his left, then his right. The howls circled him. "We need to move," Luke said to Roach. "Roach…" "*Where was Roach?*" Luke thought. He turned back, and in the distance, he saw the hobbled halfwit trying to make his escape. Luke stood and double-timed it in Roach's direction. He was on him in a flash. Luke reached out to grab Roach by the shoulder when Roach inexplicably jumped forward like a long jumper in the summer Olympics. Before Luke reacted, something snapped and crunched down on Luke's leg.

Penny raced up the hill of the ravine and through the clearing. The truck was dead ahead. "Let's go, Elvis." She sprinted to the trash truck and outstretched her arm as she reached for the door handle. She no longer cared about the dead bodies that piled up in the compactor. She gripped the door, swung it open, and climbed inside. She pulled the keys from the cup holder and was about to crank the engine when she heard Luke cry out in agony.

Luke writhed on the ground in excruciating pain. A rusted bear trap clutched his left leg. The teeth of the black metal bit down through his meaty flesh and into his bone. He let his guard down two times in as many minutes. The first time was when he let Roach out of his sight. The second was that he knew the property was booby-trapped, and he got careless.

"Karma, huh?" Roach limped to Luke's side. "She truly is a bi-atch."

"Help me," Luke gritted through blood-stained teeth.

Roach laughed and said, "Weren't you telling me a story about worms and bait?" He bent down and picked up Luke's shotgun. "Adios, motherf—"

Roach crumpled to the ground before he could finish his obscenity as Penny stood over him with a large rock in her hands.

"Luke." Penny saw the steel teeth as they tore into his calf. She dropped the stone at her side and fell to her knees. Penny tried to squeeze her fingers inside of the clamp and will herself to pull it open, to break him free. She'd always heard of stories where people showed superhuman strength in life-or-death situations. They called it hysterical strength. "I'm getting you out of here," she said as she thought of the mother who lifted a car singlehandedly to save a child. She thought of two teenage girls who lifted a tractor to save their father. And thinking of these things, she grit her teeth and pulled with all her might. She strained in agony, and her face started to turn purple.

"You can't." Luke placed his hand on the side of Penny's cheek.

"But if you stand, I can help you." Penny traced a chain attached to the bear trap. Its steel links were a half inch thick around and tied to a stake that was cemented into the frozen ground. Penny yanked and tugged and pulled with all her might, but the stake didn't budge. She fell backward and released her grip as the color drained from her defeated face. Shadows danced in the trees; the howlers stalked them. These things, these— creatures, were upon them and en masse. "You have to leave to leave me here."

"No."

"Go back to the truck. You still have time."

"But you'll—they'll." Penny wouldn't bring herself to say the words.

"It doesn't matter what happens to me now," said Luke as Penny started to cry. "What matters is your mom's alive. And you're gonna find her."

Penny shook her head no. "Not without you."

"You have to." Luke wiped Penny's tears from her chin. "Go on." Penny didn't budge. "Go!" Luke urged her away.

Reluctantly, Penny stood and shuffled back a few steps. "Luke, I can't, I–"

"It's okay, Penny. It has to be this way. I need to know you're alright. Please, just get to the truck and don't turn back."

Penny sniffled in a fit of tears, spun slowly on her back heel, and started to walk away. Luke nodded as she moved further from him. "Good," he said under his breath as he watched a girl who began this journey as a foul-mouthed stranger disappear as his daughter. Luke laid back on the cold, wet dirt and closed his eyes. He took long deep breaths and waited for the inevitable.

"I may not be the family you were born into," Penny's voice jolted Luke to an upright position, "but I'm all you got left." Luke's eyes snapped open to see Penny towering over him.

"I told you to go."

"And I didn't listen. Figured you'd be used to that by now. Penny bent down and slid the shotgun to

Luke's side. "Family sticks. And I'm all you have left right now. You got me?" Penny smiled through her tears, and Luke returned a heartfelt grin, but the touching moment was cut short as howlers charged toward them.

Thunderous footsteps pounded the earth like armored infantry as the rabid banshee-like cries surrounded them. Luke and Penny fired shots into the mist at everything that moved. They huddled close together. Luke still winced in pain as his leg went numb.

"Last chance to change your mind," Luke warned.

"Fuck off, old man."

"Watch your mouth, young lady."

The duo unleashed a torrent of lead in all directions, but one howler slipped through. The howler raced toward Luke and Penny and closed in fast until Elvis leapt up and sunk his teeth into its leg.

"On your left!" Luke yelled. Penny unloaded all the rounds in her handgun into a Howler's chest. It skidded to a grinding halt at their feet and gave them a front-row seat of its horror. The man, if you want to call it a man, was burned beyond recognition. The Howler's waxy charred skin clung to his bones like paper mâché. Its fingernails were three inches long and sharp enough to tear the hide from a buffalo. In particular, this howler had a robotic arm, and its left eye was that of an ocular implant, as black as the eyes of a doll. The howler's mouth was permanently drawn open and full of carbon fiber razors capable of chewing through any substance. And more shocking than any of the physical features of these former human's turned psycho-killers was that Walnut's source appeared to be correct. These Howlers were half-man, half bio-mech, and all nightmare."

"Reloading." Penny popped her empty clip, grabbed another from the bag, and snapped it into place. She continued to fire rounds, struck a Howler between its eyes, and blew half its skull into oblivion.

Luke steadied his hands as another Howler bound toward him, charging on all fours like a gorilla. The fiend lifted his arms upright and started to swing down. Its deadly claws inched closer just as Luke blasted out another round from his shotgun. The shells shredded the Howler's chest like Swiss cheese and sent him backward into a tree. Luke pulled the trigger again as two more approached on his right. *Click, click.*

"I'm out." Luke tossed the gun aside and reached for the bag, his fingertips barely kissing the outer edge of the handle. "Penny. The bag. I need ammo."

Penny continued to fire and drop enemies until her gun jammed. "Shit." She cleared the chamber and pulled again, only for it to jam a second time. She heard a noise overhead and looked up. A Howler was perched on the highest branch of a tree, just waiting to strike. It screeched and jumped down with reckless abandon. The beast plunged fast, but before it landed, Elvis intercepted it and sunk his teeth into the Howler's neck. Elvis heaved it away while he continued to rip its throat from side to side. Penny spun around to see two Howlers coming in fast as three more flanked them. The first sprang toward Penny but didn't attack. Instead, it picked up the gun bag that held their ammo and carried it far from Luke's fingertips.

The remaining four stopped just inches from Penny and Luke. They hovered over them like a dark cloud.

"Luke," Penny cried out with uncertainty as the villains flashed their claws and teeth and showed just how hideous they truly were as they stalked them.

"Don't look at 'em." Luke reached out with both arms and pulled Penny in close. "Close your eyes."

"But—"

"Close your eyes," he said again. "I got you," he said. Just as he did on the day of the attacks and just as he did the day on the football field. Luke pulled Penny tight against his chest and held her close. She began to shake and weep in his arms, and there was nothing he could do about it. The only thing that Luke did is pray. Pray for a quick death. Pray they took her fast and without suffering.

The Howler nearest Luke was massive. Its arms were the size of tree trunks. Luke closed his eyes and said, "I love you, Penny."

Penny looked up at him, and through her tears, she saw the Howler. She saw its swing rain down and saw its claws aim right for Luke's neck. He'd be dead within a second. And her soon after. Then, out of nowhere, Penny saw the light. A bright beam of light followed by the roar of an engine. The Howlers saw and heard it too, but not before it was too late.

"Luke, duck!" she screamed and pulled him down as the howlers were plowed into by a '67 Cadillac DeVille. The creatures smashed against the car's grill. Three of them bounced off the windshield and flew skyward, with one still lodged in the glass. The Cadillac ground to a rumbling halt as gore splattered down the quarter panels like flame decals. The car's headlights haloed through the mist.

The howlers landed inches from Luke and Penny, three of them dead as hell, while the fourth still twitched.

Ed Decker, better known as Walnut, stepped out of his car, somehow unchanged by the apocalypse. He wore his bucket hat, cargo shorts, work boots, and a Hawaiian shirt. Although, he did have a tactical shotgun strapped to his back and a Magnum in each hand. Walnut paraded over to the twitching science experiment gone wrong and put his boot to its chest. He aimed both Magnums at the creature's head and fired two rounds. The kick of the guns caused Walnut to stumble backward. He fell and landed in the mud with an embarrassing thunk.

Penny and Luke stared at Walnut in awe. They watched as he got to his feet and marched to Luke's side. He looked over the carnage and graveyard of Howlers that surrounded them. "Jesus Christ, these things are ugly as sin." He turned his attention to Luke and his leg. "Uh, partner. I hate to tell you this, but that was meant for a bear."

"We left the bear at Target," Penny noted. Walnut cocked his head in confusion. "Long story."

Some time later, after Walnut had pried Luke free of the bear trap and dressed his wounds, he, Luke, Penny, and Elvis stood over Roach as he woke.

"What's with numb-nuts here?" Walnut said.

"That's my Dad."

"And what do we do with him?"

"Throw him in the trunk," Penny said.

"Wha—" Roach mumbled in a daze, just before Penny delivered a heel to his forehead and sent him back to dreamland.

Walnut shrugged, bent over, grabbed Roach by the arms, and carried him to the car.

Luke hobbled to Penny's side and watched as Elvis dug a hole to bury a Howler's arm in the ground.

"So. Grand Junction?" Penny faced Luke and stared up at him. A numbness fell over her. Though she knew her mother was alive and they had her location, deep within, it felt as if they were somehow starting over. And now, with Roach along for the ride, there was a shadow from Penny's past that loomed overhead. A shadow that she fought tooth and nail to rid herself of for so many years.

"Unless you got other plans," Luke said.

Penny grinned and put her arm around Luke. She helped him stagger to the car as Walnut closed the trunk on Roach.

Walnut entered first and stared out of the giant hole in his windshield. Luke ducked into the passenger side, and Penny dove into the back seat. She called for Elvis, and as soon as he jumped in, she closed the door behind him.

"Walnut," Luke asked, "how'd you find us? Of all the days we could have come here. I mean, we were as good as dead, and you just, just—How'd you do it?"

"Your walkie. I tried to tell ya, but you don't never listen."

"Don't you even start with me, Decker. *Channel twelve. Every morning at eight mountain time*," Luke mocked. "We called, just like you said, but you didn't pick up."

"We was supposed to use Mountain Time?"

301

Luke inhaled, drawing a slither of fury through his nostrils. "Save the dramatics and just tell us. If you was on the walkie at the wrong damn time, how'd you find us?" He glared at Walnut expectantly, waiting for the conspiracy nut to drop some knowledge or come up with another excuse for his absence from the radio chatter, but instead, Walnut simply smirked with a toothy grin and replied –

"Government-sanctioned geo-tracking, my dude."

"Walnut," Penny said.

"Yeah?"

"Don't ever say my dude again."

The Cadillac lumbered through the field and eventually snaked its way to the gravel road. Together, they traveled west until they reached the highway that would take them straight to Jess; straight into the lion's den; straight into the Prophet's lair.

END OF BOOK ONE

ABOUT THE AUTHOR

Jeff Carr is a father of two, an elementary school teacher, a first time novelist and a produced screenwriter. The first screenplay co-written by Jeff was an ambitious horror film. However, he quickly found out, you can't make the next Conjuring film on an off-brand can-of-beans budget. The second produced film was a documentary on the Italian Mafia. This resulted in threats from a prominent mob boss's ex-wife. Jeff didn't know whether to be frightened or flattered. And although Jeff is an experienced swimmer, he'd prefer not to sleep with the fishes.